SHOOTING SCRIPT

BOOKS BY ELSA KLENSCH

Style

Live at 10:00, Dead at 10:15

Shooting Script

SHOOTING SCRIPT

Elsa Klensch

A TOM DOHERTY ASSOCIATES BOOK

New York

SHOOTING SCRIPT

A Forge Book
Published by Tom Doherty Associates, LLC
175 Fifth Avenue
New York, NY 10010

www.tor.com

Forge® is a registered trademark of Tom Doherty Associates, LLC.

Library of Congress Cataloging-in-Publication Data

Klensch, Elsa.
    Shooting script / Elsa Klensch.
        p. cm.
    ISBN 0-765-30765-0
    EAN 978-0-765-30765-1
    1. Women journalists—Fiction. 2. Remarried people—Crimes against—Fiction. 3. Family
reunions—Fiction. 4. Health resorts—Fiction. 5. Hawaii—Fiction. I. Title.

PS3611.L46 S56 2005
813'.6—dc22

                                                                                            2005047308

First Edition: October 2005

Printed in the United States of America

0   9   8   7   6   5   4   3   2   1

To my sister Pamela Lemon
who is always there

Acknowledgments

Without the critical encouragement of my longtime advisor and friend, Jerry Krone ... the care and concern of my agent, Kay McCauley ... the thoughtful nurturing of my editor, Melissa Singer ... and the love and support of my husband, Charles ... this book would not have been possible.

And special thanks to my friend Pat Salmon, who showed me the wonders of the Big Island.

SHOOTING SCRIPT

Chapter **1**

The Big Island, Hawaii
Saturday, 8:00 A.M.

It was strangely hot. No breeze stirred the palm fronds. Even the surf seemed listless as it drifted over the dark volcanic sand of the Hawaiian island.

Sonya Iverson glanced at Perry Dalton, her cameraman. They were shooting on a wide stone terrace that overlooked the sweep of the bay. Perry's eye was pressed to the viewfinder; she could see sweat forming beads on his forehead. The bushy, prickly mustache that dominated his face was beginning to drip.

Sonya turned her attention again to the small TV monitor placed on one of the bamboo chairs. Like many TV producers, she used the monitor to direct Perry's camera movements, though after five years of working together, Perry often instinctively knew what Sonya wanted.

She watched him shoot Lara Swanson as Lara bent her blond head, picked up a golden hibiscus blossom from the table, and breathed in its delicate fragrance. The camera followed as she placed it among the other flowers in the low glass bowl.

Lara was cool, Sonya thought. Each movement was deliberate. Lara Swanson knew what she wanted.

Perry finished his shot by zooming in to the open heart of the flower.

"Perfect," he said, lifting his head and smiling. Sonya saw that the beautiful, long-haired Lara had won him over. That was unusual. Perry was tough, a veteran of 15 years covering news for network TV.

Lara smiled right back at him.

"Thank you," she said. "What do you want to do next? I only have about 30 minutes. I must check on . . . well, everything." She gave a slight, embarrassed laugh. "And I have to get Errol up and ready for the guests."

Sonya glanced at her watch. It was barely eight o'clock. The party to celebrate the opening of the Swanson spa was to start at noon. Surely Lara, with her large, well-trained staff, had no need to rush.

The newspaper and magazine press had arrived the day before and been installed in luxuriously appointed bungalows. Built of Hawaiian woods and surrounded by native trees, the small buildings all but disappeared into the landscape. For most of the reporters, this morning was a time to sleep in, their only chance in a hectic weekend to recover from the 10-hour flight from New York.

Sonya and Perry had arrived three days earlier, on Wednesday, to do a feature for the *Donna Fuller Show.*

Donna's TV magazine program, one of the top-rated in the country, covered both hard news and light features. It ran twice a week—Tuesday and Thursday nights at 10:00. It was an hour long or, as Sonya reminded herself, about 44 minutes, depending on the number of commercials.

Donna Fuller was a highly respected journalist, at times a tough one, who fought for what she wanted. She demanded that her staff look for unexpected twists in stories that aired. She'd flown in on Friday in the network's private plane, along with makeup artist Sabrina and Sonya's boss, executive producer Matt Richards.

The reason for the spa coverage, Sonya knew, was that Errol Swanson, Lara's husband, was a former chairman of the media conglomerate that owned the network. Sonya was fascinated by the unlikely relationship between Errol and Lara, a 30-year-old former nutritionist. Lara was Errol's third wife. She strongly believed that love could cure all. Her philosophy began with love of self and extended into all aspects of life. A pure heart was essential. Love must be unconditional; nothing could be expected in return.

While Sonya felt the appeal of these beliefs, she wondered what Errol, a hard-nosed, cold-blooded executive, thought of them. That led her to question Lara's sincerity.

In addition to the press, Lara had invited Errol's two ex-wives and his two grown children to the spa. Errol's aunt had arrived from Mexico, a male attendant in tow. And finally, there was Lara's alcoholic mother, who was divorced from her accountant husband.

From what Sonya had seen, it was a dysfunctional family. However strong Lara's belief in the power of love, it wasn't working.

Sonya came to herself with a start. Perry and Lara were waiting for directions.

"Sorry," she said, recovering, "I was just thinking about the next shot. We need to get some wide views of the party setup, but I don't want to hold you up, Lara. We'll do the spa, follow you to the kitchen, get some shots of you with the chef, then come back and finish shooting here."

"The table does look beautiful, doesn't it?" Lara made it more of a statement than a question.

"It sure does," Perry came back quickly. "You and the view and the flowers."

The tables were spread throughout the dining room and the outside terrace. Lara had used soft warm colors for the table settings. The centerpieces were clear bowls of golden flowers. Each seemed to capture a ray of sunlight.

"It's serene and beautiful," Sonya said, echoing Perry's comment. She suddenly realized that Lara had used the colors that best set off her pale beauty, both for the decor and when she'd chosen the soft cream shift she wore. It was high-waisted, with a flowing skirt designed to conceal her pregnancy.

"Once we turn on the air conditioning, it will be cool," Lara said, turning to Perry. "I'm so sorry you're hot. The flowers like the natural heat, they will open spectacularly in a few hours. Right in time for the party."

"We can cool down with an iced papaya juice. You'll find it the most refreshing drink you've ever had."

"I'm fine," said Perry. "I'd say this is paradise, compared with some of the jobs I've done."

Sonya interrupted, "Let's get on with it. And, Lara, I need you for a reverse shot. It will just take a moment."

Perry picked up the camera and tripod and carried them to the other side of the table so the beach would be in the background. Lara stepped into position and picked up another hibiscus. Perry put his eye to the viewfinder. But instead of focusing on the flower, he lifted his head in irritation.

"Errol's daughter is wading in the water," he said. "There, in the shallows."

Lara turned toward the beach. "Yes, that's Christy. She loves the water. Errol says she was a brilliant swimmer as a child. She's sweet."

Perry shifted his weight. "Well, she looks goofy in that white dress. I don't want her in the shot. She's too distracting. I'll have to wait until she goes."

Sonya looked toward Christy. Her hands were trailing, her head shaking from side to side. Something must have set her off. Doing research for the story, Sonya had learned Christy was a schizophrenic, and she knew schizophrenics were unpredictable.

"I'll get her out of the way," Lara said. She turned and waved to Christy, motioning her to move along the beach. Christy saw her and ran out of the water, toward the steps that led to the terrace.

Perry looked at Sonya with a raised eyebrow. She nodded. As usual, she wanted him to keep shooting. It was often the unexpected shot that could make a story exciting.

Together they watched Christy, holding her wet dress in her hands, clamber up the rough, stone steps in her bare feet. Her hair had escaped its combs and hung in wet strands around the square, angular face she had inherited from her father. She was talking to herself in a low voice, repeating the same words over and over again.

"What is that? Is she singing?" Lara was confused. "I can't make out a word she's saying." Lara's face showed none of the frustration she must be feeling at this interruption.

"She's trying to tell us something," Sonya said.

They watched silently as Christy came near, her wet dress clinging to her thin, bony body. At the top of the steps she ran to Lara, grasping both her hands.

"We know he's dead, really, really dead," she said in a singsong quaver, swinging her arms and Lara's back and forth. Her eyes were wide, almost unseeing. Her breath came in gasps.

Lara tried to calm her, to stop Christy's frantic movements.

"Christy, be still. You must stop imagining things. Stop listening to the voices in your head. You know it is not good for you. No one is dead. You are safe here. This is not a place of death, but one of love and harmony."

"He's really dead." Christy pulled on Lara's hand. "Come and see."

For the first time Lara's voice rose. "Come and see what?"

"Come and see the body." Christy was insistent.

There was something ominous about the scene. Sonya realized that whatever Christy had witnessed had deeply disturbed her.

"All right, I'll come," Lara reluctantly agreed.

Had Lara caught the urgency in Christy's voice? Or was she just embarrassed and eager to get rid of Christy? Whatever the reason, she let Christy guide her toward the path that led to the Swansons' private quarters.

Perry looked at Sonya. She nodded. He took the camera off the tripod, swung it onto his shoulder, and set off after them. Wordlessly they followed the path, then stepped into a shaded courtyard at the center of the complex that Lara had designed for Errol, herself, and the child they were expecting in a few months.

Lara looked back and saw Perry and his camera. She flushed. Her pale, almost transparent skin became a rough, angry red. Her blue eyes narrowed. Her face twisted. She let go of Christy's hand and turned toward them.

"Please, Sonya," she said. "No photography here. This is a sacred place. The place where our family lives and meditates together."

"Of course," Sonya said. "Perry, we're out of here."

Before they could go, Christy sprang forward and pushed open a door.

She screamed, "It's not my voices. I'm not crazy. There he is. And he is really dead."

Lara moved quickly to close the door, but Christy threw her weight against it.

"Come see, come see, come see." She waved them in.

Sonya hesitated. She caught a glimpse of Errol Swanson on a blood-spattered bed.

Should she go in and get a shot? If she didn't, she could miss the best one of the story. If she did, she could lay herself open to criticism for invading the Swansons' privacy.

What would Donna Fuller want her to do?

"Get the story," she told herself. "Always get the story."

She took a deep breath, put her hand on Perry's shoulder, and pressed him into the room.

Errol Swanson lay on his back on the four-poster bed, his body covered by a crumpled sheet. His head had rolled toward the door, and Sonya could see the bullet hole in the center of his forehead. Blood had poured from it over the embroidered pillowcase.

There was so much blood. The smell hung in the air, thick and heavy. She felt bile rise. She closed her eyes and breathed hard, fighting to control it.

"My God, Sonya, look." Perry's voice was rough.

Sonya opened her eyes. Errol Swanson's hands and feet had been tied to the bedposts with the fine sarongs Lara had placed in each of the spa's rooms. There was no sign of a struggle.

He had been helpless, with no way to defend himself. How ironic, Sonya thought, that the sarongs were printed with words that Lara so often used: Love, Serenity, Peace, Tranquility.

Lara stepped quickly into the room, pushing Perry and his camera out of the way.

"Christy," she said, "untie these scarves immediately. He can't be found this way. I will call Jackie and the police. And you two, get out. Surely you've had enough for one morning."

Sonya looked at Lara. Her angry flush had faded. Suddenly she was as calm as she had been on the terrace.

Why no shock, grief, or even surprise at finding his body?

Sonya followed Perry into the courtyard. A cool breeze suddenly blew Sonya's red curls across her face. She put her hand up and thoughtfully brushed it away. Yes, she told herself, Lara's calm was strange. It was almost as though she had arranged the scene.

Chapter 2

Honolulu
The previous Wednesday, noon

No sooner had the executive jet lifted off than the co-pilot put his head around the cabin door.

"The flight's only 40 minutes to the Big Island, but I can still offer you a drink. My name is Bruce," he said, smiling.

As he spoke, his eyes lingered lasciviously on Sonya's shapely bare legs crossed under her white Bermuda shorts.

"Make mine a Coke," Perry said brusquely, annoyed at the man's obvious interest in Sonya.

"And make mine diet," Sonya said quickly.

The co-pilot turned and stared at Perry lounging in the beige leather armchair that took up almost half the width of the narrow eight-seater jet. Perry wore his usual T-shirt and well-worn jeans. His baseball cap was pulled down over his eyes, shielding them from the sunlight that streamed in.

"Whatever you wish," the co-pilot replied as he opened the bar and reached for the fridge. "We're well equipped. From champagne to mineral water and everything in between. Like I said, anything you want, anything."

He added with a smirk, "Are you sure you wouldn't prefer a glass of icy-cold champagne, Ms. Iverson? Mrs. Swanson usually has a split when she comes aboard after a long day's shopping in Honolulu. She says it prepares her for the change of pace on the Big Island."

Sonya smiled and shook her head. "Just diet."

But Perry wouldn't leave it alone. "You island boys know how to come on fast," he said.

"We call it aloha or, to you, sir, island hospitality," the co-pilot replied stiffly, staring at Sonya.

"Okay," Sonya interrupted, "let's concentrate on the drinks."

She knew Perry was tired after the flight from New York, and she knew it irritated him when she wasn't treated with the respect she deserved—especially by young jerks.

The co-pilot put drinks and bowls of macadamia nuts in front of them and skulked away. He did his best to slam shut the heavy door that divided the passenger cabin from the cockpit.

Sonya took a sip of her drink, then turned to Perry. "Cool it, Perry," she said. "Get yourself in the mood for the surf, the sun, and the beaches of the Big Island of Hawaii."

"Yeah, I know. And I'm glad you asked me to do this shoot with you." Perry had his own way of apologizing.

He went on, "Like everyone else at the network, I despise Errol Swanson. I don't welcome the idea of following him and his new wife as they show off the multimillion-dollar spa he built for her as a wedding present. Swanson should be in jail, not sitting by the Pacific enjoying the sun."

"He's a tough man," Sonya stated, trying to soothe Perry.

"More than tough. He's a greedy bloodsucker who did every-thing to destroy the network for his own gain. Ever count how many people he fired?"

"Yes, I know, Perry," Sonya said.

But Perry would not be stopped. "And how much money did he get as a golden parachute when he left? How much money did he pile up in stock options over the years?"

"He must be worth more than half a billion while hundreds of the people he fired are still looking for jobs."

"Cool it, Perry." Sonya had rarely seen him this angry.

"I want to know why Donna agreed to do this story in the first place. What's in it for her?"

Sonya shrugged. "Donna took a long time to say 'yes.'"

Sonya, too, had been troubled by Donna's decision, and there was one possible explanation she didn't want to discuss with Perry. There were rumors that Donna had had an affair with Errol Swanson and suggestions that the affair was the reason Donna had gotten her own show. Sonya could accept that there might have been an affair, but not that Donna had gotten her show be-cause of it. No, not Donna.

She continued, "I guess it was pressure from all those executives on the nineteenth floor."

"But Swanson is out. He doesn't run the network anymore. He left four years ago," Perry reasoned.

"He's still on the board," Sonya replied, "and he still knows where the bodies are buried."

Sonya looked out the window. She was getting tired of Perry's questions. He was hitting her on a sore spot. As he knew, she hadn't wanted to do the story, and had agreed only after Donna insisted.

To refuse would have angered Donna, something Sonya wanted to avoid. Donna was her mentor. She had guided and even protected Sonya countless times. Their relationship was invaluable to Sonya in the tough male-chauvinistic life of the TV network.

She had argued with Donna that the Swanson story was just a puff piece with palm trees. Similar luxurious hideaway spas existed around the world. What was there to make this one worth time on the highly rated *Donna Fuller Show*?

Donna had laughed. "That's for you to find out. Do the research. You're a producer. That's your job."

But after days of work, the only angle she could find was the extraordinary life of Errol Swanson, a man who overcame a disturbing childhood to become a world-class force in business.

It was easy to say that most executives were motivated by greed and power. But something deeper seemed to drive Errol. He was cold, brutal, almost inhuman in the way he treated his staff. He seemed to take a perverse joy in the misery he created.

Sonya's research showed that Swanson treated his family in much the same way. His first two marriages had failed. One of his children was dead, and one apparently had significant psychological problems. The third child was, as far as Sonya could tell, completely estranged from his father.

Now there was Lara, a woman the magazines were calling Errol's "trophy" wife. What was this marriage about? What was the long-range plan for the spa? It would hardly be much of a money maker by itself.

Of course, Errol might plan to get a large amount of publicity and then introduce a line of products to market on a global stage.

Maybe Lara had dreams of becoming the Estée Lauder of the twenty-first century.

Sonya picked up the monogrammed napkin the co-pilot had given her with her drink. The initials LSE were beautifully entwined—obviously the work of a professional designer.

It would be a classy logo for a perfume, she thought.

Well, Sonya told herself, she would preinterview Errol and work up a list of questions for Donna to ask. Maybe Donna could figure out an angle that would justify airing the feature. Donna was the best—quick-witted, experienced. And she probably knew more about Errol Swanson than she let on.

Sonya dug her hands deep into the pockets of her jacket and relaxed her shoulders.

"Swanson's childhood made him the man he is," she insisted. "He really had a rough time growing up, Perry."

Perry snorted in disbelief.

"He may have been one of the wonder boys of the Chicago business world in the '80s," Sonya continued, "and he was certainly a high roller when he moved to New York and took over the network. But his early life was no picnic.

"His father was a World War II hero. Charles Swanson's name was practically a household word, but he suffered a lot of psychological damage. When he first came home, after almost two years of fighting, he didn't recognize his wife. Errol had been born while he was away and the man didn't believe Errol was his son."

Perry was unsympathetic. "The father must have been hospitalized and treated."

Sonya gave him a quick look. "Spare him a bit of compassion, Perry. Treatment for mental illness was limited in those days. Of course they put him in hospital and after a time he was able to go home. But that didn't necessarily mean he was well or that his family didn't suffer."

"How do you know all this?"

"From my research. Charles Swanson was one of the subjects in a study done by psychologists at a Chicago university. I read several articles about the study in medical magazines."

"What did he do for a living?"

"He wanted to be a doctor but medical school was too tough for him and he turned to dentistry. He hated it and apparently felt that life had cheated him." Sonya shook her head. "He died a year or so after Errol started college."

Sonya turned to look out the window, signaling to Perry that the conversation was over. The sky was blue and so was the ocean that seemed to stretch to the rim of the world. On all counts it was a glorious day.

Nevertheless, she felt tears coming. Her father, too, had died young, and Sonya knew how deep such a loss could be. It had changed her life forever.

Damaged though his father was, Errol Swanson still must have loved him. And must have suffered. Nothing could alter that.

Perry sensed her sadness. He broke the silence with a casual question.

"So how were your three days on Oahu? How was swimming at Waikiki? Did you see everything you planned?"

"And more." Sonya grinned at him. Perry, for all his size and ruggedness, could be sensitive. Sometimes it seemed as if he could read her mind. Perry smiled in return, then reached out, took a handful of her nuts, and tossed them into his mouth.

"There's a good reason you call me 'Ms. Control,'" Sonya joked.

"I made a list of the things I wanted to do, the places I wanted to see. I hired a car, got a good map, and saw every one." She said it proudly, hiding the fact that she'd rather work than try to have a social life.

She had spent little time on the beach. The fair skin that went with her curly red hair burned too quickly. Usually all she got were painful blisters and ugly peeling skin. And freckles.

But there had been the Bishop Museum and the Art Institute, both of them as fascinating as they were cool.

The leather creaked as Perry slid down to be more comfortable in his chair. He reached for another handful of nuts and chewed thoughtfully.

"You'll never make me believe you spent three days without doing any work."

"Well, I did do some," Sonya confessed. "Lara Swanson claims in her press release that she built her spa on ground sacred to the early Hawaiians. She says it's the site of ancient rituals and that the fire goddess Pele watches over it.

"So I spent a few hours in the Bishop Museum library, and found out that her claims could be true. Pele is one of the powerful figures in Hawaiian folklore. She's been important down the centuries, probably because she was—as goddesses go—very young."

"How young?" Perry teased. "Will I want to date her if I meet her?"

Perry's humor was often odd, but Sonya played along.

"That depends where you meet her. Her big claim to fame is that she controls Kilauea, the volcano that is still active on the Big Island.

"The Hawaiians say that she will appear as a beautiful young woman in the mountains and as a very old and ugly woman on the seashore.

"There's an old Hawaiian saying, 'Always be nice to an old woman. It might be Pele.'"

Perry blinked. "Sounds like she'd make an interesting date. Are you really into this stuff?"

"Don't laugh. Lara Swanson takes this very seriously and so do lots of other people. You say you like strong women, and Pele was strong—as fiery and impetuous as her volcano. It was dangerous to cross her. And almost as dangerous to be loved by her. So watch out, Perry."

"Trying to scare me off? You're worried I'll get tangled with a goddess?"

Perry laughed and pulled the cap over his face to avoid her eyes. He took the last handful of nuts from Sonya's bowl.

"These are good." He chewed them hungrily. "I must admit that Errol, with all his faults, is treating us in style. Does everyone get this treatment? I like this private plane bit."

"Yes, this is part of the spa deal. The guests fly to Honolulu's main airport, then Errol's jet takes them to the Big Island. It's quicker and it gives them a taste of the luxury to come. VIPs with their own jets can fly from the mainland, since the runway is long enough."

Perry took a good look around the cabin. Its eight chairs were covered in padded beige leather. "A pity he didn't send it to New York for us. Business class was never this comfortable."

Sonya nodded. She picked up her drink and sipped it. The ice clinked in the crystal glass as the plane circled the airport prior to landing. The airstrip was a stripe of soft gray in the bright green of the plants.

As the plane turned, Sonya watched the shadow of its wings dip over the beach and the wide stretch of water that formed the bay.

The co-pilot put his head around the door.

"The wind's picked up," he warned. "Make sure your seat belts are fastened securely. We're in for a bumpy landing. But don't be concerned. The weather in Hawaii is always unpredictable."

In those few minutes the vista had changed dramatically. Heavy dark clouds streaked against the sky. The palms bent nearly halfway to the ground against the wind; crested waves crashed on the ugly jagged rocks below the cliff.

The Big Island looked primordial. Sonya reminded herself that life here was constant change. The island had been formed by lava that had first bubbled up from the seabed some 70 million years ago. The lava was still coming, rising to the surface and making the island bigger every day.

The plane nosed down. The runway came rushing toward them. Sonya closed her eyes and sighed in relief.

Suddenly the plane jerked up. The pilot turned at the last moment and circled for another pass.

Sonya felt the jerk in the pit of her stomach. Her heart began to race. She forced herself to breathe deeply.

The pilot's voice came calmly over the speaker. "Sorry. The wind is stronger than I thought. We'll have another go."

It took two more passes before the plane came to rest on the tarmac.

Sonya's face was drained as she unclipped her seat belt and stood up. It was eerie the way the wind had sprung up so quickly.

She put her hand on the back of Perry's chair to steady herself.

"Do you think the goddess Pele was trying to stop strangers from coming to her beautiful bay?" she asked.

Perry turned and grinned. "I doubt it," he said. "I don't think she'd give a thought about us after all these centuries."

But Sonya shuddered. This place seemed to have a force of its own, a force beyond anyone's control.

Then she laughed at herself. She was always imagining things.

Chapter 3

"Raise your hands if you've lost weight this week. Come on. Be proud of it. Remember, it doesn't matter if it is an ounce or a pound. You are already a slimmer, happier person."

How many times had she heard those words?

Joan Swanson felt her depression deepen. She was about to start it all again. Another 90 pounds to lose. Another two years of watching every bite.

Counselor Jenny Shaw was slim and neat in her dark gray suit. She knew what she was doing, and her strong, high-pitched voice, with its slight Midwestern twang, made what she said a command.

Three hands reached up above smiling faces.

"Now you three weight losers stand up and let us applaud you."

Joan Swanson strained her neck to look over her shoulder and watch the obese women grip the back of their seats and struggle to rise. With the dozen other members in the class, she began clapping.

"Hang in there," she told herself. "It's only a few minutes. You can take it."

This was the fourth diet therapy group she had joined. She had left the other three when she'd gained back every ounce she lost. Now she was heavier than ever, and her doctor was adamant that she lose weight.

"My dear Joan, you must face it. You are considered obese," he said. "You are only five-foot-three and you weigh 230 pounds. That means you are wide open to diabetes, heart attacks, strokes, and I could go on. You've already had an operation on one knee. You can expect trouble with the other one."

He looked at her over his half-glasses, his bald head shining as the light caught it.

"You must lose weight, Joan."

Joan had bent her head as the shame swept through her. How could the doctor have any respect for her? She had none for her-self. She had failed so often.

"Oh, Dr. Stevens, you know I've tried," she appealed. "But when I'm worried or anxious I can't stop eating. It's like an addiction. It is the only comfort I have." She bit her lip to force back the tears.

Then he suggested a new concept. In this program, meetings are held once a week for women of about the same age. Studies show that these women relate to each other better than groups of women of mixed ages. And the support they offer is more effective.

"Apparently it succeeds best with women in their fifties. They are willing to share their experiences, to discuss their problems with husbands and children. And, of course, menopause and the problems that come with aging.

"If you go to the meetings regularly, it could work for you."

Eight weeks ago Errol had made his claims for money from Joan's toy business. That call from her attorney, telling her of Errol's demands, had set off one long binge.

Joan felt that deep hollow inside that only eating could satisfy. She had gained five pounds in what seemed to have been only a few days. None of her clothes fit. She would have to start buying an even bigger "fat wardrobe."

In the four weeks since she'd joined this group Joan had attended only one meeting. She was here today only because Jenny Shaw had called to tell her she must have private sessions.

Joan had agreed to come to the meeting and see her afterward. The counselor had greeted her at the door and seated her in the front row in one of the wide, armless chairs that were designed to hold overweight bodies in comfort.

"Now, ladies," counselor Shaw said, turning her head so she included them all. "Let's talk about what went wrong."

"Everything," Joan whispered to herself. "Just everything." She felt tears welling up and bowed her head to hide them. But the counselor had heard her.

"What did you say, Joan?" she said. "Tell us about it."

"Everything went wrong, so I binged. I binged and binged and binged. I drove to the mall on Saturday and Sunday to shop. But what I really did was go from dispenser to dispenser buying candy bars and cramming them into my mouth.

"Tonight when I left the office, I stopped at the newspaper stand and practically bought them out of chocolate. I told the guy behind the counter I was having a birthday party for my niece and had forgotten to stock up. I finished them all on my way here."

The counselor put her hand up in sympathy.

"Tell me more about the experience. Did the man in the store know you were buying the candy for yourself?"

"Of course he knew. He has no respect for me. I've done the same thing a dozen times."

"Was it such a degrading experience?" The counselor glanced around the room as if to harness sympathy for her.

"Yes, it was. That skinny guy stays as far away from me as possible. He doesn't like to even touch my hand. As if being fat was repulsive or contagious."

"And, of course, all this binging made you gain?"

"Yes, 15 pounds in the four weeks since I was last here." Joan was almost defiant in her desire to let the truth out.

"Would you like to tell us what started this round of binging?" The counselor's voice was consoling.

"It's my ex-husband," Joan said, wiping the tears from her cheeks with the back of her hand. A groan, half laughter and half sympathy, went up around the room.

"Come on, Joan, tell us more. I'm sure you'll get plenty of understanding on that score." The counselor could see her distress and obviously wanted to encourage her.

Joan closed her eyes and rested for a moment against the back of her chair.

"We've been divorced for more than 20 years, but he still wants to punish me. Not for the divorce, but because I married him under what he believes were false pretenses. He claims he is entitled to half of my business and he wants the money."

"Have you seen a lawyer?"

Joan paused before she could answer. She was close to tears again. She nodded.

"Yes, I've seen a lawyer, but the law always seems to be on the side of men. It's hard for women in business." She opened her handbag, grabbed a tissue, and blew her nose.

"I'm sorry," she said. "But my marriage was a complete disaster. I've lost both my children. My son was dead at 19; my daughter is schizophrenic and is lost to me."

The room was still. Joan paused, feeling a wave of sympathy and understanding. It compelled her to push on with her story.

"Now my ex says he'll force me to sell my business, my family toy business. I struggled for years to make it a success, and now that it's doing well he wants it. Why? He doesn't need it. It's only to punish me."

Joan collapsed. Sobs shook her body and made the waistband of her pants bite into her stomach. The taste of the chocolate bars she had eaten flooded her mouth. She felt she was about to throw up in front of them all.

The woman in the seat next to her put an arm around her.

"Let it all out," she said. "We understand what it's like."

"I've never had control of my life." Joan had to stop herself from screaming. "I lived with my parents until I got married at 19. Errol persuaded me to marry him because he thought my family had money.

"I had my twins nine months after the wedding. Now my son is dead.

"My daughter was a beautiful child. She could have been a champion swimmer but she was ashamed of me even as a child. My husband delighted in throwing that in my face."

Joan clutched her hands to her chest. Her body was icy cold. She stood up as quickly as she could.

"I'm going to be sick."

Counselor Shaw opened the bathroom door.

"When you feel better," she said, "go into my office and rest. There's bottled water in the fridge. I'll join you when the session ends."

The counselor's office was small, dark, and comforting. Joan sank into a chair, took a handful of tissues, and wiped her face. She wanted to cry until the guilt melted away. How could she have humiliated herself in front of all those women?

The silence of the room comforted her. She felt released from her problems and anxieties.

Counselor Shaw's voice was equally comforting when she quietly opened the door and entered the room.

"How are you feeling?" she asked.

"As crazy as it sounds, that outburst calmed me." Joan ran her hands through her short blond hair as if to reinforce her statement. "I know it is easy to apologize for getting out of control. But the effort of coming to the meeting devastated me. There was no other way to get here but to let myself binge."

"I understand," Jenny Shaw said as she sat in the chair opposite. "Let's forget it for now, and talk about when and why you first gained weight. Were you heavy as a child?"

"No," Joan shook her head, "not particularly. My family was close-knit. We owned the toy shop and everyone had to contribute. I worked hard. After school, at weekends, and right through the Christmas holidays.

"Food was important to us, but no one in the family was obese."

Shaw leaned forward in her seat and looked at Joan.

"So when did you start overeating?"

"When I was pregnant, more than 30 years ago. I didn't realize at first how much weight I was piling on, and when I did, I found it impossible to stay on the diet my doctor recommended.

"Then, the week I found out I was having twins, my father had a stroke. I moved back home to be with my mother while my brother took over the business. I was tense and angry all the time.

"To top it off, my husband demanded I move back with him. The only time I felt secure was when I walked into my mother's kitchen, opened the fridge door, and saw the food inside. I'd tell myself not to eat, but then I'd lose control."

"And like many pregnant women, you told yourself that as soon as you had the babies you'd lose all the weight?" Counselor Shaw smiled as she spoke.

"Of course. At 20 everything seemed possible. I hadn't wanted to get pregnant so soon, but I looked forward to my twins and wanted to give them as much love and support as they needed.

"But it didn't work out. I gave up college and worked part-time in the store. The babies slept beside me in the office as I did the books. Things were so bad I didn't ask to be paid. That made Errol furious. He expected me to be home and care for him, not to be the unpaid slave of a rich family, as he called us.

"When I came home I got into the habit of looking in the mirror, getting depressed at what I saw, and heading straight for the kitchen. I told myself I'd be able to cope when I got older. But here I am, weighing 230 pounds."

"What's your next step?"

"Now that I'm comfortable with you, I'll try to come every week." She lowered her head and looked away. Joan wanted desperately to talk to this woman about Christy, but it was hard to start.

"I have another problem and I'd like your advice," she said in a voice so low it was almost a whisper. "Errol and his third wife have built a luxury spa in Hawaii. His wife has invited my daughter and me to come to the opening."

"How do you feel about it?"

"Well, my attorney said I should go and try to talk to Errol about the toy business."

"That sounds sensible, but only if you feel you can cope with the stress."

"The problem is my daughter. If I go she will want to come with me. I'm not sure how she'll react when she sees her father with a new wife. She can have a fit and be out of control in seconds." She paused. "Of course I'll make sure she takes her medication. But we have never gotten along. She resents everything I ask her to do."

"Look on the bright side. You are a clever woman. You have proved that in business. With a little more confidence, a little more belief in yourself, you could find a way to stop your ex-husband."

"Stop him?" Joan looked at the counselor. When she spoke again, her voice was steel. "No one can stop Errol Swanson. Whatever he wants, he gets. He'll be that way until the day he dies."

Chapter 4

Manhattan
Wednesday, 4:00 P.M.

Frank O'Neill dropped his packed bag near the front door of his Greenwich Village apartment. Then he went back to his study to make sure he'd taken all his notes. He'd need them to work on the book. With any luck he should be able to get down a few hundred words before the plane landed in Chicago. "Now," he told himself, "do a quick check of the rest of apartment and be off."

In the bedroom he looked down at the unmade bed. It was here that he had first seduced Lara Swanson.

What a night it had been. His beautiful Lara had lain there naked, her arms stretched out for him. And he had come to her, loved her, and watched her fall gently asleep in his arms. He put his hand over his eyes as if to hold the memory.

Yes, she had loved him then, and for six months they had been together, the happiest time of his life. She was so responsive and giving. Just being near her excited him. Her body was round and soft, her breasts sweetly perfect. He sat on the bed and buried his head in his hands. Those nights, were they gone forever?

The house phone shrilled.

"It's Joe, the doorman. Your car has arrived to take you to the airport."

"I'm ready and on my way down. Tell him to wait, not circle the block."

The sleek black limousine double-parked at the curb surprised him. "This is style," he said, with a wink to Joe. "It looks like the old days at the network."

He walked to the trunk of the car, motioned the driver to unlock it, and stowed his bag. Then he opened the door and slid into the back seat.

"Good to see you again, Frank," the driver said. "Remember me? Andy? I used to drive you sometimes when you were doing those commentaries on that Sunday show. Now I'm the Swansons' driver."

Frank was pleased that the driver had recognized him.

"Of course I know you," Frank leaned forward and patted the man on the shoulder. "It's great you're here. I just didn't expect a network limo."

"Mrs. Swanson's assistant Jackie arranged it from Honolulu. She said I was to pick you up, get you to the airport on time, and provide you with refreshments." He laughed. "There's scotch, ice, and soda in the fridge."

Frank O'Neill opened the small refrigerator, for a moment feeling uncomfortable. Did Errol Swanson know he was getting this treatment? He laughed. What the hell, it was almost cocktail hour. He leaned forward and poured himself a drink. The whiskey trickled down his throat and immediately he felt relieved.

Frank sank back into the comforting leather of the seat and looked out the window. Third Avenue was gridlocked with traffic fighting to get to the Midtown Tunnel. Let Andy handle it. Frank would go back to thinking about Lara Swanson.

He'd been astounded when he received the invitation to the opening of the spa. Errol Swanson had fired him from the network in the most humiliating way, yet Lara was inviting him to the spa opening as her guest. Why? What did she want from him? Would she expect him to pretend there had never been anything between them? At first he'd told himself not to go.

Then came the request from the travel magazine to write a story on the spa. It would mean a good fee, and he needed the money. Going to the spa would also give him a chance to get more background for the unauthorized biography of Errol he was secretly writing. Still he hesitated. How would he manage being near Lara?

Then her e-mail had arrived. Frank slipped his hand into the inside breast pocket of his sports jacket and pulled out the printed copy of Lara's message. It was simple and direct. He had read it over and over.

"Frank, please come. I DESPERATELY need your help." That was not like Lara. She always seemed so confident. She kept her insecurities private.

He'd called her immediately.

"Yes," he assured her, "of course I'll come. But what's the problem? What do you mean by 'desperate'?"

Her reply was cool and formal. "Errol and I will be so glad to see to you." Then her voice faded to a whisper, as if someone were listening. "I can only say I need to discuss things with someone, and you are the only person I can trust. I will explain when you're here."

An assistant picked up to arrange the details.

What was the beautiful Lara so worried about? It had to be a problem with Errol. Frank had used every argument he knew to talk her out of the marriage, but she had been adamant that it was what she wanted.

"Errol loves me," she had told him the last time they had dinner together. "True, he's hurt people in the past. I know what he did to you, Frank. But he tells me that since we met, his life has taken on new meaning. And I believe him."

She had put her hand across the white tablecloth and touched his arm. "I truly believe he has changed."

"Do you really think that anything can change a man as evil as Errol is?" he asked.

"Yes, I do," she replied and withdrew her hand. "My philosophy teaches that love will conquer. With me, Errol Swanson will become a different person."

Frank shook his head. Lara was deluding herself. Errol Swanson would never change.

"And what about you, Lara?" he'd asked. "He's almost 30 years older than you. What kind of future will you have? Money, yes. But what else? You will never convince me that you are in love with him."

"I wouldn't marry a man I didn't love in some way. To me, Errol has been kind and loving, and he will give me the thing I want most."

Frank laughed.

"Oh, Lara, I know him too well. Yes, Errol will give you your spa. But you will pay a price for it. And in the end, it may not be worth it."

Now that she was in trouble, he thought again of his warning.

But if anyone paid the price, he would do his utmost to make sure it was Errol Swanson.

As he sat back, Andy caught his eye in the rearview mirror.

"You know I'm Mr. and Mrs. Swanson's personal driver," the man said as Frank dropped a couple of ice cubes into his glass.

"It was part of the deal he got when he left the network. A car and driver have to be available whenever he wants. It's okay by me. I pick them up at the airport when they arrive, and drive them around as long as they stay. That's how Mrs. Swanson arranged for me to drive you."

Andy laughed. "She's a honey. She's been mighty busy building that spa. She's told me a lot about it."

Frank made an encouraging noise, hoping Andy would keep talking. "Sounds like it's the most beautiful place in the world, but you know how women are, going on and on about things. You're headed for the opening?"

"Yes, I have to spend a day in Chicago doing some research, then it's off to Hawaii—and Lara's magnificent spa," Frank added with a tinge of sarcasm.

Lara had told him she'd dreamed about the spa since she was a teenager. Now she had it. And in a few months she would have Errol's baby. Yes, Errol was giving her everything she wanted.

So why should she be "desperate"?

Frank knew her better than most people did, yet he had no idea.

He had met Lara six years ago after she had returned from working in London as a nutritionist. She got a job with a group of New York doctors. She was so successful she had plans to start her own practice.

He was doing a story for a New York magazine on the growth of diet fads in the city. He had just been fired from the network, and he was pleased that the magazine had asked him to do the story as social commentary.

As he researched the diet story, Lara's name kept surfacing. She had a reputation for being bright and witty and having a perspective on the latest crazes.

From the moment they met he felt an immediate attraction, and she let him know that she returned it.

It was nothing she said, just the way she looked at him as she answered his questions, the casual brush of her hand across his as she reached for a glass of water.

She was intellectually impressive, too. She had graduated with an honors degree in science from the University of California. She had continued her studies in London. Then she had come home to work.

She'd looked sensational in the photograph they had run on the magazine cover.

He had asked her out to dinner to celebrate, and she had plied him with questions about the magazine, the other nutritionists he'd interviewed, and what he had learned about their work. She was an ambitious, competitive woman.

He left her at her apartment door that night knowing that he was already in love with her. In the next month, he had seen her many times. But, unlike his usual pattern with women, he didn't pressure her for sex. She was different. They became better friends each time. His love grew, and then finally he had taken her to bed.

Frank smiled to himself, and gently stroked his empty glass. Then he poured himself another drink.

The traffic on the expressway came to a halt and he noticed Andy eyeing him again in the rearview mirror.

"That's good scotch, isn't it?"

"Yes," Frank said. "The very best. I'm glad you bought it for me."

"It's Mr. Swanson's favorite. He likes single malt."

"Well, you can thank him for that, if nothing else. Mr. Swanson is not what you'd call a friend of mine, but I will drink his scotch." There seemed to be nowhere he could hide from Errol Swanson.

Andy was curious. "I heard that when Mr. Swanson fired you that Sunday, just as you were about to go on air, he locked you out of your office so you couldn't get your things. Everyone talked about it."

The anger of that day came back to Frank.

"Everyone *should* have been talking about it! Swanson is an ab-solute bastard. He's a swine. Just remember that when you're driv-ing him around to fancy places."

How could Lara have married Swanson? He felt the jealousy that whiskey couldn't dull. He finished his drink in one gulp, re-membering bitterly how shocked he'd been at Lara's initial de-cision to date Errol. He had pleaded with her not to become involved with that lousy, evil man.

The traffic started to move. Andy went on, "Maybe you don't like him because he fired you."

"He fired me because he didn't like some of my political views—and because he was interested in my girlfriend. Lara Swanson was my girlfriend. I tried to protect her from him."

"How did she and Swanson meet?" Andy asked.

"He saw her photo on a magazine cover for a story I did. He tracked her down pretty easily."

"So in a way, you're responsible for the marriage, right?" Andy laughed. "You can only blame yourself."

"Goddamnit, that's a hell of a way to put it. That man fired hundreds of people in what he called a budget cut, and he moved in on the woman I love."

"Sorry, sorry," said Andy. "I was just joking."

"It's no joke. All Swanson cared about was power and the size of the bonus he got," Frank continued. "He didn't care about good programming. Damn it, I'm a writer. A good one. A prize-winner. And he threw me out!

"He destroys whatever the fuck he touches. He's an evil man. That sums him up."

Andy started to reply, but Frank stopped him.

"Just drive."

Frank rested his forehead on his hand and stared at the empty whiskey glass. The last time he'd seen Lara had been a few hours after she'd told him that Errol had agreed to build the spa in Hawaii and they were getting married. Frank had still been furious when Lara arrived at his apartment later that night in response to his demands.

"You are nothing but a manipulating bitch," he had shouted as he threw her on the bed and held her there. "I won't lose you. Not to him."

"No, you never will," she had whispered as she arched her body up to his. "I'll marry him, but I'll always feel love for you."

Shaking his head, Frank dismissed the memory. He had to put Lara behind him.

"This is the last time I run to her," he said to himself. "I want her out of my life."

But not until he had finished with Errol.

Chapter 5

The Big Island
Wednesday, 1:30 P.M.

Lara was waiting at the entrance to greet Sonya and Perry when they arrived at the spa. When the manager said he would escort Sonya to her bungalow, she spoke sharply. "You look after Perry. I want to explain to Sonya about my philosophy in building the spa."

The manager and Perry moved away and Sonya followed Lara. Despite the apparent warmth of her welcome, Sonya saw that Lara's back was stiff with anger and her knuckles, on the hand clutching the key, were white.

"Of course the spa is luxurious. But it is my concept of luxury. Mine and no one else's," Lara said, pausing beside a flowering shrub. She held up one of its bell-shaped purple flowers, bent her head, and drank in the fragrance. Then she offered it to Sonya to smell. "The Hawaiian climate is perfect; almost any plant will flourish here."

As they walked, she brushed aside Sonya's questions about the problems of building an opulent spa at such a remote spot on the island. She focused instead on the natural setting. "She's smart," thought Sonya. "The flowers, the shrubs, the beach will look great on video."

Lara seemed to read her mind. She stopped again. "You will be able to get beautiful pictures everywhere you go. Look at this plant. It's a frangipani and its flowers are precious. We thread them to make our traditional leis." She motioned to Sonya. "Smell them. They are so sweet. I wanted fragrant plants lining the paths so that every step our guests take is a welcoming one. Believe me, this is true luxury, not gaudy gilt taps in bathrooms."

Sonya adjusted the bag that was weighing on her shoulder so she could smell the flower. Its scent was intoxicating.

Sonya said, "It is amazing. I'm relaxed already."

"That's exactly the response I want," Lara said, her voice quickening with pleasure. "Our guests must feel the power of nature the moment they arrive. Nothing is more relaxing than beauty. And true beauty comes from nature. That's an important part of my philosophy."

Sonya returned to her original concerns. "How did you get it done so quickly?"

Lara smiled. "I began working on it the moment we became engaged. After all, this spa was Errol's wedding gift to me. Of course, my love of Hawaii started a long time before I met Errol. It began in one of my former lives. Long before my rebirth in this body, I once lived here as a princess, the daughter of a Hawaiian chief when the Polynesians first came to the Islands. I have known this since I was a child. I am related to the great goddess Pele."

Sonya found it difficult to accept Lara's ideas. She looked away.

"You are embarrassed, Sonya. Don't be. I'm used to people finding my beliefs unusual. But I think reincarnation is just one part of the endless cycle of love. I hope you will come to understand this while you are here."

Sonya tried to imagine Errol Swanson married to this woman, but it was impossible. They seemed to be complete opposites. Then again, she told herself, that could be the attraction between them.

Lara continued, "I've studied the history of the islands for years. I never knew why I was I attracted to Hawaii, but the reason lay deep inside my consciousness. This spa is something I have been planning for centuries, through many of my former lives. It is a way to heal the brutal suffering of my ancestors.

"I am driven to do what I do, and I will continue doing it while there is breath in my lungs."

Sonya changed the subject. "Did your parents understand your fascination with Hawaii?"

Lara laughed. "As a child I ignored Cinderella for Hawaiian myths. I guess that was pretty hard to take. My father, who is English and an accountant, used to joke about my dreams. He called me 'Pele's princess.'

"He doesn't admit it, but I know he is amazed at what I have done. He'll come to the spa sometime after the opening. He doesn't want to be here at the same time as my mother. That makes me so very sad. For me, family is everything. I believe love of family extends outward endlessly to the family of mankind."

"So your mother will be here?"

Lara gave a half nod. "I'm not sure. She's unpredictable, but she's creative and full of fun. If you meet her you'll adore her, as I do."

Sonya considered Lara's belief in family love as a possible angle for her story, something that could be threaded through the interviews she planned to set up with Errol's relatives. It was intriguing to think of what this collection of ex-wives and grown children might have to say about Errol Swanson and love.

"When did you first visit Hawaii?" Sonya asked.

"When I was a teenager I came with a school group. I loved the mystery of the Islands so much I deliberately missed the plane home. I guess you could call me a problem teenager. My mother had to come and bring me back. I begged to go to college here, but my father insisted that I study first in California and then in London. He considered the British educational standards higher. He told me I could come back after I graduated.

"I'm an only child and I was spoiled. In my father's eyes I could do no wrong. I think he would have given in and moved to Hawaii if he had found a job here. Anything to make his sixteen-year-old daughter happy."

Sonya doubted that Errol was as devoted to her needs. She asked, "How does Errol feel about being here?"

She sensed Lara's hesitation before she answered, "Oh, he's happy for me."

Then she quickly pointed ahead. "Look, there is your bungalow. It's hard to see because it's completely closed in with shrubs. In the front garden is a statue of one of our ancient Hawaiian gods. I have the staff leave fresh flowers at its feet every morning. But if you decide to pick some for a little ceremony of your own, I think it will give you an unexpected pleasure."

Lara stood back and let Sonya enter the front garden.

"It's really lovely," she said in true admiration.

"And that's not all." Lara opened the door and quickly walked through the living room. She slid open another door, then stepped back to allow Sonya through.

"Here is the back garden, with its own beautiful pool, a plunge pool, small but deep. This sanctuary is not meant for swimming but for floating, relaxing, looking at the stars and dreaming. I got the idea when Errol took me to Bali on our first holiday together."

Sonya walked to the side of the pool. It was about six feet wide and about twice as long—just enough to swim a few strokes. Its blue tiles reflected the light and made it seem much bigger. A scattering of white flowers floated on the water.

"A plunge pool is a way to free yourself," Lara encouraged her. "Take off your clothes and plunge naked into the pool. The water will caress you. It's like going back to the womb."

"How deep it is?"

"About four and a half feet. It is quite safe. Do a plunge when you get up in the morning and each time you come back to the bungalow. It's addictive, I promise you."

"Just make sure the gate is locked," laughed Sonya.

Lara joined in. "There is no gate in the back—there are bamboo fences among the shrubs. Don't be concerned. It's against the Polynesian culture to intrude."

Lara walked back inside. "Now I'll show you my magic." She pressed several switches and the blinds around the room rose slowly, revealing the muted green décor of the living room.

"It *is* magic." Sonya was surprised at its beauty. "It's as if the colors have been washed by moonlight."

"Thank you," said Lara. "When I started I decided the sea would be my inspiration for the colors. Not the blue of the ocean, but that myriad of colors you see as the waves break on the shore. We used more than a dozen different shades of green." She laughed with real pleasure.

"Now to other matters. I have given you a two-bedroom bunga-low, as I know you want to be with Donna's makeup artist. You each have a bathroom, but you share the living room."

Sonya looked around. "I'm sure we won't have any trouble. There seem to be plenty of surfaces for the TV equipment."

"Yes, I think you will find everything you will need. If you don't, please call." She paused as she moved to the door. "I am looking forward to your story. I hope you will tell Donna Fuller you are happy here. You know it is important that people understand that my philosophy is reflected in my spa."

Sonya was amazed at how easily Lara had managed to make a case for a positive story.

"Yes, I will tell her just how I feel. Thank you for your hospital-ity and the walk through the grounds."

Lara turned then stepped back into the room. "Just one more thing," she said. "I have a list of the staff for you in case you want information and I am not available."

She picked up a folder from the desk and handed Sonya a list of names. "These people are responsible for different areas of the spa. You can call any one of them. They all know you are here and what you are doing. But the person who will be most useful to you is Jackie Olsen. She is my right hand. She knows everything about the place and will help you with anything you need."

Sonya looked at the list. Lara had underlined Jackie Olsen's name and written in a cell number for her.

"I see," she said, "but she's listed here as the director of the ma-rina."

"Yes, I know. She insists on calling herself the captain of our boat. But there is nothing Jackie can't do or fix. I don't know what

I would do without her." She gave Sonya a quick smile and walked to the door.

Sonya said, "So I should call her, rather than the manager?"

"Exactly." Lara was firm. "Jackie knows where I am every minute. Now just relax, unpack, and explore." Lara smiled again and left.

"That's a practiced smile," thought Sonya as she watched her go. "It's impossible to tell how sincere she is."

Sonya told herself she was here to work. Sure, it was nice to be surrounded by luxury, but she needed a room that functioned as an office. That exquisite lacquered desk and cupboard next to it made her anxious. They looked too precious. Could she pile her tapes, computer, and other gear on it?

She went to the desk and experimentally put her hand under its heavy top. A computer table swung out. Perfect for her laptop. She opened a cupboard door, revealing a laser printer, complete with fax and scanner, next to a stack of printer paper. Lara had been a working woman, too. She knew how to get an office together.

Sonya went into the dressing area, where the porter had placed her suitcase. The symphony of greens continued here and in the adjacent bathroom. Even the coat hangers were the same pale celadon as the inside of the closet. The bathroom had the biggest shower Sonya had ever encountered, but the real luxury was the small fridge on the counter next to the sink. Inside was the makeup collection that Lara had designed for the spa.

It was worth a try. Sonya reached in, took out the cleansing cream, and smoothed it over her face. She wiped it off with cool wet tissue, then applied the protection cream. She checked her face in the mirror. Not only did she feel better, she looked it. This was going to be fun, especially when Sabrina arrived.

She grinned to herself. Maybe there was something to be said for the life of luxury. She unpacked, then stripped and plunged into the pool. It was as wonderful as Lara had promised. Sonya decided to show her gratitude by gathering a few flowers and laying them at the statue's feet. It would be a sweet thing to do. And considering how tough the television business was, it couldn't hurt to be on the right side of the gods. There was no doubt she could use a little help dealing with her executive producer, Matt Richards.

She climbed out of the pool, dried herself, and put on a light linen robe. Then she went into the front garden to pay homage to the goddess. The flowers that the staff had left that morning were wilting in the sun.

"Pele needs fresh blossoms," she said aloud to the statue as she tossed the old ones to the ground. She plucked a hibiscus and placed it at the goddess's feet.

"Let's hope your offering will prevent Pele's new lava flow from doing damage." Perry's voice startled her. "Kilauea is erupting."

Sonya felt embarrassed at being caught. "The volcano? Erupting? How do you know?"

"The manager told me when he showed me around my bungalow. I want to get some shots of it. If we can't use them, maybe the news department can."

"Okay." Sonya was glad. The shots would certainly add drama to the piece. "Just let me throw my jeans on and I'll be with you." Perry followed her into the bungalow and relaxed into a lounge chair while she went to the bedroom to change.

"That manager is weird," Perry called to her. "Errol hired him, but he thinks Errol was a fool to invest his money here. The locals believe the spa won't make it. Two others have failed here before. And guess why? The land is cursed."

"Cursed?"

"It goes something like this. An ancient warrior chief invaded the island and was betrayed by his son. As he died, he cursed the place. The curse won't be lifted until the old chief's bones are taken back to his home island. But no one knows where the bones are hidden. How's that for a story?"

Sonya came out of the bedroom, pulling her hair into a ponytail. "Maybe there is some truth to it. For all its beauty, the island has real force. It makes me feel like—like we're a long way from Manhattan."

Sonya went to the bar and got a bottle of water. She took a long drink.

"Have you settled in?" she asked Perry.

Perry complained, "All I have is a bedroom about half the size of yours. It's the usual stupid approach. The working guy with the equipment never gets the big space. There aren't enough desks or tables to put things on. There was nowhere to store the tapes, so I had to put them on the floor near the bathroom door.

"Then the water overflowed when I took a shower. Well, bottom line, it flooded the bedroom floor and the cartons of videotape."

"Are the tapes okay? They were still in their plastic wraps?"

"Yeah, we have all the tapes and the staff has mopped up. But the cartons are ruined. I'll have to get new ones to ship the tapes back."

"That shouldn't be a problem. Just let me get my bag."

For some reason she felt uneasy. While she'd agreed to shoot the volcanic eruption, she also wanted to find out what was really going on at the spa. She already had too many unanswered questions.

Chapter **6**

Tracey Swanson had never felt so vulnerable, and for no good reason. Her friend would arrive from the airport at any minute.

Roger McCoy, that giant of a man, had insisted on flying to Mexico to see her. He would protect her, and her money from Errol. After all, Roger was the most brilliant trust attorney in Chicago.

Tracey sat on the beige silk sofa, trying to relax in the golden light that filled the room. Trembling, she picked up one of the antique tapestry cushions and pressed it to her chest, feeling her heart race.

She was being ridiculous. Roger was a good friend as well as her attorney. He would be aghast if he knew how stressed she was at the thought of seeing him. She must stop the panic and talk over her problems calmly.

Roger would give his point of view firmly, but he wouldn't force her to accept it. He never had. And anyway, whatever he suggested, there was no need to act immediately. She was not 70 yet, and she was well and strong enough to remain in Mexico for at least a few more years. All she was doing was getting her plans in order.

Dropping the pillow, Tracey picked up the invitation she'd received from Errol and Lara Swanson to join their family celebration in Hawaii. Receiving it had brought things to a head. Now she had an opportunity to rebuild the bond she had once had with Errol, a bond that was essential for her plans.

Roger had suggested at their last meeting that she buy into a retirement community. He wanted her to settle in Chicago where she could be close to the best in medical treatment, to her family, and, of course, to him. She knew that as of now he didn't mind his quick trips to see her in Mexico, but the time would come when he, too, would want to retire.

Tracey stood up. She must be at the entrance to welcome Roger, to show him how much she appreciated his being there.

She walked to the fireplace and stared above it, into the huge mirror with a carved gilt frame that was the highlight of the room's Spanish décor. Her reflection in the antique glass pleased her. Her skin was smooth under the makeup and her eyes were as clear as they had ever been. The fitted linen jacket that matched her beige jeans emphasized her slimness.

"The weight I lost in the hospital makes me look younger," she told herself.

She glanced anxiously at her watch. She had sent her car and driver to collect Roger at the Acapulco airport. The plane was on time; he would be here at any moment.

She was lucky to have him and the care he gave so willingly. The trust fund he managed for her was nowhere near as big as most he handled.

Donald Simpson, the married man she had given her life to, had been Roger's best friend. She touched the heavy gold chain at her neck. Donald had given it to her on the tenth anniversary of their meeting. She had worn it every day since.

She and Donald had been sitting close together in this very room when he told her that with Roger's help he had set up a trust to give her an income for life.

"You can expect trouble from my daughters if I die before you," he told her that sunny morning. "They still resent my love for you. They may try to prevent you from inheriting anything. But don't worry, I've taken good care of them. This will be *your* money. You are to do anything you like with it."

Strange that now she had nothing to fear from his family, only her own. "Donald, how I wish you were here," she said, speaking out loud as if he were still sitting beside her. "But you always said to follow my gut feeling, and that's what I'll do."

No matter what happened, she wanted her niece, Christy, to have enough income to support her for the rest of her life. She had deserted Christy once; she would not do it again. Even if Errol arranged to have Christy declared mentally incompetent, Tracey would make certain he could not touch a cent of the money Tracey was going to leave her. Roger must set up an unbreakable trust to prevent it.

Yes, Roger McCoy would see to it all. But changing her will was only one of the reasons she'd called him.

She heard the car coming up the long, curving drive. She went quickly down the hall and was standing in the doorway when Roger climbed out of the back seat. He stood for a moment, looking around. His handsome head was bent to one side, the usual quizzical look on his face.

She smiled. He was doing as he always did, making a quick assessment of the condition of the place.

"Roger," she called, "I'm here, in the doorway."

"I can't see you; you're standing in the shade," he replied in his calm, measured voice. He got his briefcase out of the car and started up the wide steps that led to the veranda. Roger was dressed conservatively, as usual. His rimless glasses perched on his nose; his graying hair was parted at the side. Tracey went to greet him and stretched up to kiss him on the cheek.

"Oh, Roger, you are so solid," she said with relief. "I don't think I have ever been more pleased to see you."

He set down his briefcase and put both his hands on her shoulders, holding her at arm's length.

"As an attorney I'm always glad to hear that, and as your friend even happier," he said. "Now let me look at you. You're thinner than ever. How much weight have you lost?"

"Only a little. From the allergy to the anesthetic."

"You were in the coma for how long? A day?"

"Yes, but that's behind me." She drew a long, deep breath. She had to be calm.

"It's the panic attacks that frighten me. I had one just before you arrived. They started a few days after I left the hospital. They come on so suddenly for no reason. I'm afraid something dreadful is about to happen."

She moved closer to him and rested her head on his shoulder. He put his arm around her waist and led her through the doorway.

"Come now, Tracey," he said. "It's not like you to be so upset. Let's go inside so you can tell me everything."

Signaling to the maid to bring coffee and sandwiches, Tracey led Roger to the small sitting room at the top of the stairs. It had a long view of her garden, and was where she was most comfortable. It would be easier for them both to talk there.

"It's so good of you to come," she said as they sat together on the sofa. "Don was right when he told me I could always rely on you. You have become the mainstay of my life, the only person I can really talk to." She paused for a moment. "I told you on the phone that Errol's invitation to the spa opening has brought back all the old family problems. Thinking about them has exhausted me. In fact, it may be the reason I get these wretched panic attacks."

He was sympathetic, as she expected.

"Tracey, I have a feeling you need rest more than advice. First of all, you are being hard on yourself. I'm not surprised you're confused. You knew Errol when he was an ambitious young man. Now he's an aging multimillionaire starting a new life with a trophy bride years younger than he is. It amazes me that she wants you at the opening of their spa."

"I tell myself that the invitation arrived at an opportune moment. And there are good reasons for me to go. But I'm afraid of Errol. There is so much bad blood between us."

"Then don't go."

"But Roger, you know they are the only family I have." Tracey paused, thinking back over her life. "I would like to be part of their lives again. As I've told you, I wasn't fond of Joan when Errol married her. But times have changed. Her father controlled her—her money and her opinions. He is long dead, and Joan today must be a different woman."

"And you really care about Christy." Roger paused as the maid entered the room with a tray and placed it on the table. He waited while Tracey poured two cups of coffee, then picked up a sand-wich and bit into it. "Is she really the cause of the bad blood be-tween you and Errol?"

Tracey sipped her coffee. "There were so many things. It all hap-pened so long ago, and it seems ridiculous that it mattered so much."

Roger went on. "I know you were raised together as brother and sister, but remember, you're only his aunt."

"That's right, but my parents died when I was seven, and Errol's mother took me in. Errol was only two, so while I lost my parents, I gained a baby brother." She looked at Roger and smiled. "Yes, I was devoted to my kid brother, as I was proud to call him."

"I never really heard all the details, but I remember you saying he had a lot of difficulty with his father."

"Yes, and since the invitation arrived I've done nothing but go over the past. The battles in that home were fierce. Both father and son were strong-willed, very much like each other. It must have been terrible for both of them." She paused. "Roger, I was desper-ate to get away from them. To have my own life. I moved out as soon as I graduated from business school and got a job."

"What was the last time you were really close to Errol?" he asked.

"A long time ago, when he was about 19. He'd had a bitter argu-ment with his father, who wanted Errol to study dentistry and eventually take over his practice. Errol refused and moved out."

"He stayed with you?"

"Yes, for a few weeks. When things settled down he moved back home. He had to; I couldn't afford to support him. But in those weeks we were closer than we had ever been. I had a tiny apart-ment with a closet kitchen, but every night I cooked dinner for him. Afterward we would go to the movies or walk along the lakeside, discussing our dreams."

"You sound as if were his friend. Do you really think there's such a problem between the two of you?"

"Well, I was angry with him for marrying Joan. Back then, I thought there were many good reasons against the marriage. He was too young, he had to finish college, the crowd he ran with was anti-Semitic and Joan was Jewish. And then they had the twins. Problem after problem."

"Still, he stayed with them and got a job good enough to support them. Didn't that please you?"

"Oh, yes, he did well enough. But I think the reason they stayed together was Joan's family. They had the toy store and she was always running there. Her family gave her the financial and emotional support she needed."

"You told me once that Joan forced Errol to marry her. Do you still believe that?"

Tracey pressed her hands together and shook her head.

"I was wrong, so wrong about many things." she said. "The truth was that Errol manipulated Joan into marrying him. He thought she was rich and he expected her family to support them. He was just as desperate to get away from his father's rages as I was."

"And he didn't stop to consider that she was Jewish?"

Tracey sighed. "Roger, can you remember what it was like to be young and foolish? The anti-Semitism became a problem when Joan's family insisted the twins be raised as Jews. He resented it terribly, but he wouldn't let it show. Their money was too important."

Roger placed his coffee cup back on the tray and poured himself a refill. "How did you get along with Errol after he married?"

"I didn't. He was always working. But I spent as much time as I could with Joan and the twins. Joan favored Craig and I became close to Christy. She was a withdrawn child and I looked for some way to give her a little confidence. When I saw she had a natural talent for swimming, I encouraged her. I've told you about the weekends I spent taking her to kids' swimming carnivals, but I never told you that Joan hated them. She constantly used the excuse of having to work in the toy shop to avoid coming."

"What about Errol? Did he go?"

"Only once that I remember. It was a district competition and very important to Christy. By qualifying she proved she was champion material. I insisted both her parents come. Errol looked like the up-and-coming young executive in his white pants and tailored shirt, but Joan was clearly out of place.

"When Joan offered Errol a glass of her mother's homemade lemonade, to toast Christy's success, he knocked it out of her hand and stormed away. We didn't see him again that afternoon. Joan was upset and Christy was devastated." Tracey sighed.

Roger said, "Bad as that must have been, it's not worse than what many families go through."

"I know," Tracey admitted, "but it seemed to have a great effect on Christy. Looking back, I realize it was not long after that that she began to act oddly."

Tracey stood and walked to the window. "She was still a young adult when she was diagnosed, after she was arrested for shoplifting in a department store. Oh, Roger, I've always kept that secret before." Tracey looked at Roger. "When she was questioned by the police she said her voices had told her to do it. She was hospitalized, given drugs, and then allowed to go home. Errol refused to deal with her problem. He didn't visit her in hospital, wouldn't go to the meetings with her psychiatrist, just turned his back on her.

"Christy has had to fight too many battles in her life. I want to spare her any more, you understand?" She shook her head as if to rid herself of the memories. "I'm sure Donald would agree with me."

Roger joined her at the window and put his hand on her shoulder.

"Now that I understand how fragile Christy is, you have my word that I will protect her," he said. "Tell me more about this invitation from Errol."

"Errol would never want to have us all there unless he has an ulterior motive. This invitation must be his wife's idea. I read she is a spiritual woman who calls herself 'a guru of love.' "

"You can't be serous," interrupted Roger.

"Yes, yes, I am serious. But I don't care what the rumors are. I must go there to see what this marriage will mean for Christy's future."

Roger shook his head. "Surely it's not wise to visit Errol right now. Better wait until things calm down. Find out more about the wife and then go."

Tracey felt her chest tighten again. She forced herself to face the reality that it wasn't the trip was causing her panic attacks. It was what she had to do when she arrived.

"Roger, you've helped me make up my mind," she said. "I want to go. I want to be there with the whole family. This is the time for us all to be together."

"But, Tracey . . ."

"I'm going. Don't worry, I'll take Ramos with me." She hesitated for a moment, deciding what would sound plausible. "He is young and strong and takes good care of me. Now, let's have lunch and get on with our discussion of Christy's trust fund."

"Ramos?" Roger stroked his chin. Tracey recognized the gesture, it meant that Roger was not happy with her decision. "Do you really think that's wise? With his history? Surely it would be better to take your maid?"

"No, Ramos it is. I've already discussed it with him and he is eager to go. He'll be discreet. He'll stay in the background and do exactly what I ask." She laughed. "I'll tell them that I have been ill and need him to care for me. I may really need someone to push a wheelchair if my knee acts up."

Roger shook his head. "I don't think it is wise to go, and I think if you take Ramos you are asking for trouble. I just don't trust him."

"Oh, Roger, don't be such an old stick-in-the-mud. I trust him. And so do you. You've known him almost as long as I have."

"I give up. I'll say one thing, you may be a foolish woman, but you're also a brave one."

Chapter 7

Tomas Swanson placed the gift on his mother's desk, stood back, and smiled, his face glowing with pride and pleasure.

"I know I'll get a scolding for buying this. But don't start on me until you've opened it," he said. "I think it is absolutely you. I bought it because I love you, Mother, and to say I appreciate how you always help me."

"Oh, Tomas," Margot Didot said, looking into the blue eyes of her handsome son, "this is too much. You must stop buying me gifts. You must start saving your money. Or at least start spending it on yourself."

Even as she spoke, she reached for her ebony paper knife and eagerly slit open the silver wrapping paper.

Tomas perched himself on the side of the desk, then bent over and kissed her on the forehead. She caught a whiff of his after-shave lotion and smiled. He had splashed on the spicy men's fragrance she had just introduced under her Margot Didot label.

"And," he said, "I wanted to buy you something to say thank you for agreeing to go with me to Hawaii for the opening. I know it's not going to be easy for you.

"Being able to confront Dad face-to-face means so much to me. He always has an excuse to avoid talking on the phone. But if I am standing in the same room, he has to listen to me. He has to acknowledge that I am gay and accept me for what I am." His voice trembled as he added, "I am 19, and I want some sort of relationship with my father."

Margo was silent. The box under the silver wrapping paper was sturdily constructed and covered in deep blue silk. It was obviously custom-made for the object inside. Tomas's gift was precious and probably antique.

She placed her surprisingly strong hands on the box, the dark burgundy nails filed to make her square-tipped fingers look longer.

"Tomas," she sighed, "I don't want to be cruel, but you must give up the idea of getting your father's affection. He won't let you be close to him. It's too late. He'll never admit he has a gay son. It would be an admission of weakness. I'm happy we're going together, but you mustn't dream about a reconciliation with your father.

"Just tell yourself that we're going to Hawaii on the advice of my attorney. That is the truth."

"Yes, Mother, I know, but—"

"The attorney says it will show goodwill on my part. If we work out a deal, I'll use the money your father owes me to bolster the business. Money is what this trip is about. Nothing else."

"I don't want to go over all that again." Tomas tried to force the pain out of his voice. "Just open the box and see what's inside. It's a treasure, I promise you."

Margot looked at her son and sighed. "It is my fault. I tried too hard to protect you from his violence."

"Oh, stop the guilt trip," Tomas interjected. "Just open your present."

Inside the box lay a gleaming crystal caviar dish on a heavy silver stand. The pure lines spelled the most sought-after design style of the twentieth century, Art Deco.

"It's an Otto Grabow original, isn't it?" Margot held up the dish, turning it and examining its shape against the light. "It is superb. It's impossible to find these today. Any museum would die for it. Where on earth did you find it?

"And, Tomas, tell me the truth. How much did you pay for it?"

"Those two secrets I'll keep," laughed Tomas, "but you can imagine my joy when it was offered to me. It was pure chance. But I'm not telling you about it. At least not now."

Margot Didot Swanson had been collecting elegant Art Deco crystal since she'd first gone to Paris as a student. Her much-admired collection was the theme for the décor in her sleek Manhattan apartment.

"Well, you'd better not tell your secrets to your father when you're confronting him face to face," she laughed. "If he finds out how much you make as a model, he'll stop your allowance altogether."

Tomas laughed back at her, swooped down, and picked up the box.

"I'm going home. I'll take this with me, to serve you caviar from it before dinner."

As he reached the door, he turned and blew her a kiss. "I'm going to buy some beluga. Your Otto Grabow deserves the best and so do you. Just don't be too late, Mother."

Margot Didot Swanson sat for a moment, thinking about how happy her son was and what awaited him in Hawaii. She rose and moved restlessly around her large office—the office Errol had planned for her when she started her business.

"It must be large and it must be a corner office," he said. "That spells power."

So she had crowded the design and fabrics rooms into tiny spaces at the back.

"Appearances are more important than the comfort of your staff. You can rent more space as the business grows. What is important is the image you create. You must start by giving the impression of stability and success."

When she protested, he became angry. "You keep telling me it's business sense that counts in fashion today, not creativity. So shut up and just do what I say."

He had been right in so many ways. He had insisted she arrange every award or honor she had received on the wall behind her desk.

"They will frame you and impress your visitors."

She walked back to her desk and looked at the awards. There were now so many: statues, diplomas, plaques, all carefully displayed on stands or in frames. And even a Golden IDA Award from the International Designers Association.

Errol had been at her side when she received many of them, including the IDA. Novelli had presented it. How proud she had been, how happy and how grateful to Errol. And, she remembered, how Errol had lapped up the publicity she brought him. Errol Swanson wanted to be the star, no one else.

Margot was sure he would also find a way to be the star in Hawaii, no matter how beautiful or clever his new wife. Errol was a master at working the press—just how much to say, just how to maneuver himself into every photo, every video.

She sat in her chair and picked up the pile of sketches her assistant had left on her desk. This was the most exciting part of creating fashion—playing with ideas for the materials she had chosen for the season.

But it was no use. She closed her eyes and listened to the silence of the office. She had known Tomas was gay almost from the moment she gave birth. It had never mattered to her.

Now, at 19, he faced a sure future in the world of art or design. He was everything she wished him to be. He could have whatever else he wanted, but not his father's love.

She had tried to improve their relationship over the years, but Errol insisted it was her genes, not his, that had produced a homosexual. She had almost laughed out loud, wondering what her macho geologist father would have thought.

How often, in those unhappy years of her marriage, had she accepted Errol's abuse? Protecting Tomas had been her only goal. She avoided conflict with Errol until the divorce, hanging on to get what she wanted: total control of her business and custody of Tomas.

She felt the nagging guilt come back. Had she been wrong to make so many excuses for Errol's violent behavior? Perhaps if she hadn't tried to be so protective, father and son could have built a better relationship.

How many times had she said, "Your father is a brilliant businessman. He has a company to run. He just can't spend that much time with us."

She told herself that was in the past.

Now she needed the money Errol owed her. It belonged to her and she would take her attorney's advice and sue Errol if she had to.

But Tomas still came first. She had to make sure he could protect himself if Errol became violent. There was only one way to do that.

Margot walked to the étagère on the opposite side of the room, knelt on the floor, and pulled out the heavy books that lined the bottom shelf.

Tucked behind them was a rosewood box. She took it to her desk, pressed a hidden button, and slid open the flat lid.

Inside lay a revolver, a Colt that had belonged to her geologist father. He had taken it for protection when he traveled into rough country. She picked it up and examined it carefully. Her father had been a cautious man, and he had taught her about guns.

She put it back with the bullets. Carefully she closed the box.

She had planned to give it to Tomas on his twenty-first birthday, but now was the right time. She would ship it to Hawaii to avoid security at the airport. It would be waiting for them when they arrived.

Tomas was still young and vulnerable, but she would protect him whatever happened.

Chapter 8

The Big Island
Wednesday, 4:00 P.M.

Sonya wiped the perspiration from her forehead, her impatience growing with each step as she trudged up the path behind Perry.

If only Pele had had the grace to wait a few days before erupting. And if only Sonya hadn't agreed so readily with Perry's demand to shoot the stream of molten lava.

In the three hours since their plane had made its bumpy landing on the Big Island, the only work she had done was to unpack her laptop.

She glared at Perry's sweaty back. It was his fault.

Perry knew better than anyone else the amount of work she had to do, but he had gone ahead and arranged for them to get to the eruption even though the eruption had nothing whatever to do with their spa story.

Being a TV producer meant more than traveling around with a cameraman. That was the easy part. She had to set up schedules, do preinterviews, make lists of questions for Donna, and locate the best shots of the spa. Finally, she had to do an outline of the feature and lay it at the ungrateful feet of her condescending executive producer, Matt Richards. All in two days.

As often happened, Perry read her thoughts.

"Boy, are we lucky. Pele is really turning it on. She's been quiet for months and now she's spewing out lava as hot as it comes. It's something I've always wanted to shoot. The video should be spectacular, and the park's open 24 hours so we can work as late as we want."

Sonya laughed. Count your blessings, girl. The video would be spectacular. Perry was the greatest. Let him have his fun. They'd get the piece together. They always did.

"For a girl from Minnesota, this is hard going," she said. "Just drop any ideas you have of spending the night with Madam Pele. She's too hot to handle."

She followed Perry to the lawn that surrounded the main building. The glare was enough to give her a headache. The sunshine pricked her shoulders and legs. She took her sunglasses from her bag and grabbed a tissue to wipe the perspiration from her face.

A tall park ranger, trim and neat in a pristine uniform, stood beside a Jeep with a driver. As Perry approached he opened the back door.

"Hi, I'm Joe Robertson," he called in a flat, careful voice. "If you'll get in, sir, I'll explain the procedures as we go."

Sonya fumed silently. Either the ranger hadn't seen her or he assumed that because Perry was a man, he was the boss. How often had this happened to her?

She caught up with Perry and stood beside him.

"Hi, Joe," she said, extending her hand. "I'm Sonya Iverson and I'm the producer on this feature.

"Perry," she turned to him with a grin, "sit in the front as you always do. You'll have more room for the camera."

Joe turned his attention to Sonya. He seemed to be sizing her up. Then he shook his head.

"You're coming with us?"

"Is there a problem?" What was the matter with this guy?

Joe dropped his head. Then, almost as if reading from the park regulations, he said, "I advise you against wearing that outfit. At the very least you should have your legs covered. If you slip you could cut yourself badly. The hardened lava is as sharp as glass and cuts from it don't heal easily."

Sonya ran her hand over her shoulder and glanced down at her bare legs and feet. He looked like a stuffed shirt, but he had a job to do and he was doing it.

"Thanks, Joe, I feel the heat badly and was trying to keep cool. I'll change. Give me five minutes." Joe nodded in apparent relief.

She liked him. There was something pleasant about being told what to do by a good-looking man in uniform. Some of Perry's enthusiasm started to rub off on her.

As she hurried off, he turned to Perry. "You'd better make sure you have enough batteries. Flat batteries are a problem on the lava fields. The heat absorbs their power fast."

Joe was sitting in the back seat when she hurried back. He nodded his approval and she felt foolishly pleased. Now, in her jeans and white shirt, she was one of the troops and ready for action. She climbed in beside him. "You really are on top of things. Thanks for warning Perry about the batteries."

He put his hand on her chin and turned her face toward his. He looked into her eyes. Sonya felt herself blush; this was not the time or place to start a flirtation. She blinked and looked away.

"You're wearing contact lenses, aren't you?"

"Well, yes, I always do. Is it a problem?"

"It depends how hot it gets. Many people who wear contacts find their eyes are irritated by the heat and the sulfur fumes. You'll need drops to protect them."

"I have some in my bag." She searched until she found her small emergency pack. She felt like a little girl when she held the drops up to reassure him. "Sonya," she told herself, "stop trying to please him. Get back to business."

"How hot does it get?"

"It depends. The problem is not just the heat, it's also the wind. With the wind at my back I've stood a yard from the flow and felt comfortable. The next day at the same spot but with a wind from the other direction I felt as though I'd burst into flames."

Perry arrived carrying two battery bricks and looking worried.

"I put them on fast charge the moment I got to the bungalow. I just hope we'll have enough power to get everything we want."

Sonya leaned forward and patted the driver on the shoulder. "Let's go."

Perry turned to speak to them over the rumble of the jeep on the rough road. "How often does Kilauea erupt?" he asked.

Sonya reached for her notebook. "Yes, Joe, give us the facts."

"Madame Pele is a bit of a tease. The lava from Kilauea can stop flowing for months and then suddenly start up again. It also shifts from place to place. Sometimes it forms an underground tube and goes straight into the ocean so we never see it."

"But not this time?" Sonya heard a catch of anxiety in her voice. She didn't want Perry to be disappointed, and she, too, was counting on those shots to beef up the piece.

"Rest assured, Kilauea is putting on a flawless show, and more important, one that's easy to get to."

Sonya smelled the lava flow before she saw it. Sulfur. It hung in the air the way it did in chemistry class—rotten-egg gas.

Then the Jeep turned a corner and the lava stream stretched before them. It bubbled, groaned, rumbled, detonated, rushed, hissed, and splashed. The red flare was brighter than any furnace. It destroyed everything in its path.

Sonya was mesmerized. She stood beside Perry in silence.

Joe broke the spell. "There are not many places on this planet where you can walk on ground that is younger than you are. Right now we are seeing the creation of the world. It is almost impossible not to watch it."

But after two hours Sonya had seen enough. She was ready to leave. They had enough shots for the spa piece and the news department. But Perry wanted more. "Let's get closer to the flow for a final few dissolves. If I get a really good one, you could use it to end the piece."

Sonya didn't object. There was something about good cameramen that relished peril. Perry seemed unaware of the heat, ash, and smoke—or the danger. And Joe was clearly too proud of the volcano's wrath to suggest they finish.

She bent over and idly picked up a small piece of smooth black lava. It was a treasure—an oval shape with a smooth glassy surface that shone like lacquer in the glow of the lava. She held it up to show Joe.

"It is beautiful. I think I'll take it back to New York as a souvenir."

Joe smiled at her enthusiasm.

"We call them Pele's teardrops. They're globs of molten glass formed when the lava explodes. But please put it back. We ask visitors not to take anything at all from the park. We like the lava to be replaced exactly where it was found."

Sonya stepped toward him, the lava still in her hand. "But I want to keep it."

As she moved, the wind picked up. She felt its force on her back, pushing her forward. Her ankle twisted, and she lost her balance and slipped toward the river of red that seemed only a few feet away. The lava under her body was hot.

Then Joe was behind her. His strong arms grabbed her. As she turned in his grasp, she could see the alarm in his face. But one tug and she was on her feet, clinging to him. She couldn't help herself. She put her head against his chest and burst into tears.

"It was only a few seconds, but I seemed so close to it," she blurted out. "The wind twisted; when I was falling, it changed direction and brought the stench and heat toward me. It was suffocating."

She gasped for air. Her lungs felt scorched. Gaining control wasn't easy. She wanted to stay in his arms and cry her heart out.

Then, with one hand still on his arm, she took an unsteady step back from him.

"Thank you. I'm sorry, but I got such a shock."

"Where is Pele's teardrop? I'll put it back for you." Perry was by her side. "People say that Pele brings bad luck to those who remove a piece of her lava. I don't want to risk your slipping again."

Sonya managed a laugh. "She's got it back already. It flew right out of my hand. There's a lot to admire on this island, but I'm learning it's important to tread warily.

"You have my word, Joe. I'll never pick up another piece of lava."

Joe kept his arm around her. "Let me steady you. It's time we went back to the Jeep. And don't think twice about crying. A number of women weep when they see the flow. Men, too. The volcano is an enigma. It touches us in different ways."

"I owe you dinner for all that work," Sonya said to Perry as they waved goodbye to Joe and walked back along the path to their bungalows. "You can plunge in your own pool, and then come to my bungalow. I'll have a medium steak waiting in, say, 40 minutes."

She stopped before a yellow oleander shrub and gathered a handful of the trumpet-shaped flowers. "Appease the gods," she told herself, "especially Pele. She's a girl who knows her own mind." Then, as she floated among the sweet-smelling frangipani in the plunge pool, Sonya pushed away the memory of the angry lava bubbling from center of the earth. The stars were bright, and from here the wrath of Pele and her fire-breathing volcano seemed light-years away. Hawaii was an island of many moods.

Perry was hungry and surprisingly, so was Sonya. They wolfed down their steaks and fries in silence. Perry had beer and Sonya a half bottle of red wine.

"That hit the spot," Perry said at last, wiping his mustache with his napkin. "I've got enough energy now to keep going all night. How about seeing what night shots we can get of the spa?"

"Okay," Sonya agreed. "I think the best place to try would be on the hill by the Swansons' home. The view there is sensational." The night was radiantly beautiful. It would be good to try and capture it, and if anyone could, it would be Perry.

They walked back to his bungalow, collected the camera and

tripod, and climbed the rise to Errol and Lara's home. Perry put the tripod on a mound and focused on the lights of the spa and the white fringe of the surf curling on the beach. "Look," he said. "I think I've got it." Sonya looked into the viewfinder and okayed the shot. "Try a zoom into the waves as they break on the sand. It's wonderfully romantic."

"It's going to take time. I'll have to steady the tripod and play with the exposure."

Sonya left him and walked along the path toward the pine trees that surrounded the house. Maybe Perry could get a shot of the stars through some of the branches. They would give form to the sky and contrast the brilliance of the stars. She grinned to herself. The wine was making her artsy.

As she drew closer to the house, she stopped. She could hear voices—Errol and Lara Swanson, arguing. She must be close to their bedroom.

Errol was pleading with his wife.

"Please, I need you to do it for me. Tonight. Now."

Lara's voice was firm. "No, Errol, I've had enough. I'm pregnant. I'm tired. I'm finished. You can't force me."

"Damn it, Lara, we had an understanding."

"Errol, enough is enough. I will not."

Errol's voice rose in anger. "I'm your husband; you'll do what I say. Do you understand that? Now or anytime."

Sonya turned away. Errol Swanson's rages were legendary. She and Perry should leave before they were seen.

Chapter 9

Chicago
Thursday, 8:00 A.M.

"No, once and for all, *no!* You cannot come to Hawaii with me. I have business to talk over with your father. That's trouble enough."

Christy Swanson put her hand over the mouthpiece. She would not interrupt her mother. She would just wait until her mother stopped talking.

"Christy." Joan's voice took on a desperate note, "I want you to try and understand. Your father and I have had a serious disagreement about money. I'm not fooling you. It really is serious. If I don't win, it will affect our futures drastically."

Christy closed her eyes. The same old story. How many times had she heard it in her life? Mother the martyr.

"Are you there, Christy? Are you listening to me?"

"Yes, Mother, I hear you."

"You know how hard I've worked to make your future secure. I don't want you ever to have to rely on your father for money."

Joan paused and Christy listened to the silence. How would her mother attack her father this time? It was her favorite sport, bad-mouthing the man she had married 40 years ago. Though, Christy knew, her mother had wanted the divorce as much as Errol.

When her mother spoke again it was relief, not anger, that Christy heard in her voice.

"I might as well tell you the facts. You will have to face reality one day and it might as well be now. Errol is trying to take the toy business away from us."

"Why, Mother? Why would he want our toy business?"

"He doesn't need the money, but he wants to control everything. We don't have millions. The toy business provides our income. It pays for your apartment, your doctor bills your allowance. Every cent you spend comes from it. While I have control you will always be cared for.

"But if your father gets hold of it . . . well, I don't trust him. He will manipulate things until he pushes me out. Then he will decide where the money goes."

Christy felt a moment of fear. She had always disliked the toy shop. But their money came from it, had come from it for as long as she could remember. As a child she had seen her grandfather give bills to her mother, who had greedily stuffed them into her purse.

Then she got a grip on herself. This was just another of her mother's schemes to turn her away from her father. She had always wanted to crush the love Christy had for him.

"Oh, Mother," she cried, "do you really think that Daddy would put us out on the street?"

"Christy, I know you love and believe in your father and I have never wanted to destroy those feelings. But he has many other re-sponsibilities. He has Margot and Tomas, and now a new wife who is expecting a baby. You must come to terms with that. You are almost 40, and he no longer looks on you as 'his little girl.' "

Joan stopped. Christy sensed she was gathering her forces to continue the attack.

Her heart started to race. Her mother was so unfair. Her father had never been a demonstrative man, but he had loved her when she was a child. At night she would listen for his car and run to the door so she would be the first to greet him. She would put her arms around his leg and hug it with all her might. He would put down his briefcase, pick her up, and nuzzle her neck. "My little girl is always waiting for me." Then he would reach into his pocket and give her a piece of candy. She knew he picked up the candy from the jar on the office receptionist's desk. She had seen it there. But still, he remembered every night.

"Oh, Mother, don't start again. You have always come between Daddy and me. I can't hate him the way you do. Why should I? He is my father and I love him, you can't change that."

Christy had chosen her words carefully. She knew how to build her mother's guilt. The more guilty she could make her feel, the faster Joan would relent, and Christy would get what she wanted.

It was a game they had played for years, ever since Craig ran away from home and she had been put in the hospital.

Christy bent her head and sighed into the phone. "Daddy left us because of you, not because of me. Okay, I got sick. But I couldn't help it. You know what the doctor said. But you still blame me. You never loved me the way you loved Craig." She started to sob.

"Christy, Christy." Her mother's voice rose with despair. "Stop it, Christy. Don't upset yourself. You know too well what will happen. You don't want to get sick again, do you?"

Christy couldn't stop. She didn't want to stop. She let the sobs wrack her body. She was her mother's unwanted, unloved daughter and always had been.

The party in Hawaii was just another affair she was excluded from. The truth was that Joan was ashamed of her and always had been. She had never wanted to admit that her daughter was schizophrenic.

But it went deeper than that. Almost from the time she could first remember, Christy had felt she was the forgotten member of the family, the weak link in a sturdy chain.

She remembered, as a child, being told to play in the back while her mother worked in the busy toy shop. Craig was allowed to help, to stack the shelves, run messages, talk to the kids who walked, starry-eyed, into the store.

"Craig is the best salesman we've ever had," her mother had boasted.

Yes, Joan was so proud of him. How often had she praised him to the customers, patting him on the head, laughing at his jokes, even seeing that he got the biggest slice of the chocolate cake for afternoon tea.

Christy remembered watching them together from her favorite hiding spot, under the counter. She learned how to close the sliding door and lie down so that she could watch the customers through a crack in the paneling.

One afternoon she fell asleep.

When she woke up the store was closed and she was alone. Only the neon sign flickering outside broke the darkness. She had backed into the corner of the counter, keeping her head down, wrapping her arms around her knees, crying silently.

It seemed hours before they came to find her. And then, when they did, she wouldn't come out. She knew her mother would be angry, but her grandfather would be worse, he would be furious. He would punish her as he always did—send Craig to get a switch from the willow tree in the back, then give her three lashes with it. Often he would add a few extra, "to stop her being so stubborn."

She decided to come out when she heard her brother calling. "Don't be afraid, Christy, I know where you are. I've come to get you, so we can play together."

Her mother told her she hid under the counter only to cause trouble. Joan did not see the fear that flooded Christy before she took Craig's hand and let him lead her into the light.

Christy told herself she must forget the past, even though she could never forgive her mother. She got up from the sofa, walked across the room to the window, and watched the fan-shaped leaves of the gingko trees dancing in the early autumn breeze. She had moved to this apartment not because it was close to her mother's, but because of the ginkgos that lined the street. She had read that ginkgos had survived for 20 thousand years and were the oldest surviving tree species. Usually she found that thought comforting, but not this morning.

"Mother, it is you who is sick," she almost shouted into the phone. "And Grandfather, why didn't you stop him?"

"Christy," Joan interrupted, for God's sake, I don't need to hear this again."

But Christy was not to be stopped.

"Didn't you realize that evil old man was taking out his frustrations on me? You've spent your life telling me how bad I was compared to Craig. Craig ran away because of the way the family treated me. He told me he couldn't take it anymore."

Joan was incensed. "Don't you make accusations about your grandfather. He was doing what he thought best for you. He treated Craig in exactly the same way. He got as many beatings as you did."

"Oh no, he didn't. I counted the strokes. I always got more than Craig. And Craig didn't have pull down his pants, as I did."

Her mother was silent for a long moment.

"Christy." Joan's voice startled her. "Your grandfather gave me the same treatment when I was a girl. Smacking children was the natural thing to do. I don't hold a grudge. Neither should you."

"No, Mother, he was the one with the grudge. He resented me from the moment I was born. He had no time for me. Only for Craig."

When she was eight, her grandparents had given her a doll for Christmas. A beautiful doll. The most expensive in the store. She had taken it out of the box with disbelief.

"Is it a baby sister for me to play with?" she had asked her grandmother. The old woman had patted her on the head. "Do you want a sister that badly?"

Embarrassed by the question, Christy had hung her head and shyly turned to her grandfather.

"Is it really a baby? Does it have a heart?" she had asked him.

"You silly girl. All babies have hearts. Just like all of us, like me, like you." He brushed aside her question and turned to look at Craig's airplane.

Christy had kept the doll on her lap right through the long holiday dinner. It was something to hold, something to love.

"Do you think it really has a heart?" she had asked Craig on the way home in the back seat of the car.

"There's only one way to find out—cut it open and have a look." Craig had been too busy with his own presents to be interested.

And so she did, later that night, alone in the room she shared with Craig. She pulled the doll apart, searching through the stuffing to find its heart.

"But Grandpa told me it had a heart, just like him, just like all of us. You told me the heart was the center of love. I wanted to find out if it really was there," she had tried to explain to her mother when she found the broken doll.

But Joan wouldn't listen. "Why did you destroy your grandparents' present? How do you expect me to explain this to them? Why do you torment me? Do you know how much that doll cost? How lucky you were to get it? Oh, Christy, you are impossible. What did I ever do to deserve you?"

Christy had cried her heart out. When her mother had the doll repaired and returned it to her, she had barely managed a thank you. The only time she had picked up the doll again was when her grandmother asked to see it.

When her next birthday came she received a silver heart on a black velvet ribbon.

"Did Daddy chose it? Is it a real heart?"

"How can it be real? You couldn't wear a real heart around your neck," her mother replied. "But it is real silver, that means it's valuable. And yes, Daddy helped me choose it for you. He knew how upset you were not finding a heart in your doll."

Christy had knotted the black ribbon tightly around her neck.

When she looked back, it seemed as if she had built her whole world around that silver heart. She refused to take it off, even in the bath. She fought with her mother about what she wore with it. Only her special clothes were good enough.

One morning Joan had screamed, "I chose the stupid locket for you in the store. Your grandfather let me have it. Your father wasn't even interested in looking at it. He never is."

At first Christy thought her mother was lying. As she grew older she realized that Errol would never have had anything to do with it. He was ashamed of the toy store and everyone in it. He would never have spared the time to choose a locket. Work was so much more important.

She sobbed as she remembered. She must put it behind her, as her mother so frequently told her, and get on with her life. But the damage was deep. She would never forget. The heartache would linger forever.

Her mother was right. If she went to Hawaii it would bring back the bad memories.

She sobbed into the phone.

"All right, I give up. I won't go." She hung up and sank into the sofa again. She would stay home, take her medicine, and make her visits to her doctor.

What if Craig wasn't dead? How else could his voice keep telling her what to do? His voice was always with her, wherever she was. She knew they would be together one day. He would come to her, he would take care of her as he always promised.

The phone rang.

Christy didn't hear it. She was lost in the fantasy of being with her twin again. Her mother left a message.

"Christy, you can go to Hawaii—on two conditions: one, you will never be alone with your father, and two, you will never mention your brother's name."

Chapter **10**

It was the start of another brilliant day. The sun would soon melt the soft puff of clouds that lingered on the horizon. In a few hours, the sky would be a blaze of blue and the island would buzz with life.

Errol Swanson stepped out into the courtyard and felt the coolness of the weathered stones under his bare feet. The sun had not risen far enough to penetrate the heavy branches of the pine trees, and their tangy perfume hung in the air. He tightened his pajama pants around his waist. This was his domain. Nothing should disturb him here.

He had wakened with a jolt from a nightmare that left him twisted with fear. He remembered few details, just the horror. When his heart stopped racing, he reached for Lara. If he had cried out in his dream, as he often did, he must have disturbed her.

She turned from him, stretched, and continued her calm, shallow breathing. She was asleep.

He got up and walked around the bed to check on her. She lay on her side, one hand pressed against her forehead, as if she were worrying over a problem.

He pushed the hair back from her face. He felt he was losing the woman he had fallen so desperately in love with. He had given her so much. Now that she was pregnant, she thought she could manipulate him to get even more. She was wrong. It amused him to watch her play the games he knew so well. He was still in command.

He walked to the edge of the courtyard and looked down at the swimming pool, a strip of deep jade in the early morning light. It was carved out of lava rock and lay between the beach and the garden, which led to the dining room terrace.

He had insisted it was a brilliant design. Lara had disagreed, saying the pool was too geometric and so big that it jutted out and spoiled the fine curve of the beach.

"Don't worry about it," he had told her. "If people are paying top dollar for a spa like this, they want a real pool to swim in, not a bathtub."

They had compromised. Lara got the plunge pools for the romantic souls who wanted to float nude under the stars. Errol got the big pool for the swimmers.

It was a saltwater "infinity" pool that not only echoed the coastline but formed a double horizon. It looked as expensive as it was.

As he watched, Sonya Iverson came down the shadowy path from the terrace, paused, and then ran to the diving board. In a moment she was in the water.

He admired her style, the way she knifed her way cleanly lap after lap. Her body was lean and strong, in a bare black swimsuit. But she was feminine enough, with that smattering of freckles on her arms and shoulders. He wondered how her curly red hair would feel in his hand, crisp or soft. She was a woman of experience, too. She had to be.

He had checked her personnel file. She was divorced and almost 40, 10 years older than she looked. A face-lift accounted for that. She was no frightened little chick who would back off at first touch.

He glanced at his watch. It was still early. Sonya had plenty of energy. He knew her plans. She was shooting the spa in the morning light and then would do a preinterview with him before lunch. So he would be alone with her in a few hours. Well, who knew what could happen? Maybe she was as bored as he was.

Sonya walked into Errol Swanson's study and sat down in the armchair across from his desk. She wore white pants and a beige silk shirt that she had closed primly to the top button.

"You look so cool and professional. The epitome of a network producer," Errol said when he opened the door to greet her. "I hope your questions are not going to be too tough. Remember, I'm a retired executive now. My days on the nineteenth floor are over."

She laughed and said she would prefer to do the interview outside, in the cool shade of the pine trees. But he replied, "I don't think so. It will be quieter here in my study, and I have all the facts and figures here."

She hesitated. "This is only a preinterview. I just want to get a few ideas for questions for Donna. You know how she insists on being well prepared. She's a great lady for details."

"Yes," he said. "You may not know it, but Donna and I go way back. I can't imagine what she doesn't know about me already. You don't have to worry about that."

He knew he had put her in her place when he saw a faint blush creep up her face.

"Well, it's your new life we are interested in, not your past," she said. "First of all, how are you enjoying life at the spa?"

"It's great."

"Was it hard to adjust to island life after being so busy in New York, heading one of the world's largest media companies?"

"I did miss New York. Not the frustration, the people. But Lara keeps me busy here. The spa is a new business for me and I find it fascinating. It has opened many new worlds. I am never bored."

Errol could see she was getting frustrated. His answers were exactly what she didn't want, the usual clichés of a wary executive. He was a master at spinning a story just the way he wanted.

He watched her expression with half-closed eyes. She was frowning, playing with the pen poised over her notebook, thinking of a way to tackle him. Then she looked up, shook her red hair back from her face, and smiled at him.

He liked her. The way she leaned forward and looked straight into his eyes gave him a sense of power. He could tell she was attracted to him. Maybe he should open up, keep the conversation going. After all, he wasn't being taped.

"I like being interviewed by you," he said, to relieve the tension. "So let me tell you the facts. What I have now is a real family life. That is something I gave up in my previous marriages. Both my ex-wives worked away from home, so our time together was always limited. That is very hard on a marriage. And, of course, very tough on children."

"Lara is your third wife." Her voice was matter-of-fact, but in it he thought he detected a note of envy.

"Yes."

"And she is pregnant. Do you want a boy or a girl?"

Errol gave a quick smile of encouragement. "Here's the usual answer, but for me it is absolutely true. We decided not to ask. A boy or a girl, either will do. I'll just be grateful for a healthy baby. I am absolutely committed to Lara and her beliefs. Whatever she wants, I'll go for. She considers family life to be important above everything, and a real family is something I've always wanted."

He dropped his head back, thinking. There was no harm in telling Sonya the truth, or something near the truth. It would please her to think she had gotten him to reveal something special. Anyway, Donna knew most of his life story already.

"I rushed into my first marriage; I knew Joan's brother in high school and that's how we got together. We were babies, just 19. Our twins were born nine months after our wedding day. Joan came from a wonderful family, and with their help we struggled through college. Her parents owned a toy business and Joan was involved in it all her life. Now it's a successful chain—thanks largely to my help."

"But the marriage didn't work out?" He heard a note of interest in Sonya's quiet voice.

"I was always busy with my career, so Joan packed up the twins and took them to the store while she worked. We slowly grew apart. When I look back I realize our marriage failed because we both worked too hard, at everything but our relationship. Sonya, it just wasn't fun. The sixties was a great decade, the most exhilarating of the century, but it swept by us so fast we didn't know what was happening."

"Your son's disappearance can't have helped."

"Oh, you know about that? Well, of course it was a tragedy. Craig was a brilliant boy, but sensitive."

Sonya checked her notes.

"You were then the international sales manager for the company, based in Chicago. Quite a job."

"Actually I was only sales manager for South America. But it was my first big break. I was absorbed in the job. You have to be if you want to succeed.

"Craig and I were planning a trip to Argentina and Brazil, but somehow it didn't come off. I didn't realize how upset he was until he disappeared. All we ever received from him were two postcards, telling his mother he was okay and not to worry."

"The police never found a trace of him?"

"No, runaway teenagers are a dime a dozen. It seems to be part of the modern way of growing up."

"And then they discovered his body in Guatemala?"

"Joan went to try to identify it, but it was impossible. The body had been badly mangled in an explosion, and there was no DNA science in those days. I kept an eye on our daughter, who couldn't deal with the death of her twin. It was a devastating experience for all of us. It destroyed the family."

Errol closed his eyes for a brief second. He usually avoided talking about Craig. It had all happened so long ago. But even so, his disappearance had received much publicity. His death and the reason for it were common knowledge. Better she get the story from him.

Sonya took the initiative.

"What about your family? The records show that your father was ill when he came back from the Pacific in World War II."

Errol looked out the window. How far back had she gone? What did she know about his father? Who had she been talking to?

But as he turned back to her, she smiled, and that smile convinced him that she was a caring woman. She wanted to hear about his past because she was fascinated by him. He wished he had known her better at the network.

"My father, Charles, suffered from severe periods of depression. When the worst of them came on he would lock himself, practically barricade himself, in the garage."

"How frightening," exclaimed Sonya.

"Sometimes he was in there for days. No amount of pleading from my mother, his friends, or the doctors could get him out. At times he didn't speak. The police had to be called more than once to break in the door."

"It must have been dreadful for you."

"Yes, they tried to hide it from me, but I always knew what was going on."

"He eventually became a dentist?"

"Yes, he was, but not a happy man. I think he would have liked to be a doctor. In fact, it was his problems with his work that made me decide to take a different course."

"He had a problem in a malpractice case? I read about that."

"It was an accident. The drill slipped and he damaged a nerve in a woman's tongue. She couldn't control her saliva. One look at her and the jury was convinced Dad was guilty."

"That was the truth?"

A wave of pity for his father filled him; he wanted to share his feelings with Sonya.

"Yes, he was guilty. But if you had seen the psychological wreck he was when he returned from the Pacific, you would pardon him.

I can still see him on the day he came home from the hospital. He stumbled out of the car into the sunlight. My mother pushed me forward and he patted my head, but he had no idea who I was."

"Did he ever talk about his experiences?"

"No. He fought on Okinawa, in some of the worst battles of the war. The belief that the emperor was god was so strong that hundreds of Japanese women and children drank poison rather than surrender to the Americans. Dad was one of the U.S. soldiers who dug their graves."

"It must have been appalling." Errol heard sympathy in her voice.

"Years afterward we would wake up to his screams in the night."

"He died just after you finished college? He never saw you as a powerful TV executive?"

"Right. He said often that he was a failure and that his life was not worth living. I'm sure it would have thrilled him to know about my success."

Errol found it difficult to talk about the past. All his life he had taught himself to concentrate on the future. And now he had told this woman more than he had confessed to Lara.

For a moment there was silence.

He continued, "But then I found a new kind of life with Margot. We met in Paris, and she taught me to relax and enjoy myself.

"Margot had dreams of having her own fashion house. She wanted to open it in Paris, but I persuaded her that New York was the best place to make money. And I was right. She has done very well."

He gave a cynical laugh.

"That's one point you can make in your story. In both my marriages, I taught my wives a lot about the art of making money. They would never have been so successful if they hadn't married me."

"Margot also gave you a son."

"Yes. And what a son. Tomas is a faggot, and all because of his mother. He was her pet, her plaything, her prodigy child. She couldn't bear to be parted from him. She took him with her to work, out shopping, to the theater," he raged on. "I kept telling her she should let him be a boy, let him play soccer with the other kids. She would never listen. We fought about his education, his clothes, the way he walked. She taught him French so she could speak to him without my knowing what they were saying."

"But he is your son."

For a moment, Errol felt that Sonya was judging him.

He smiled at her. "Of course he is. And he will always be. I'm sure he will have a brilliant future once he straightens himself out—if he ever does."

Then he looked toward the door. Lara was standing there, a bunch of gardenias in her hand.

"Darling," she said. "I don't want to interrupt, but we're having lunch early today. I have to spend the afternoon in the spa shooting with Sonya." She smiled and left.

"Thank you, Errol," Sonya said as she rose to go. "I appreciate the time you gave me for this interview. Now I should get to work on my notes."

Errol walked Sonya to the door, determined not to let her go so abruptly.

"Now you know a lot about me," he said, putting his hand on her shoulder and caressing it so his arm touched her breast. "But there's one thing you don't know, and that's what a swimmer I am.

How about I meet you after dinner at the pool and give you a race?"

He watched her face as she thought about his invitation. By the way her body moved toward him, he was certain she was attracted to him.

Then she stepped back.

"I'll have to see how the day goes," she said. "I have a lot of tapes to view and logging to do. I must have a list of questions ready for Donna when she arrives."

He stood in the door, watching as she walked away, her narrow hips snaking in her tight pants. He'd aroused her.

"Yes. I've got her hooked," he told himself. "A woman her age always finds it tough to get a man. She'll be at the pool tonight."

Chapter **11**

Tomas Swanson stopped at the end of the runway and posed for a full 30 seconds so the photographers could get the shots they wanted. Then he turned and started to walk back. But the press wanted more of him.

"Give us those muscles, Tomas," a cameraman shouted over the blare of the music.

He grinned and held up both arms, letting his muscles ripple in a winning-boxer stance.

He'd made it. The press couldn't get enough of him. He had no doubts. He was this season's top male model. And he had done it himself. No influence from his designer mother or his billionaire father.

His brief outfit, a hand-stitched black suede vest and a pair of snug cutoff jeans, flattered his young body. The olive skin he had inherited from his mother gleamed with gel. His blue eyes flashed under his dark, blond-streaked hair.

He gave the photographers a quick wink, then strode back and pulled designer Burt Jenkins from backstage.

Tears streamed down Jenkins's face. He was out of control, with a mix of fear, joy, and, Tomas knew, cocaine. Tomas put his arm around the trembling designer's waist and half carried him down to the cameras at the end of the runway.

The audience roared its approval. There was no doubt that the show was a hit. Burt Jenkins was on top of a major fashion trend with his expensive, hand-crafted pieces. They were the height of slick urban sophistication, and yet casual enough to be paired with that uniform of the twenty-first century—jeans.

Tomas knew he was perfect for the mood of the clothes. After all, they had not only been designed on him, but for him. He had worked as a model for Burt for three seasons and done the Burt Jenkins advertising campaign in the fall. Sales had soared. The question now was whether it was due to the image he projected or to Jenkins's designs or even to the hyped-up show. The bets were on Tomas.

Undoubtedly Burt was talented, but he had a long way to go to prove himself before the real money would pour in. He certainly wasn't rich enough for Tomas to sign an exclusive contract with him. And for Tomas it would be stupid to tie himself up with one designer at the beginning of his career. He had looks, brains, and youth. The whole world was waiting for him.

To disassociate himself from Burt, Tomas gently pushed him forward to take the bows alone, to be the star of his own show. But Burt clung desperately to Tomas. Then, to Tomas's horror, put his head on his shoulder and began to sob.

"I owe it all to you. I love you, I love you," he repeated over and over again.

Tomas froze. This was too much. He knew Burt was in love with him, and so did most of the fashion crowd. But Tomas was only Burt's friend. The cameras were still rolling. He had to make the relationship seem as professional as he could. He lifted Burt's head off his shoulder and, with his hands on the designer's waist, stepped behind him and pushed him forward. It was the action of an associate, nothing more.

Burt's display of passion ruled out any chance that Tomas would linger at his big celebratory party that night. Yes, he would stop by, but only for a moment. He'd give Burt a high-five, have a quick martini, and be on his way.

Making excuses would be easy, but Tomas knew he would infuriate Burt. His success with Burt's ad had brought him bookings from three other houses. But because of his trip to Honolulu, he had to do fittings that evening for the clothes he would wear for shoots the following week. The designers wanted him to look perfect. But more important, so did he.

He felt guilty, but competition was the name of the game in Manhattan.

It was 11 o'clock before Tomas opened the door of his apartment. He was glad to be away from the party and done with the fittings. The scent of lilies from the bowl on the coffee table greeted him. His mother knew they were his favorite, and he knew she had bought them especially for him.

The apartment had been cleaned, dusted, and polished that morning, every book, every scrap of paper neatly squared off. As usual, it looked like a spread in a classy decorating magazine.

It was just as well he was as neat and orderly as his mother, Tomas told himself, otherwise she would have driven him mad.

And just as well he was gay. No straight man could have put up with her need to control.

He put his backpack down on the parquet floor, then went into the kitchen, where he knew a half-cooked meal was waiting. A quick zap in the microwave and his dinner would be ready.

Tomas's Manhattan apartment was next to his mother's, over-looking the East River. Margot had bought it years ago, claiming it was an investment. Then, when her tenant's lease was up, she quietly redecorated it. When Tomas's eighteenth birthday came around, she had placed the key to the apartment in a greeting card.

"That's all you're getting," she laughed, "because it is all you need."

To him it was perfect. She had thought of everything. The small second bedroom had been turned into a gym; comfortable chairs were arranged around the large-screen TV in the living room; and she had managed to fit a steam box into the second bathroom. Okay, it meant that his mother was too close at certain times, but she often worked late or went to the theater.

On the reverse side of the coin, his mother's housekeeper, Miranda, was at his disposal. She had looked after him since he was eight and there was nothing she wouldn't do for him. He knew he took full advantage of her love.

"With all the work you're getting, you need carbohydrates to keep up your energy. It's pasta every night this week," she had told him on Monday morning. "I'll slightly undercook it so it will be perfect after you microwave it. And I'll make an extra portion in case you bring home a friend. The salad will be ready in the fridge and I'll put the dressing beside it."

Tomas had put his arms around her and given her a hug and a

thank-you kiss on the cheek. Words were not necessary between them. After all those years with him and his mother, Miranda knew everything—the fights, the violence between his parents, and the eventual divorce. How many times had he run to her for comfort when the anger in the home had overwhelmed him?

He heated his spaghetti primavera and took it to the living room to eat while he worked at his desk. He smiled as he remembered how many times Miranda had instructed him not to read while he ate. She said it would destroy his digestion.

But he had work to do. He wanted an approximate idea of how much he'd earned that week. It gave him infinite pleasure to think that he could earn five times as much in a week as his father had earned in a year at the same age.

He totaled the four days' earnings, making deductions for his agent's 15 percent, taxes, and the expenses of the car he hired to rush him from show to show. At most, he would be left with $50,000. Not as much as he had hoped.

The trip to Hawaii meant he had to cancel two shows on Friday, the last day of the season. The major designers held out for that day. And major designers paid the big money.

He shrugged. It was worth a few thousand dollars to talk face to face with his father.

But although he knew he'd made the right decision to go to Hawaii, Tomas couldn't shake off the feeling that something was wrong. The truth was, he should be in New York tomorrow to face the backlash of Burt's open declaration of love on the runway. The fashion world fed on gossip. If he didn't appear in any other shows, the rumor would start that Burt Jenkins had signed him exclusively to promote his collection. Or worse, gone off with him for a passionate weekend.

If that appeared in the press, his mother would be furious. It could also mean that he would lose some of his bookings for the upcoming Paris shows, and that was last thing he wanted. He planned to stay freelance until he was famous enough for an international designer to pay him top bucks for exclusivity.

He picked up the phone and dialed a number of one of the city's newspapers. The editor of the gossip page was nobody's friend, but she liked a scoop. What's more, she had taken his mother's side in her divorce from his father.

Her answering machine gave the usual message. He waited for the beep, then spoke, making his voice loud and clear. "This is Tomas Swanson calling to thank you for the help you've given me. And to tell you I won't be at the shows tomorrow as I'm flying to Hawaii to be with Mummy at the opening of Dad's spa. Keep your fingers crossed for us. Hope I see you in Milan or Paris. Again, thanks for everything."

The columnist could verify the trip with a call to his agent. With luck, the story would appear in the paper on Friday. That would help allay any gossip.

He got up and saw the package lying on the coffee table. It was addressed to him in his mother's hand. He knew what was in it—the box with the revolver she had given to him in her office.

She had wrapped and sealed it. While they both trusted Miranda with their lives, a gun was a gun, and it was better she knew nothing about it.

Inside was a note in his mother's spidery hand on her pale blue paper.

"Good news, Tomas," she wrote. "I've managed to get hold of a friend's company plane to take us to Hawaii. We'll have to refuel in L.A., but it will still be a faster trip. More important, we won't go through airport security, so I won't need to send this gun separately. Just put it in your suitcase.

"I plan to talk to your father and demand the money he owes me. I want to have the gun to threaten him—to have the upper hand for once.

"The car will pick us up at 8:30 in the morning, so get some sleep. I'll call to wake you at 7:30. Love as usual, M."

His mother was right to take the gun. Not for a moment did he doubt her decision. His father was a violent man. Tomas had seen the bruises Errol had left on her body. And has seen how they grew larger as his father hit harder and harder. Even as a small child Tomas had wakened in the night to hear his father's drunken voice shouting, threatening his mother. She would weep hysterically, begging him to stop. At times she would run into Tomas's room, climb into bed with him, and clutch him to her. He would try to soothe her, telling her how he loved her and would protect her all his life. Eventually her sobbing would cease and she would drift off to sleep. But he would lie awake, fighting the rage against his father. Yes, his mother had every right to fear his father. He was glad to pack the gun.

Tomas opened the box and flipped through the registration papers that lay on top. His grandfather had been a meticulous man. Everything was neatly placed in order. He had even included a list of the countries he had taken it to in his work as a geologist. The gun was nested in the padded box; the bullets were beside it.

Tomas ran his hands through his blond streaks. He should be meticulous, too. And the first thing was to get rid of his mother's note. He went into the kitchen, lit it at the stove, and burned it over the sink. No good could come of anyone knowing how deeply Margot hated his father or how vengeful she was.

He had to calm down and stop worrying about his mother. He would cope with whatever happened. If it came to violence, he was young and strong, a good match for a man in his fifties.

He picked up the gun and took it to his bedroom, hefting it to get the feel and checking to make sure it was empty. Then he lifted his arm and pointed the gun at his father's photo on the chest of drawers. He pulled the trigger once, then stood back and dry-fired it again. And again. And again. And again.

Finally his rage was spent.

He put the gun back into the rosewood box and placed it in the center of his suitcase. He would pack his clothes around it so that no harm could come to it.

Chapter **12**

The Big Island
Thursday, 1:00 P.M.

Sonya had only half believed the stories that circulated about Errol Swanson, as gossip was so much part of network life. Now, after her interview, she was convinced every rumor was true.

Errol Swanson was a monster. He had brushed aside Lara, his pregnant wife, and made a blatant pass at Sonya, while Lara could hear.

Sonya felt anger and disgust swell in her. Anger at herself because she hadn't had the nerve to slap his face. Disgust with the old-boy system. Errol had left the network more than three years ago and still had more than enough clout to get a prime-time story glorifying his spa. Errol was balding and almost 60, but he still thought any woman who came his way was fair game.

"Just forget it," she told herself. "All you can do is bide your time. You can't let your anger show. Not now."

She strolled as casually as she could to the pond in the center of the Swansons' courtyard. She trailed her fingers in the water and watched the lazy grace of a golden carp as it moved slowly among the lily pads. The sun was high and the heat almost overpowering. Even the fish must feel it.

She took sunglasses from her bag, put them on, and glanced back at the house. Lara was at a window, watching. Her pale dress was caught by the light. Sonya made a gesture of farewell, but Lara ignored her and moved away. To Sonya, Lara looked as if she'd had a fright, almost as if she'd been trapped.

What was happening between the Swansons? Of course, there must be tension from opening the spa. But it seemed to be more than that. Was the marriage failing? So soon? From the conversation Sonya had overheard last night, she knew Errol wanted something Lara wasn't prepared to give. But what?

Last night Lara had been in control. Her refusal had been firm and steady. But today the roles had reversed. Errol was in command and was dead set on showing it. Lara had lost the battle and now was taking the punishment. Errol had forced her back into the role of a dutiful, grateful wife.

Sonya shook the water from her hand before moving away from the pond. Let the Swansons solve their own problems; she had to think about the story she had to produce. What she needed now was a long soak in her bungalow's plunge pool. That would wash away her disgust.

Lunch, a plate of cold cuts and salad, was as cool and refreshing as the water in the pool. She ate as she watched the news on CNN. Being connected to the buzz of the international world usually brought her back to herself, but today was different. Errol's arrogance still bugged her. Instead of interesting her, CNN's hard news stories reminded her of how easily she been manipulated into coming to Hawaii. She hated herself for not insisting on using her talent to its full potential.

She had to pull herself together. "You're here to do a job that's all," she told herself. Just then there was a knock.

Perry pushed open the door and stood blinking in the sudden dark of the room.

"I've got news for you," he said. "We'll have to shoot this afternoon without Lara. She's tied up with Errol, discussing plans for the opening."

"They didn't call me." Sonya let her annoyance show.

"They did but you didn't answer, at least that's what they told me."

"I did take a long time in the pool." She paused, puzzled. "But I checked for messages when I came in. There weren't any." She glanced at the phone. The message light was dark.

"I ran into Jackie Olsen—she said she was coming to speak to you directly, but I told her that I was on my way here and would give you the message. She said not to worry about a thing; Lara had made sure the spa was set up for us to shoot."

"Jackie." Sonya was curious. "Lara told me she was her right hand. She's that close to Lara?"

"Apparently Jackie is quite a girl, and Lara's very good friend. They met years ago in London. The word is that Errol doesn't like her, and she doesn't like Errol."

"I can understand that," Sonya broke in. "I am so angry at him. Can you believe it? He made a pass at me. He wants me to go swimming with him after dinner."

"His pool or yours?" Perry joked. "I'll bring the camera."

"You'll bring the camera, all right. But you'll be showing me the video you shot this morning while I was with Errol."

"What a happy threesome we'll make," Perry laughed. In a few moments Sonya joined in. He always could make her laugh. Life was easier with Perry around.

She knew what she'd do about the date Errol had forced on her. She had worked out a routine for amorous husbands years ago—pretend ignorance. When she saw Errol the next day she'd just smile at him as if she hadn't understood what he said. It would make her look like a ditz, but it shouldn't hurt his ego.

Meanwhile she'd have to set up another appointment to shoot Lara at the spa. That was essential. Lara's New Age treatments were a critical part of the story.

She picked up the phone and dialed Lara's number. The operator answered and suggested that she leave a message. As she spoke she heard the chimes announcing someone was at her door.

Perry opened it with mock drama. Outside stood a sweet-faced maid awkwardly holding a pot of glorious golden orchids. The pot seemed about to crash to the ground. Perry moved fast, took hold, brought it into the room, and put it on the table.

"Mr. Swanson told me to bring it to you immediately," the maid lisped in a singsong voice.

"Mr. Swanson?" Perry gave Sonya a quick look.

"Yes," said the maid, "and Mrs. Swanson. Orchids are her favorite. She always sends them. Even to people in London that she knew when she was living there."

"Really, how nice," Sonya replied. "Well, thank you for bringing them to me. They are absolutely magnificent."

They were, too. Hothouse orchids. Not the small unsophisticated natives of Hawaii, but glorious giants bred from orchids found deep in the jungles of South America.

One or both of the Swansons were trying to make amends.

Sonya slit open the note wedged between two stems.

"It's from Lara," she said to Perry. "She's apologizing for not turning up this afternoon. She says Errol wants to check all her plans for the party, as there is so little time. Errol suggests that if we must do the treatment rooms today, we could catch them there together an hour or so before dinner.

"Lara adds that we could use the boat this afternoon; we just have to make arrangements with Jackie."

"So Errol wants to get in on the act." Perry sounded resigned. "I expected it. He wants to show the world what he's got now. He may have lost a network, but he gained a beautiful blonde and a glorious home. Not to mention a new business."

"We can't shoot in the treatment rooms at night," Sonya sighed. "It just won't work. The rooms are practically all windows and in the dark they'll reflect our lights. The only time to shoot is during the day. And think how Errol would look surrounded by jars of cream, makeup, and the rest of the paraphernalia. He'll look like what he is—a jealous husband who insists on being part of the act. Pathetic."

"Yeah," agreed Perry. "And Lara will look as if she is showing Daddy what a clever girl she is." He thought for moment. "Maybe that's what they were fighting about last night."

Sonya shrugged and put the note back among the orchids. "Who knows, and at this stage, who cares? We'll stay with our original plan—shoot the treatment and exercise rooms now. We can do it so that if we get Lara there for half an hour tomorrow, we can cut her into the video. It'll be hard work in postproduction, but better than having Errol in it.

"You go and set up while I call the spa and tell them what we want to do."

"Okay," Perry said. "But please, book the boat so we can go out and get some shots after we finish at the spa."

Shooting the spa was easy, thanks to Lara's efficiency. She had arranged for all the treatments to be set up, from salt rubs for removing flaky skin to water massages for aching backs. The technicians were ready and waiting. And so were the slim, attractive girls who acted as models.

Sonya watched as Perry worked fast and effortlessly. She knew he had one thing on his mind—the boat.

As they finished the last exterior shot, Jackie Olsen strode up. In her cap and nautical whites she looked the very picture of a boat captain. She took Sonya's hand and gave it a quick, hard shake.

"You don't have to call me captain, just Jackie," she said in a British accent. "My father sailed and I've been messing around in boats since I was a kid. Running the marina is the favorite of my many jobs at the spa."

Then she turned to Perry, who had started to pack his gear.

"Here, let me give you a hand with that," she said. "I've worked with TV crews; I know how to handle the gear."

Sonya looked at Jackie as she bent to pick up some batteries. She was a strong woman, thin and muscular. Her hair was short and swept back from her tanned face.

"Thanks," said Perry as Jackie folded one of the light stands and handed it to him to put in its case. "It's good to have some help."

"Call on me anytime," she replied with a grin. "I'm at your service."

Yes, Sonya decided, Jackie would be good to have around. She was calm, friendly, and efficient. And decidedly close to Lara. She must know the truth about Lara's problems with Errol.

Then Jackie spoke, almost as if she had read Sonya's mind.

"Let me tell you, Lara is absolutely devastated she wasn't able to show you around the spa today. She is the only person capable of explaining how it all works. But Errol is Errol and he insisted she do it his way."

Sonya heard a twinge of resentment in her voice.

"Well, we missed her, of course," said Sonya, "but we got the guts of it. The shoot was amazingly well set up. We had no problems at all. I wish every job went as easily."

Jackie nodded, then gave her a wide approving grin.

"Of course, the models were great, photogenic and cooperative." Sonya went on, "but it's essential we get shots of Lara in the treatment rooms. The story doesn't add up without her. I'm hoping she will spare some time for us in the morning."

"Don't give it a thought," Jackie interrupted. "Lara asked me to tell you to schedule it whenever you want. She's prepared to spend as much time as you need. After you finish with her, you can shoot one of the bungalows. We'll make it look great. Fill it with orchids. And anything else you want."

"Thanks," Sonya said. "You've worked with Lara before?"

"Not exactly, but I was one of the first people she approached when she decided to open the spa."

Ignoring Perry's protests, Jackie took the tripod from him, slung it over her shoulder, and led them down the path toward the marina. Her long, fast strides made it hard for Sonya to keep up with her. She took a deep breath and said to Jackie, "You sound as if you've known Lara for a long time."

"Of course. We are as close as sisters. I met her in London. She was still at school, just a kid but extremely ambitious. We used to hang out and talk about what we wanted from life. I thought she was just a dreamer. How wrong I was."

Jackie wanted to talk, and Sonya was happy to encourage her.

"Yes," she said sympathetically, "Lara told me how she had always dreamed of living in Hawaii."

"The spa is what's important, and it is only the beginning of her plan."

"Really? Tell me more."

For a second Jackie hesitated. "Well, I have to ask you not to make too much use of this in your story," she said. "But Lara plans to become an international queen of style. She'll build a chain of spas, and then manufacture products that cover everything— home, fashion, travel, beauty."

"And the concept will be Hawaiian?"

"Yes, from here, where life is still beginning. Where land is still being formed. The world is fascinated by the beauty and mystery of the Hawaiian Islands."

Jackie stopped when they reached the entrance to the dock, and looked across the bay.

"It's getting choppy," she said to Perry. "Do you have a rain cover for the camera?"

"Yes," Perry said. "Do you think the spray will come so high I'll need it?"

"Don't risk it. I don't want any harm to come to you or the camera."

Without a pause she turned back to Sonya. "You like the idea?"

"Yes, it's fascinating. Tell me more.

"Lara will concentrate first on Asia," Jackie said. "Its young population is demanding a better lifestyle. Those kids want everything that is available in the West, yet they are bored with the heavily promoted European brands. They want fresh products, products with a new edge. And that's what Lara will give them. From Asia she'll move into the States and then to Europe."

"That's some plan. You must have a lot of faith in her."

"I've seen her in action. Her looks help a lot, but apart from that she has one great talent. She knows how to manipulate men. She's ambitious and she gets what she wants. Just take a look around you."

Sonya was glad to hear Lara's plans, but starting a huge international business from this minute spot in the Pacific was a tough order, one that might make even Errol Swanson think twice.

"Is Errol behind these plans?" she asked. "It sounds to me as if it will take a lot of people and a lot of capital to get it going."

"She lets him think they're his ideas. Errol had no idea how brilliant Lara was until after he married her. Now he's jealous of her. He's lost his power in the business world, so he's fighting to get complete control of the spa. He thought it wouldn't make a dime. Now he realizes just how wrong he was. He wants this to be his spa, but he won't get it. We'll see to that."

Sonya was not convinced. "But Errol has all the money. You can't deny that."

"I don't. But once we have the spa running, we won't need it. Lara has already had offers to open spas in China. There's plenty of money there, and plenty of businessmen looking for new ways to invest it."

Sonya interrupted. "Jackie, Lara is having Errol's baby. There still must be some love between them."

"The baby is another good reason not to worry about money. Lara is having Errol's son. That's what he wanted from her more than anything. He'll hang in with her."

Perry finished strapping the waterproof cover on the camera and came over to them. Together they walked to the gangway. The yacht was beautiful, its clean lines silhouetted against the deep blue of the ocean. It was as big as Sonya had expected.

Jackie took the tripod off her shoulder and handed it up the rail to a crew member. "Let's get on board. We'll head around the coast to get the shots of Pele's lava crashing into the sea."

Before she could move, Sonya grabbed her arm.

"Jackie, Errol told me he and Lara didn't know whether the baby is a boy or a girl."

Jackie threw her head back and laughed. "Errol only knows what Lara wants him to know. Make no mistake about that. There's a lot about Lara he has to learn. Wait and see."

Chapter **13**

Chicago
Thursday, 5:00 P.M.

She was late, as usual. Probably sitting on the bed with her clothes strewn around her, her suitcase empty while she debated what to pack. That was Christy, never able to make a decision.

Joan Swanson walked toward Gate A12 at O'Hare Airport. She had told Christy that she was old enough, at 39, to get there by herself. Joan would meet her at the gate and get her aboard. If she missed the plane, too bad; Christy wouldn't see her father in Hawaii.

As Joan wove her way through the crowded terminal, she knew she'd made a mistake. If Christy didn't make the plane, she was likely to create a scene at the gate. She'd done it before.

Joan should have followed her usual plan: gone to Christy's apartment an hour early, helped her pack, and taken her to the airport. That was the only way to be certain Christy would make the flight.

But so what if Christy didn't make it? The thought filled her with sudden relief. It was true she'd have to listen to a weepy, hysterical Christy on the phone. But to be by herself, in a bungalow by the sea, would be bliss. No faxes, no e-mails, no business calls. No Christy. A chance to have some sort of peace.

Christy had a support system in Chicago. Joan had worked hard enough to set it up for her. Let Christy's expensive doctors take care of her.

Joan couldn't remember a time when she hadn't been Christy's watchdog. When she first went to school, each morning Joan had to force her to dress. First Christy would say she wanted to wear one thing, then another. How often Joan had watched her lie on the floor, screaming with rage.

Craig would leave for the school bus as soon as he was ready, eager to get away from the two bickering females. Christy would argue until she missed the bus and Joan had to drive her to school.

Joan sighed. She could understand why Christy put on those terrible scenes. Was it to antagonize her, or was it some part of her illness? It must be the illness, Joan comforted herself. She believed she had done everything she could to avoid the fights.

Christy's problems became worse as she grew older. No matter which treatment she was under, she was never at peace with herself. In her teens, the shoplifting and the episode with the police taught Joan to stand guard over her daughter when they went into a store. She even checked Christy's bag when she came out of a fitting room, to make sure she hadn't slipped anything in.

"You are so hard on your daughter," a sales assistant said to her one afternoon. "Can't you give her a break?"

"You don't know what you're talking about," Joan had snapped back. "She's been arrested once for taking things. I won't go through that again."

The assistant had shrugged and walked away. But Christy wouldn't let it end there. She turned to her mother and slapped her.

"Did you hear what she said? She said you were too tough on me. She's right. I need a break. I need a break away from you." Joan said nothing. At such times she wished Christy had never been born.

Joan stopped. She was only at Gate A4. Her breath came heavily as she tried to bring herself back to the present. An advertisement of a young dark-haired man riding a bike caught her eye. It was a painful reminder of the disappearance of Christy's twin, Craig. Christy couldn't let go of him. She fantasized he was still alive and living in Chicago.

It was heartrending to see her grief. Christy searched for him night and day. She stopped young men in the street, stared into their faces, and asked if they were her brother. It didn't matter whether or not the men resembled Craig, as long as they had dark curly hair.

Most of the men were confused by her demands, some were angry, and some even threatened to call the police. Joan hated having to make the apologies and even more the scenes after she demanded Christy leave the men alone.

Christy's search was still going on despite years of sessions with her psychiatrist. Sadly, Christy still believed her twin would come back to her one day.

"It's tough for me to bear," Joan told herself, "but it must be even more so for Christy."

Joan reached the boarding gate and stood there undecided. Should she tell the woman at the gate that Christy might turn up after the flight had left? Joan had become accustomed to handling these situations. To tell the truth, Christy was unpredictable. She decided to let the gate agent know.

The agent was an African American whose hair was done up in sophisticated cornrow braiding. The badge pinned to the lapel of her well-pressed uniform identified her as Rose. She looked as though she could handle Christy.

When she saw the worried look on Joan's face and heard the story, she clucked in sympathy.

"Don't worry," she said. "I have a daughter. I know what it's like. She's always late, but she usually makes it. I'll keep my eye out for yours and rush her aboard at the last minute if it is possible."

Joan was curious: "How old is your daughter?"

"She's a typical teenager, she turned 13 last October."

"Mine is 39 but she never grew up. Mentally she never left her teens. She's just one big problem." Joan's eyes filled with tears.

The man standing in line behind Joan spoke up. "Ladies, how about continuing the soap opera another time? I'm waiting."

The agent ignored him and looked at Joan. "Are you all right?"

"Yes," she said. "I'm all right. It's just that sometimes the worry gets the better of me." She paused to gain self-control. "The board says the plane is 10 minutes late?"

"Yes, and that 10 minutes will grow to at least 20. She has time."

"Thanks, and enjoy your daughter," added Joan. "Time goes by so quickly."

"And now, sir, how can I help you?" Rose said to the waiting man with forced politeness.

Joan moved away and looked wistfully at the line of chairs. She longed to sit down. Sit and do nothing. Just let it happen. But those extra 20 minutes meant she could head back to look for Christy. Perhaps she was having trouble at security.

She walked down the corridor studying the passersby, looking for Christy's blond hair. Christy was fair, like her father, and had the same square jaw. Although Errol had been handsome as a young man, his good looks didn't translate well on Christy. She was tall, angular, and unfeminine.

How strange that the twins were so different.

Craig took after Joan's father—dark with curly black hair, sturdy, strong-minded, yet sensitive. Her family had adored Craig from the moment they saw his tousled black curls in the hospital.

As he grew, the resemblance grew and so did the family's affection for him. Craig was the darling, the spoiled one.

She let her mind float back. How her father had loved Craig and how she had loved them both.

"Father was the man I respected most," she told herself. "I was stupid not to realize what a good man he was. If only I'd listened to him I wouldn't have ruined my life by marrying Errol."

Her father had disliked Errol from the moment she brought him to the toy shop. And he never wavered in his resistance to the marriage.

"No, you are too young," he said over and over again. "You have no idea of what the world is about. You are a young Jewish girl who has been provided for and protected all her life. Now you want to marry a stranger from outside our faith. He's not even a man. He's just a boy—a boy with no background, no religion, no education."

For the first time in her life, she didn't listen to him. She was desperately in love. She dreamed of Errol night and day.

Her father did everything he could to stop the marriage. He threatened to cut her off from the family, to forbid her mother to speak to her. But deep down, they both knew that would never happen. She was his daughter. He called her his "right hand," and she knew she was indispensable to him. His love for her was so strong he could never abandon her.

They had planned together for her to take over the business. From the time she was a toddler he took her to the manufacturer showrooms and let her pick out toys for the store.

"She has a better eye than I have," he would joke with the salesmen.

At first he refused to go to the wedding her mother had hastily arranged. But he gave in and she walked down the aisle on his arm. That moment was the happiest of her life.

But he never got over his dislike of Errol, and he let the bitterness show. The one thing he could never forgive was that she had married out of her faith.

Now when she looked back, she wondered about the stroke her father had suffered shortly after the twins were born. Was it brought on by the feeling that finally he had lost her to Errol? Was it a subconscious desire to get her back?

When her mother had called with the news about her father, she had rushed to the hospital. She spent days at his bedside, begging him to get well. She promised she would never leave him and that she would do everything to keep the business going.

"Mother will take care of the twins," she assured him. "Errol will not interfere. There is nothing for you to worry about."

"You are the one to take over," he whispered to her, making a great effort to speak. "No one understands the store as you do."

"I'll not only take over the store, I'll expand it for you," she said. "We'll end up with a chain of stores, each one bigger than the next."

From that day on she took the twins to her mother and worked full-time at the store.

She didn't take a salary until she knew the business was back on track. All she allowed herself were the expenses for taxis and the part-time babysitter.

It infuriated Errol.

"I'm putting food into your mouth while you work for nothing for your rich family," he complained constantly. She tried to explain that the medical bills were overwhelming. But Errol didn't want to hear it. "I've had enough problems with my own father. I didn't marry you to take care of yours."

One night he made her so angry, she hit him. He hit her back, time and time again, with a savage rage that terrified her. She knew then that her marriage was over.

To escape from him, she worked longer hours at the store. The harder she worked, the angrier he became. In a way, she told herself, the store was the only home she had really known. She had spent her childhood playing on the floor and watching the customers.

She had watched her parents remove the cash from the register and hide it in a secret drawer beneath the counter. She learned just where the special nail was that released the drawer. Her father had designed it, and as a sign of his confidence, to her delight, he let her open it each night.

How the store had changed. Customers now paid with credit cards that they slid through a groove in a card reader.

But Joan hadn't changed. She still loved the toy business. It gave her the feeling that she was doing something for the community. The toys amused children, but also taught them and encouraged good citizenship. The store built a reputation on her energy and her beliefs.

In the last years of their marriage, the business was the only subject that she and Errol could discuss with civility.

"Believe in what you are doing, put your heart and soul into the store, and you'll succeed," he had told her during what he called their weekly Sunday night "business sessions." Despite the problems in their relationship, she looked forward to those Sunday evenings. She relied on his advice and he gave it unstintingly.

It was he who encouraged her to open a second store, and then another, until the Toy Biz chain grew to 12.

Now Errol wanted to take it all away from her, and that thought sent a cold shiver down her spine.

She was panting as she reached the end of the boarding-gate corridor. Ahead were the security machines and a jumble of people huddled around tables while guards searched through their bags.

A wave of guilt swept over her. Christy was mentally ill. How could she have expected her to deal with this confusion? Her daughter, who had never finished school, who had never worked or faced the realities of day-to-day living, could not be expected to cope with the stress of security screening.

But Christy was there, already through security, sitting in a plastic chair with her sneakers beside her. The table in front of her was strewn with clothing, makeup, and jewelry.

Joan rushed to her, half in relief, half in anger. "Christy, you made it."

Christy looked up. "Mother," she said surprised to hear Joan's voice. "Of course I made it. I'd be at the gate, except the man wanted to go through my bag to find my scissors. He was a nice man, but he took them away from me."

"Get your sneakers on while I repack for you." Joan stuffed the things in the bag. "Didn't I tell you not to bring scissors onto the plane?"

"I guess you did. But I put them in with my nail file. I just forgot."

"Christy, it's time you learned to remember. You're lucky the plane is delayed, otherwise you would have missed it."

"Of course, Mother. I'm in the wrong, as always."

Joan didn't listen. As she pulled the zipper to close the bag, it caught on the lace edge of a nightdress and stuck fast.

"Christy, why on earth did you put your lace nightdress in your carry-on bag?"

Christy was bent over struggling to lace up her sneakers, but she stood up and faced Joan.

"Because you told me to," she said her voice rising. "You said if my luggage got lost I would need something to sleep in. I always try to do what you tell me."

"Then what about the scissors? You didn't do what I said with them." Joan was joking. But Christy was beyond jokes. She grabbed the case from her mother, tore the nightdress from the zipper, and threw it to the floor.

"There. Does that satisfy you? I've lost the scissors and now I've thrown away the nightdress. Why can't you ever leave me alone? That's what Daddy always said. You never let me alone.

"The man wasn't angry with me about the scissors. He was nice. He said lots of people forget, and he was sorry he had to take them."

Christy pointed at a dark-headed inspector. "There he is, that's the one. It's Craig."

"Craig? Christy, what did you say to him?"

"I asked him if his name was Craig. He nodded and smiled at me."

"Oh, Christy, please, you promised me that if I let you come you wouldn't talk about your brother."

"I didn't break my promise; I just asked if his name was Craig."

Joan looked over at the inspector, who glanced at her, smiled, and went back to his work. Then she turned to Christy, about to challenge her again.

Christy's eyes were wide, staring, her head jerking from side to side. Joan's heart sank.

Christy had stopped taking her medication. Anything could happen.

"Don't panic," Joan told herself. "You've been through this before."

She picked up the torn nightdress, folded it, put it back in the bag, and slung the bag over her shoulder.

"I'm sorry, Christy, I shouldn't have teased you," she said, keeping her voice low and soothing. "Be a good girl now. Remember, we are going to Hawaii to see your father. Let's not disappoint him."

Christy hesitated. Joan could sense the emotional turmoil she was going through. Christy was close to walking back through security and out of the airport.

Instead she reached out and took her bag from her mother. Together they walked to the gate.

Chapter 14

The Big Island
Thursday, 4:00 P.M.

"She was conceived during my honeymoon in Tibet. That's why her spirit is so powerful. She was blessed by Buddha.

"Lara will always get what she wants. You'll see. The spa will be extremely popular. Nothing to do with Errol. All to do with Lara. She attracts life. That's the gift I gave her."

Sonya saw that Margaret Halstead's envy of her daughter was eating into her soul. It was painful to listen to, and Sonya wanted none of it. Mothers and daughters spoke their own languages. She was grateful her own mother was so independent. Mrs. Iverson was proud of Sonya and delighted in her success.

"Be noncommittal," she told herself.

Sonya murmured a polite "Really?" and left it at that.

But Margaret Halstead wasn't about to stop.

"Lara goes on with this craziness about how she was a Hawaiian princess in another life. Rubbish. Everything comes to her because I conceived her in Tibet. All Errol has given her is money."

She looked hard at Sonya, and Sonya knew she desperately wanted her to agree.

Sonya could not meet her eyes. She thought quickly, then said, "I guess in some ways you could say she is a lucky woman to have married such a wealthy man."

Mrs. Halstead went at it again, her voice rising with every word. "Haven't you listened? I just told you Lara's success has nothing to do with Errol and his money. It has to do with power I gave her."

As she spat out the last words, Sonya gave a half laugh of embarrassment. She said, "Yes, I do understand what you are saying." Then, to change the subject, she added. "Well, it is easy to see where she got her beauty. It is amazing how she resembles you. You could be sisters."

It was only a half truth. Margaret Halstead had none of Lara's shining health, although her coloring and bone structure were much the same. She was thin, with the ravaged look of an alcoholic. Her skin was gray and tired. Cut in a chin-length pageboy, with the edges of the gray-blond fringe dyed a deep purple, her hairstyle gave her an eccentric, of-the-moment look.

She brushed off Sonya's compliment. "Beauty is only skin-deep. I have given Lara power. The power of the East."

Sonya closed her eyes. She wanted the power to get away from this woman. But how could she do it without offending Lara?

She felt a wave of nausea. The sail on the boat had been a joy for Perry, but the choppy sea had left Sonya with queasy stomach. When the boat had moored, she'd been happy to leave him showing Jackie some of the shots he'd taken. All she wanted was to get back to her bed and rest for 10 minutes until the world settled down.

But as she had passed the main building, she had run into Lara and her mother. Mrs. Halstead had apparently arrived early, and it was easy to see Lara wasn't thrilled.

"Oh, Sonya, I hope you liked the orchids," Lara had called out. "I feel bad about not working with you this afternoon. But I was busy with Errol and then Mother arrived unexpectedly. Come meet her and join us on a tour of my house. You haven't had a chance to see it yet."

Sonya hesitated. She desperately wanted to lie down. But if she saw the Swanson home now, it would save time later. Maybe Donna would want to do her interview there. She should look around for the best site.

"Thank you, that's a great idea," she said as she held out her hand to Mrs. Halstead. To her amazement, the woman squeezed it tightly and then held onto it.

"Come walk with us," she said, pulling Sonya along the path. "Lara is going to show me everything. You know, this is the very first time I've been here. My very first invitation. Yes, my first from my daughter and her rich husband."

Lara ignored her comment and led them to the house, explaining the flowering shrubs to her mother as she had to Sonya. Mrs. Halstead smiled in excited pleasure at each point Lara made. Then she squeezed Sonya's hand as if to make sure she had understood.

Sonya was beginning to understand why Lara kept her mother away from the spa. Her hand was hot and sweaty in the humidity, but Mrs. Halstead held on with a viselike grip. It was only when they stepped singly into the courtyard that Sonya managed to free herself.

"Yes, yes, it is all very beautiful," she said, bizarrely anxious to cover any slight Mrs. Halstead might feel.

Mrs. Halstead beamed at her. "Only a woman with Lara's power could do it."

Lara took them into the living room, where Mrs. Halstead became so excited at the view of the ocean that she clapped her hands. She was right, Sonya thought, the view and the simple elegance of the room were well worth applauding. Below, a ribbon of black, jagged rocks stretched along the cliff. The ocean roared unceasingly, thrusting its waves against the rocks in a magnificent display of force.

"We'll start here, because this is my favorite room. The view is so amazing, I felt nothing could compete with it, so I kept everything simple both in color and design. But it is comfortable. One of my great joys is to sit here and watch the ocean. Its power makes any problem seem small and unimportant."

Lara's cell phone rang. She opened it and spoke briefly.

Then she turned to them. "I am so sorry, I have to leave you for a few minutes. Errol needs me. He is still working on the plans we were discussing when Mother arrived. I'll have to check some facts with him, but it won't be long."

Sonya signaled that she would leave, too, but Lara held her back.

"Stay with Mother please. There's coffee in the kitchenette near Errol's study. Have some, and pour me a cup, too." She laughed. "I'll need it after discussing figures with Errol."

Mrs. Halstead ignored her suggestion and walked to the window, motioning Sonya to follow. She pointed to a bronze statue of Buddha that stood in the center of the terrace below.

"Why?" she said. "I want you to tell me why. If she believes she was a Hawaiian princess in a former life, why would she put a statue of Buddha there? Why? It's the first thing she sees when she wakes and the last thing she sees at night. I tell you, Buddha is important to her, and that comes from me. From my influence on her.

"Another thing—why does she have a tattoo of Buddha on her left breast? Why?"

Mrs. Halstead paused, then whispered. "She doesn't think I know about it, but I do. I watched her through the door as she was stripping to take a shower. She can't hide anything from me. But she wants to. Why? I am her mother. I gave her life."

Sonya had had enough.

"Mrs. Halstead, I really don't know what you are talking about. I met Lara a few days ago. I only know her because I'm doing a story on the spa."

"So you're not one of those girls she collected in Europe and now can't bear to be without? They're the ones she confides in. I know they turned her against me. They've made her ashamed of me."

Now Sonya was angry. "Really, Mrs. Halstead, I just told you I only met Lara a few days ago. I know nothing of her private business."

Lara's mother walked back to the door. As she turned to look at Sonya, she seemed another woman. A hurt, fragile woman, desperately seeking the love of her daughter.

"I'm sorry. I didn't mean to accuse you of anything. It's just that Lara and I are so alike in many ways. And not just physically. We are both close to God. But Lara is envious of my strength. That's why she refuses to let me be part of this great new venture of hers."

Sonya was frantic to escape. She had work to do, calls to make, schedules to set up. She didn't have to listen to the ravings of Lara's mother. When it came to that, it was time she called her own mother. It was three days since she had spoken to her.

Mrs. Halstead looked at Sonya. "I'll get the drinks. What do you want? Coffee or something stronger?"

"Just black coffee would be perfect," Sonya glanced at her watch. The minutes were slipping away. She would drink the coffee quickly and go. That was the polite thing to do.

"Lara was always a beauty," Margaret Halstead gave Sonya a mug of coffee, then, glass in hand, sat down on the sofa and settled back to be confidential. "And always advanced for her age. We were proud of her.

"Her father is brilliant. I met him in London while he was doing his Ph.D. He wanted to sleep with me so badly, he promised me anything I wanted. I said I wanted to go to Tibet. That's why Lara was conceived there."

Mrs. Halstead laughed. "You see, I got what I wanted that time. My husband likes to win, but he didn't win that time. No indeed."

She got up and walked back to the kitchenette to refill her glass. This time Sonya took a close look. Coke laced with something. Could be rum. Or possibly vodka. Either way, Margaret Halstead was a fast drinker.

It was time to change the subject. "Will you stay with Lara until the baby is born?"

"We'll see," the older woman said. Then she caught her breath, as if holding back some deep hurt. "I was with her when her first child was born, I don't see why I shouldn't be here for the second."

"Her first child?" Sonya gave her a quick look. "Lara has had a baby?"

"Right here in the Hawaii she professes to love so much. A little dark-haired, brown-skinned baby girl. Lara was a teenager. She begged us to let her visit Hawaii with a school group. At the time it seemed such a happy idea. We thought she'd be safe, be well looked after. We never dreamed she'd get into trouble."

Sonya wasn't surprised. She knew the statistics on teenage pregnancies.

"It must have been upsetting," she said.

Mrs. Halstead played the role of shocked mother to the full. "Yes, it was. I didn't know what to say when she told me. Now she tells everyone that she fell in love with the islands and didn't want to come home. The truth is, she didn't dare."

"She stayed here until the baby was born?"

"Yes, we wanted her to have an abortion, but she wouldn't hear of it."

"Who was the baby's father?"

"One of the local guys, as dark-skinned as the baby was. Lara claimed she was unlucky, that she only had sex with him once and got pregnant immediately."

"Oh," Sonya said carefully.

"You're thinking she was raped, but she said not. Insisted. I don't even know whether she knew the boy's name; she's never mentioned it." Mrs. Halstead sighed. "Looking back, it's hard to believe that was her first sexual experience. She's sexy now and she was sexy then."

Sonya swallowed some coffee. What sort of mother was Mrs. Halstead to reveal her daughter's secrets to a member of the press? What was her purpose? To expose Lara's past to Errol? To the world? Sonya knew it would take time to check the records and find the child. But it could be done. Then again, perhaps Mrs. Halstead had already found her and was planning to produce her at the opening party. Perhaps she had made up the whole story. Whatever the truth was, Sonya knew one thing for sure—Lara's mother was as vindictive as she was crazy.

"You think I'm making it up—you don't want to believe me?" Mrs. Halstead sounded gleeful. "Well, it's true." She laughed. "Want anything more to drink?"

Without waiting for Sonya's reply, she went into the kitchenette. In seconds she was at the doorway, taking a sip from the glass.

"Of course her father believed that it wasn't her fault. When he saw a photo of the little girl, he wanted to bring her back to California, but I wasn't having any of it. I'd been through motherhood once and that was enough. We put her up for adoption. That was the end of her . . . and the end of my marriage."

Sonya looked at her. Mrs. Halstead's eyes were narrowed with hatred.

Sonya asked, "Does Errol know?"

"No, it's our little secret, Lara's and mine."

Sonya rose and stepped toward her. "Why are you telling me? I have no right to know. It is Lara's personal business."

"I'll say what I like." She waved the glass vaguely in Sonya's direction. "Lara is not the Miss America she pretends to be. She tried to stop me from coming to the spa. She said Errol didn't want me here. But I came. I'm her mother and I have rights. You'll see, he'll try to get rid of me, but I'll stay, no matter what."

Sonya moved to the window to get away from the woman and her drunkenness. It was pointless talking to her. She looked out at the Buddha, with its face so calm and peaceful. The waves crashing on the rocks below it seemed to be receiving its gentle blessing.

Just then Perry walked out of the shadows of the ridge, climbed the stairs to the terrace, and gazed at the Buddha. Jackie followed, carrying the tripod.

Perry put down the camera, took the tripod from her, and started to set it up. Perry had bonded with Jackie. Sonya could tell by the way he talked to her. That was good. She liked Perry to make friends on a job. He always wanted to be with Sonya, but there were times when she needed to get away from him.

She watched them arranging a shot of the Buddha. As Jackie turned, she saw Sonya, and waved at her to come down. Sonya turned toward Margaret Halstead. Lara's mother was sitting in a chair, her eyes closed. The empty glass was on the floor beside her. This was Sonya's chance. Without a word she took her bag and walked across the room and out the door.

Perry was pleased to see her. "I've been looking all over for you. You weren't in your bungalow or on the beach. I was about to send out a search party."

"You're a worrywart." Sonya started to laugh. Then she forced herself to stop. She felt hysterical. Mrs. Halstead had really gotten to her.

"Well, he wasn't the only one," Jackie interrupted. "That good-looking ranger from Volcano was also after you. He told me he had some information to give you. He wants to meet you at eight for a drink." Jackie handed Sonya Joe's card. "He wrote his cell number on the back."

"Thanks, Jackie, I'll give him a call."

"What's the info he wants to give you?" Perry broke in.

"Nothing important, Perry," Sonya replied with a tinge of guilt. "I'll tell you later."

"He just wants to get together with you. I know the type," Perry snorted.

Jackie shifted her weight from one leg to another, clearly wanting to change the subject. "You were with Mrs. Halstead, weren't you? How did you like her?"

"She talks a lot." Sonya was determined to be noncommittal.

"That's one way to look at it," Jackie replied. "She's a drinker with big personality problems. She drove her husband away. Lara loves them both, but her father won't attend anything if her mother is there. She's not welcome here. Her drinking causes big problems with Errol. He doesn't want her around, but Lara fights him all the way."

"Do you think she'll stay for the birth of the baby?"

"She wants to. But Errol's got a lot of emotional baggage riding on that baby. I wouldn't be surprised if he insisted on Lara having it in one of the maternity hospitals in L.A. Lara won't discuss her plans for the birth. I only know she wants her baby to be born in Hawaii.

"But her mother might get her way despite Errol. She's just as determined as Lara."

Sonya nodded in agreement. Mrs. Halstead was not an easy woman to shake off. What's more, she was determined to be part of Lara's life.

Chapter 15

The Big Island
Thursday, 6:00 P.M.

Frank O'Neill snapped his cell phone closed, then reopened it and redialed Lara Swanson's number. After six rings, the voice mail picked up. He closed the phone again. Lara knew he was at the spa. She could see his number on her caller ID. After all that urgency about his coming, why wouldn't she take his call?

He had spent Thursday morning doing research in Chicago, and the flight from O'Hare had gone like clockwork. His plane had been on time and Lara's friend and assistant, Jackie Olsen, was waiting for him at the spa.

"Welcome." Jackie's smile was wide and genuine. "I know Lara will be glad to see you. She asked me to tell you that she has left a note in your bungalow."

He rushed to the bungalow. The note was there all right, artfully placed in a bowl of purple orchids. Its message was enigmatic. "You'll find the front garden of your bungalow most satisfying. Enjoy it and the orchids. Lara."

He threw his suitcase on the bed. Lara must have mentioned the garden because she wanted him to wait for her there. He walked out the front door, frowning at the brilliant sunlight. What did she mean by "satisfying"?

The garden was filled with the usual tropical shrubs and flowers. In the center was a stone statue, and at its feet, a scattering of blossoms. He smiled. That was a Lara touch.

He sat on the stone bench to wait for her. Being close to Lara yet unable to speak to her was unbearable. He had to see her. He felt the gnawing sense of inadequacy that always overcame him when he thought of her with Swanson. How could he free her? How could he have her again?

He looked up. There she was, walking along the curved path that led past his bungalow to the marina. He closed his eyes and felt his love for her surge through him.

She wore one of her pale, floating dresses. He had often told her that in them she was at her most beautiful. A hat shaded her face as she looked at him, raised her hand, and gave him a small wave. He just stood and watched her. She still moved with that unconscious grace that set her apart.

He wanted to run to her and hold her. But instead he walked calmly to the gate and swung it open for her. He caught his breath as she walked past him and into the living room. He followed as closely as he dared.

When they were inside, she came close to him and touched his face. "I knew you would be waiting for me in the garden," she said, "that you would understand my note. Errol was standing near me when I wrote it. I couldn't say anything meaningful." She stepped back and looked at him. "Oh, Frank, it's so long since I've seen you, and so much has changed."

He put his hands on her shoulders, then leaned forward to kiss her.

She turned her face away.

He dropped his arms, uncertain. "I was expecting a warm welcome. You said you were desperate to see me."

She shook her head. "Let me calm down, Frank," she said. "I'm so confused." She took off her hat, put it on the sofa, then sat down beside it. "It took a lot of courage for me to come. If you hadn't been in the garden, I wouldn't have known what to do."

"What do you mean, courage? What's going on, Lara?"

Lara bowed her head. "You were right about Errol. He is a tyrant—he's suspicious of everything I do. And he's jealous of everyone. Oh, Frank, I never realized how frightening he could be."

Frank put his hand under her chin, lifted her head, and looked into her eyes. Surely he still had a chance with Lara. He must get her back. She was his life.

When Lara first told him about meeting Errol, he had been stung with jealousy. Had his angry warning driven Lara into Errol's grasp?

"You are not the best judge of him," she had said. "He fired you. He's different in private. He's tender and kind to me, and he respects my ideas."

"Lara, you know you're attracted to older men. You believe anything they say."

She had giggled, then kissed him. "Like you, for instance. Like you, dear jealous Frank."

She was irresistible, and he had melted.

He remembered her slight dismissive smile as she turned away.

That had been a long time ago.

Frank left Lara sitting on the sofa and went to the bar. "I'll drink to the memory of my good advice that you disregarded years ago. Would you like something?"

"Just some water, please, flat water, for the baby's sake."

"You should never have married him."

"Oh, Frank," she said as if to justify herself, "he is not the same man I married. When I first met him, he was so exciting. He had so many interests apart from his work. His every hour, every minute, was something new. And he had all that power."

Frank gave her the glass of water and sat down beside her. "He still has power. If he didn't, a network crew wouldn't be here doing a piece on your spa. You e-mailed me that you were desperate. Why?"

"I needed you. I needed someone to talk to, someone who cares for me."

"Lara, you know I still love you." Frank moved closer to her. Her body tensed, and she drew back.

"You said he still has power," she said. "Maybe that is true in New York. But here, his only real power is over me and the staff, and he doesn't trust any of us. He gets involved in every detail. He changes my orders and tells me afterward. I'm sure the new manager he hired spies on me."

Frank nodded. "Sounds like Errol. Things have to be done his way or not at all."

Lara continued, "He insists I go over every bill with him, and nothing pleases him more than when he finds a mistake. His excuse is that he is protecting my future and the baby's.

"But the worst is the way he watches me. Even when he thinks I'm asleep. He gets up early, walks to my side of the bed, and stares down at me. It's eerie. I am terrified to move in case he realizes I am awake. I lie there praying he will go away."

"My God."

"He has nightmares and cries out angrily in his sleep. Frank, I think he's speaking to me. He calls me 'whore' and 'bitch.' Some days I think he will kill me."

Frank turned to her. But her body tensed again. She needed to talk more than she needed to be held.

"Yesterday, he had an interview with Sonya Iverson, the producer from the network. Afterward he was furious, and he took his fury out on me. He said he told her more about his father than he'd meant to. And Sonya is sharp. She knew what was going on between us."

Frank shrugged. "I know Sonya from my days at the network. She's okay. You have nothing to fear from her. Anyway, sharks like Errol always have something to hide. But he's not important, Lara. You and your baby are. I want you to leave him."

He watched while Lara took her empty glass to the bar. She filled it with water and drank. When she turned to him, her attitude had changed.

"Frank," she said, ignoring his request, "tell me about the story you are doing on the spa."

"It's for a travel magazine."

"You must say that the spa was Errol's idea, not mine. Make sure you say that. He'll be furious if he isn't given full credit."

"Whatever you want, Lara." Frank walked over to her. "But you have to face some unpleasant truths about the publicity you'll get as Errol's wife. To most journalists, you are nothing but a trophy, a woman he married because she is a beautiful blonde. They'll laugh at your philosophy."

"I know, I've been told that a dozen times."

"Lara, please let me get you away from all this."

There was a long silence; finally Lara turned to him. "No, Frank. Never. I have promised Errol I will be with him as long as he lives."

"Well, then think about this: I am writing an unauthorized biography of Errol. I will tell the truth about him. I'm going to write about his questionable business tactics, his greed, his cruelty to his staff. I'll get into his personal life, his family background, his wives, his children. And you. I know a lot about him, more than you can imagine. And it will be hard for you to live with."

"Then why must you write it?"

Frank felt bitter. Why did she have to ask? The reason was obvious. To pay back Errol for the way he had fired him and dozens of his friends. The memory of that Sunday would never leave him.

He had worked as usual that morning, writing his commentary for the show. Then he had gone to his favorite Italian restaurant for lunch.

Details stuck with him. That was a blessing to him as a writer. He remembered just what he had for lunch; tortellini with peas in a cream sauce. It was a special treat. The camera made him look heavy and he was trying to lose five pounds.

He remembered he was writing part of a series he was doing on the need for gun control.

When he returned to the studio, the receptionist stopped him. She had a message from his agent. That was odd. Why wasn't it on his voice mail? The receptionist suggested he return the call right there in the lobby. Odd again.

He called his agent at home.

"Frank, I feel bad to have to deliver this message."

"What is it? What's the matter?"

"Frank, the network has let you go. You are finished."

"What? When?"

"Now."

"Now?" he shouted. "Goddamnit. Who can I talk to?"

"No one, Frank, this is Errol Swanson's decision. You know he has never liked your on-air personality, and he doesn't agree with your political views. But the reason he gave was that you've been drinking and the network can't put up with that."

"What shit. That's not true. I want to talk to him."

"No, Frank. Your desk has already been cleaned out and your electronic passkey has been revoked. You can't go back."

"Is this part of the general cutback? I could live with that."

Frank heard his agent sigh. "No, not part of that. You're getting special treatment."

"Get me a new job, Ralph."

"Face it, Frank, you're finished in television. I just hope it doesn't affect your writing career. That's what I'm going to focus on now."

Frank felt a sudden cold calm. His jaw tightened. "I promise you, I will deal with Errol Swanson. Somewhere. Some way. Good-bye."

He had tried to use his passkey to get back to his desk. His agent was right. It wasn't working.

The receptionist spoke. "Frank, I think you'll find Security waiting with your things at the loading dock." She knew he'd been fired before he did.

He'd use it all in his book, the one Lara was pleading him not to write.

He looked at her, sitting on the sofa, all beauty and grace. "The truth is, Lara, that if I don't write this book, someone else will. I spoke to my publisher last week and he told me to get it done fast.

"I have an advantage. I've worked for Errol. I know his story at the network. I knew Margot, his second wife, and I know you. He's hot right now. And I need the money."

"But you say you love me and always will. Think of me, think of my baby."

"I've told you, Lara, if I don't write the book, someone else will. And they might not be as nice to you as I will."

She turned away and wrung her hands as if to wipe away the problem.

"I have my plans for the future—my dreams. I will not let Errol Swanson's past disturb them. I will do what I have to do. Frank, please let someone else write the book. Move on to something that is more spiritual. Something that has more meaning in the world."

Frank raised a quizzical eyebrow, then laughed.

Lara picked up her hat and stood, looking at him. Tears filled her eyes.

"You have to accept the consequences of what you do. Write your exposé. But remember, if you hurt us it will come back to you."

Frank put out his hand out and touched her arm.

"Lara, I will do what I have to do. And you will bless me for it. I will make you and your baby happy and secure."

Chapter **16**

The Big Island
Thursday, 10:00 P.M.

The plane from New York landed 30 minutes early without a bump, without even the dip of a wing. "Typical," Sonya told herself. "Everything comes easily for Donna Fuller."

Donna had a star's gift for making an entrance. This sultry tropical evening, even after a 10-hour flight, she stepped from the network's private plane with the ease of a woman who had enjoyed a restful night's sleep. In her beige pants, sweater, and sneakers, she looked as if she were ready for a run.

Sonya walked toward her, amazed at the rush of affection she felt.

Donna looked her over and then brushed her cheek with a quick kiss. "Well, Sonya, you seem pleased to see me," she said. "How are things going?"

Sonya put her head back and laughed—the first real laugh she'd had since she'd arrived. It was easy to relax with Donna.

"Donna, it all seems like a bad joke," she said. "On the one hand there is no real news story; on the other there's too much story. It's like a soap opera. There's a lot going on between Lara and Errol . . . and Lara's mother." The thought of the old woman constantly squeezing her hand started her laughing again.

Matt Richards, the show's executive producer, joined them. "What's so funny? Just come from a party? Lots of time for dinner and dancing, eh? Get any work done?"

Donna put her hand on Sonya's shoulder. Sonya had stopped laughing, but before she could answer, Donna spoke. "It's girls only, Matt. It'd be too hard to explain it to you."

Sonya knew Matt was annoyed. He would never admit that he was incapable of understanding anything. Especially if it were about women.

"When do you want to meet? Or do you need to get a good night's sleep and then meet early in the morning?" Sonya asked, briskly changing the subject.

"As soon as we check in," Matt replied, "if you've got your notes together."

Sonya had learned to ignore his arrogance, but it never failed to upset her.

"Fine," she said. Matt was a creep, but a creep who was determined to rise to the top of the network. She had to be careful, to look to the future.

Matt walked back to the plane.

"We'll meet in my bungalow," Donna said. "Lara e-mailed me photos of it. It looks bigger than our studio."

"Okay, I'll meet you there," Sonya said. "And you're right, the living rooms are huge. I've got one, too."

Donna turned to her. "I'm sure Matt won't disagree. I'll be

ready in half an hour." With that she got into the limousine that was waiting for them.

Sonya walked over to greet Sabrina, who was standing by the plane, her precious makeup case on the ground beside her.

"How's it going?" she asked.

"Fine," Sonya said, careful not to reveal too much to Sabrina. Much as she liked gossiping with her, after Matt's comment she wanted to get back to the bungalow and change.

"You don't have much of a tan. I suppose that means you've done nothing but work?"

"Well, let me tell you something," Sonya said. "I just had a date with a great-looking guy, a real hunk. That why I'm dressed so sexy. I've got to race back to the bungalow to change before the meeting with Donna and Matt."

Sabrina's eyes open. "What guy?"

"I'll tell you all about him later. You know we're sharing the bungalow. We've got all night to gossip."

"Okay. I'll get a ride to the spa with the guys from the plane. See you after I've checked in."

Sonya drove the Jeep back to the spa. The early part of the evening had been a disaster and there was no time to made amends.

She'd accepted Joe Robertson's invitation for a drink at eight, two hours before Donna's flight was due to arrive. She wanted to see Joe again. He was uncomplicated, a breath of fresh air, a guy who loved nature and his job. It would be nice to be with a man who looked at her as a woman, not a TV producer.

She'd dressed carefully, choosing a long slip dress she'd bought in Honolulu. It was a floral print in the shades that suited her—a burnt orange that accented her red hair and a green that brought out the color of her eyes.

She caught her hair back with a deep green ribbon for coolness, then pulled a few strands over her forehead to soften her face.

"Wow, girl," she said as she looked in the mirror. "You've rarely looked as good." She slipped on flat sandals, put her notebook in her beige evening bag, and slipped it under her arm. She was ready for anything the evening could offer.

Joe was waiting for her in the bar. And so was Perry. They were talking up a storm. Joe owned a video camera and Perry was explaining the need to get shots from different angles for editing purposes. Sonya felt a wave of disappointment. Was she never going to escape the world of video production?

It seemed not. The three of them drank and snacked on the delicious hors d'oeuvres the bartender kept bringing. It was fun, but the usual sort of fun. Certainly not romantic. Sonya wondered if Perry had gone there deliberately, to find out what was going on between her and Joe. Then she ruled that out. She couldn't expect him to sit alone in his bungalow all night, and the obvious place to come was the bar.

When the manager came and told her that Donna's plane was about to land 30 minutes early, Sonya grabbed her bag and stood up to leave. Joe was obviously uncertain what to do. When he offered to drive her to the airport, she refused. He walked her to the door and, as she left, said, "Please give me a call. I'll be waiting for it. I want to see you again."

She had blown him a kiss before following the manager out of the bar.

And that, she had told herself, was that.

Now, as she drove back to the spa behind the limousine, she listed the things she had to do. Print three copies of her material while she changed into jeans and a tee, then race to Donna's bungalow.

Donna was ruthless about time. If she said 30 minutes, she meant 30 minutes. Sonya got everything ready in 20 minutes, stuffing the stapled pages into her evening bag along with her notebook.

She was pleased with the list she had prepared for her two bosses. It would be hard for Matt to find fault with it. She and Perry had worked long hours and covered every aspect of the spa, from the models getting seaweed treatment on their naked bodies to the long shots taken from the boat. There was also Perry's brilliant work at the volcano. The video was great. But it needed to be, the story was so weak.

She arrived before Matt. Donna called her to come in. Sonya opened the door and stood in amazement.

Lara had used dozens of different orchids to decorate Donna's suite. She had grouped pots of them on mirrored tables around the room, so the flowers with their mysterious sensuous shapes reflected endlessly. It looked surreal—like a forest of orchids.

Their colors were as gentle as those of the room—pale pink, beige, brown, and faded purples. It was romantic and luxurious, a dream room.

"The orchids are astonishing, exquisite," said Donna enthusiastically. "Lara has great taste. And I would say she was a fast learner when it comes to spending Errol's money."

"I agree," Sonya said. "But, Donna, I think there is a lot more to this story than meets the eye."

"What do you mean?"

"I haven't figured it all out, but I know the situation between

Errol and Lara is explosive. He cancels her appointments and pushes himself forward instead. There's one star in Errol's firmament and that star is Errol. But I think Lara will fight back."

Donna paused, then said, "Well, Errol's attitude is easy to understand."

"What do you mean?"

"A man like Errol is used to being the center of attention. I know him, and he must be bored to death here. Tell me, what you have found out about Lara?"

"Well, it seems she's got big plans, plans to promote the spa and its products on an international scale. I think she may be biding her time until the baby is born, then she'll ditch Errol and run with it. She may already have backing from one of the big conglomerates in China. If this marriage lasts, I'll be amazed."

"What makes you so certain?"

"Last night I overheard Lara and Errol having a bitter argument, which Lara won. Today Errol cancelled Lara's shoot with me, rearranging things so he could be part of it. He is jealous of the publicity she is getting. This afternoon I met Jackie Olsen, who calls herself the boat captain. But that's a joke; she is much more than that. I'd call her Lara's partner or aide. She knows everything that's going on. She told me of the plans for expansion and of the interest of the Chinese conglomerate."

Donna replied, "Sonya, there's no way we can get this in the story."

"No, but we shouldn't go too soft on it. The whole thing may explode any day and we'll have a lot of egg on our faces and a lot of explaining to do."

Donna started to reply, but Sonya went on with increasing

vigor. "You must know about some of this, since you've been Errol's friend for years."

"Sonya, listen to me." Donna's voice rose with anger, but she stopped as they heard Matt calling from the garden.

Sonya slid open the door for him. He was dressed in an obviously new safari jacket and proud of it. "The night is young," he sang. "I've never seen stars so beautiful."

Sonya handed him her list. "Here, you wanted to know what we've been doing between our trips to the surf and our sunbathing. This will give you some idea. We've been working our asses off."

"Sonya, that's enough," interrupted Donna. She glanced at Matt. "Did Errol get hold of you? He called here to welcome me and said he'd like to speak to you, too."

"Yeah, I spoke to him; he wanted to know the news from New York. That's what made me late." Matt sat down, took off his shoes, put his feet on the coffee table, and studied the list.

Donna settled back on the sofa. Sonya watched Matt and waited for his reaction.

"Looks okay. We've just got to get Donna's interview with Errol and then some reaction from the guests. Then, after the opening, we'll decide how to put it together."

"How long will the piece be?"

"At least 12 minutes. That means we can do justice to all the facilities and treatments that Errol told me about. It's all pretty straightforward. Nothing to worry about." Matt threw his copy of the list on the coffee table, got up, and poured himself a scotch.

"I'll have one, too," said Donna. "Let's get the interviews done with. Then we'll show how the spa works and how it can transform a tired, depressed executive into a vigorous, happy one."

Sonya sat on the sofa and pulled her notebook out of her bag.

"I've set up the interview with Errol at eleven tomorrow morning," she told Donna. "What time do you want Sabrina here for makeup?"

"Nine will be fine. She'll have to do my hair, too. It's going to need all the help it can get in this humidity."

Sonya hesitated, then decided to make her point. "I've given you a list of questions, but as I told you, there's a lot more going on than the opening of the spa."

"Like what?" Matt asked.

"Like the fact that Errol's dysfunctional family are coming. His two former wives with their children. How weird is that?"

Before she could continue, Matt slammed his fist on the table.

"Sonya, we're keeping to the simple story of a New Age spa for folks with million-dollar salaries. What I want from you is a glamour story. Nothing else. A puff piece about this place and what a great guy Errol is."

"Oh, Matt," Donna commented as she sipped her scotch, "that's too narrow. There's a romantic angle, too, about Errol the retired billionaire and his beautiful trophy bride. It's more than just a spa story. This is the story of a tough executive who worked his way up through the ranks and now, upon retirement, has found romance. Finally he has it all."

Sonya interrupted. "I told you, Donna, don't be too sure about it."

Donna was adamant. "You are way off base this time, Sonya. Errol has a young, brilliant wife, and together they've built a beautiful home in an idyllic setting, a fabulous place to entertain his friends. And with any luck a moneymaker. Not that money means much to him these days, considering what he already has."

Sonya got up and walked to the window. She didn't want Donna to see how angry she was. Tears sprang to her eyes, and she blinked quickly to get rid of them. Why was Donna so reluctant to do a story closer to the truth? It must be one of two things— blackmail or pressure from the nineteenth floor. Blackmail was impossible; Donna would never risk her reputation submitting to it. It must be pressure from the nineteenth floor.

"Donna, you're right," Matt said. As if to emphasize that the decision was made, he got up from the chair and stretched out on the sofa. "But we have to play it carefully. Errol must come out looking great. That's what is important."

"Yes, Errol is known around the country as a tough executive," said Donna, "and I've no intention of making him look like an angel. I'll lose credibility if I do. But we are not going into these relationships. There are skeletons in those closets that I don't want to see rattled."

Sonya went to the bar and poured herself a vodka and tonic. This was the first time she had been on the opposite side of an argument with Donna. Why was Donna refusing to discuss the story? Was it pressure from the network? Her old romance with Errol? Surely Donna couldn't be bribed? Whatever the reason, Sonya felt betrayed, but she was determined to have it out.

She pulled up a chair and sat face to face with Donna. Matt closed his eyes and seemed to be ignoring her, but she knew he was listening to every word.

"Donna, believe me, this goes beyond being nice to Errol. Apart from Errol's dysfunction family, Lara's mother is here. Errol didn't want her here because she is an alcoholic. But she turned up unannounced this afternoon and hit the bottle fast. Why? She's furious at Errol and she told me—a stranger and a member of the press—that Lara had a baby here in Hawaii when she was 16. I don't know if it is true.

"But why would she tell me? What is she setting up? If the press gets hold of the story, it'll make headlines. The search will be on to find that baby, who's now a dark-skinned girl of 13 or so.

"Margaret Halstead wouldn't have told me about the girl if she didn't want the world to know about it. She probably knows where the child is and could produce her at any moment."

Matt wasn't having it. "That's just the blathering of some drunken woman. I don't know why she came out with it and neither do you. My guess is that she's jealous of her daughter. And wants to be part of this."

Sonya stood firm. "I tell you, there is more here than meets the eye. Why did Errol want to have his two ex-wives come and not Lara's mother? You've got admit that's weird.

"And his children—one is gay and a model. Errol calls him a 'faggot.' He calls his daughter a 'loon'—she's a schizophrenic and has been in and out of mental institutions for years. But they are due here tomorrow. All of them to meet the press at the opening. What's it all about?" Sonya knew her voice was rising, and she knew Donna didn't like to be yelled at.

"I think you are too close to it all. You need to rest," Donna dismissed her. She picked up her glass and finished her scotch. "We can't write the story before it happens. Let's do the interview with Errol at eleven tomorrow and then decide what to do."

"Now go, both of you, get out of here. I want some sleep."

Sonya found for her bag, smiled a forced smile at Donna, and left quickly. Matt followed her through the door.

"I'll walk you to your bungalow." he said.

"No, thanks, I'm fine. I want to drop in on Perry and tell him about the time of the interview tomorrow. His bungalow is close to mine. Good night."

"Are you sure? It's getting late." Why was Matt suddenly turning on the charm? Was he feeling guilty about something? Did he want something from her?

"I just said no, and I mean no. I'm perfectly all right."

Matt shrugged and left. She would have used any excuse to get rid of him. She couldn't bear to be with him for another moment.

She knew Perry would call her early, as he always did, to go over the day's program. But right then she wanted to see him and tell him about the argument, maybe get his point of view.

He had left his door open. She walked in and found him sprawled on the sofa, sound asleep with the TV blaring.

She stood looking down at him. His head was rolled back on the cushions, his mouth was open, and his mustache quivered with every snore. After a hard day's work and a few drinks, Perry had left this world.

A few hours ago, when she'd found him monopolizing Joe in the bar, she'd been ready to cut him off. Now, she smiled to herself, she was full of gratitude for his support. He was more than a colleague, he was a good friend.

She turned off the light and left.

As she walked to her bungalow, she thought about Donna's and Matt's objections. She could understand Matt wanting to stay in favor with the network executives; he was ruthless in his ambition.

But Donna was a journalist. Why was she so determined to do a puff piece on Errol and Lara? She must see that the story of the opening of the spa could fall apart easily. Well, they were her bosses. They could gloss over the story, but they couldn't stop her from getting to the bottom of what was going on.

She had her own reputation to protect.

Chapter 17

Flying to the Big Island
Thursday, 10:30 P.M.

The pain was like a spike of red-hot steel. Tracey Swanson caught
her breath and held herself rigid. Then she put out her hand and
grasped Ramos's arm.

"My God," she said, "it's worse than a migraine."

He reached into her bag and took out a sheet of pills, broke the
seal on two, and put them between her lips.

"Just breathe slowly," he said reaching for a glass of water. "It
will pass in a moment or two. It always does. The flight has tired
you, that's why you're upset.

Tracey prayed that he was right. She was fed up with the afteref-
fects of the coma. The panic attacks and the headaches came on
without warning, and were hard to deal with.

Why was this happening? Was it serious? Something she would
have to face for the rest of her life?

Perhaps Ramos was right, she was tired. But no, she wasn't just
tired. It was more than that. She was stressed out over the decision

she had made to go to Hawaii and what would happen as a result. Could she ever be part of the family as she once was?

The flight to Hawaii involved two plane changes, first in Los Angeles and then in Honolulu. In a few moments they would land on the Big Island and ten minutes later they'd be at the spa.

She touched Ramos's hand. "Thank you, I know it is just tension. I'll be fine after a night's rest."

Ramos motioned to the steward to refill her water glass.

She took a long draft before she said, "You're a comfort to me, Ramos, I'm glad you wanted to come."

"I'll do the business of checking in when we arrive. You can wait in the car," he suggested. "I'll unpack the wheelchair and push you to your room."

"Oh, Ramos, I don't want that. It's such a long time since they've seen me. I want to look as I used to look, full of life and fun."

She had let the years pass without making an effort to see her family. Even on her visits to Chicago, she had avoided calling them. At first it was difficult; she had to harden her heart against them. But as the years slipped by, they just seemed to be people she'd known in a dream.

Joan and her straightlaced parents had objected to Tracey's affair with a married man. She remembered how Joan had told her she was ruining her life by sleeping with him.

"You think that no one knows you are sleeping with your boss," she had said one Sunday afternoon at a family brunch. "Let me tell you, everyone does. My mother and father say you are no better than a whore. They have a very clear idea of what is moral and you don't meet the test. I'm sorry to have to tell you that you are not welcome in this house. My advice is that you change your job and get away from him. If not, you'll find that no decent man will marry you after this. It may already be too late."

Tracey still felt angry when she thought of it. She wondered if Joan would remember those words and the sting they had carried. She doubted it. And what did it matter anyway? In those days Joan had simply been a dutiful daughter. Now both her parents were dead and she had enough troubles of her own. Tracey could not resist feeling a certain satisfaction.

She looked down at the pear-shaped diamond engagement ring she wore instead of a wedding band. She had made the right choice. Marriage was not for her, but that didn't matter. Her life had been filled with love. Not having children had been a trade-off she accepted.

She relaxed as the pain eased. The pills were stronger than she realized. Yes, with them and a sleeping pill she would get a good night's rest. And a good night's rest was all she needed to face the family. She was not the same woman, torn between love and guilt, that she'd been 30 years ago.

She took out her makeup kit, outlined her lips, then added a touch of gloss. Yes, she would look like the rich, sophisticated woman she was.

Low conversation in the living room roused her in the morning. Ramos had insisted that she leave her bedroom door open in case she called for him in the night. But after a bowl of clear soup and dry toast, she had slept peacefully.

"Ramos, who is it?" she called.

He appeared at her door with a pot of pale gold orchids in his hands. Blooms with centers spiked with blood red sprayed out from three large stems.

"A maid brought these from Lara Swanson. There's a note. Do you want it?"

Tracey held out her hands for orchids. "They are just magnificent. I knew there were orchid farms here, but I never thought they would produce blooms like these."

Ramos put the orchids on the bedside table and handed her the note. "I'll order your breakfast and bring you your pills."

"Hmm." Tracey picked up the note and read it. "Lara sounds sweet. She says that she is sorry she missed seeing me last night. And she's invited me for coffee at eleven. Errol won't be there. But she would like to take this opportunity to get to know me."

"Yes, very nice," Ramos replied. "It will only take a few moments for you to get there. I walked by last night after you went to sleep."

"You went there?"

"Yes, I took a long walk. I'm like, as you so often say, a dog who has to mark his territory. I'm not happy until I know my way around."

Tracey yawned and stretched her arms.

"I feel lazy. I'll have breakfast in bed and gaze at my orchids. Ramos, this morning I'll skip the coffee and just have tea and toast. Ask if they have any Hawaiian honey. It might be delicious."

When Tracey was ready, Ramos walked with her to the Swanson home. She was glad to get out of the cold air conditioning and into the warm sunlight. The gardens were beautiful and so were the views of the water. She'd always thought her own home in Acapulco was the best, but she had to give Lara her due. She had done a magnificent job.

When they arrived at the Swanson home, Lara was in the courtyard talking to an older woman.

"I'll leave you now," Ramos said. Tracey reached out to introduce him, but he was already gone.

Lara greeted her with a warm smile. "This is my mother, Margaret Halstead," she said. "I'm sending her to have head-to-toe treatments so she'll be ready for the party tomorrow." She smiled at Tracey, then added, "That's what I want you to have as soon as you are ready."

She kissed her mother on the cheek and patted her on the shoulder as she left. Then she turned back to Tracey.

"Errol chose well for wife number three," Tracey thought. "She is charming. Much more compassionate than Joan, and much more intelligent."

"How delighted I am that you've come," Lara said as she took Tracey's arm and led her inside. "Errol has told me so much about you."

Tracey studied her face. Yes, Lara was as beautiful as everyone said. But under her skillfully applied makeup, she looked tired and drawn. Lara Swanson could get herself together, but she couldn't hide her vulnerability.

"Lara, why are you doing all this? It must be so much stress. Not just the spa, but having to take care of Errol's family," she asked, surprised at her openness and urgency.

Lara was quick to reply. "For one thing, I want to show the press that the stories about Errol are not true. Of course he was a tough businessman, but that doesn't mean he's evil. I would not have married an evil man. And I felt it was important to have his entire family come together in a circle of life and peace.

"I don't think that is hard to understand. Errol is starting a new life with me and I want the world to know it."

Tracey was silent. She let Lara lead her to the terrace, where coffee cups and cookies were laid out on a low satin-brushed steel table. The china was clear celadon green, a color that Tracey had always thought was the most calming of all.

"I thought you would like to sit on the terrace because the view here is so beautiful. We designed the house around it. And here, of course, is where we placed our beautiful bronze statue of Buddha."

"Are you a Buddhist?" Tracey asked.

"I don't follow any one religion. I like to think there is love and truth in each of them.

"But Tracey, tell me about yourself. You haven't been well." Lara's interest seemed genuine.

"Unlucky rather than unwell. I was allergic to a drug, and it really knocked me out. I am fine now and I am tired of talking about it.

"Everyone seems to have had some experience with the side effects of drugs, so my story is not news."

"Then tell me about your life. You live in Mexico full-time?"

"Yes, and I love everything about it, the climate, the people, the food."

"But you are alone?"

"Yes, there has been just one man in my life, Donald Simpson, a married man who had two daughters. I started working for him in my late twenties and we fell in love. But as he couldn't get a divorce, we simply lived together during the week and he went home to his family at the weekends. Leading that kind of life is nothing special now, but 30 years ago it was a scandal. Errol and Joan called it a 'disgrace to the family.'"

"Yes, Errol told me that Joan treated you badly."

Tracey felt a sudden urge to be frank with Lara and tell her everything, even the reason behind her decision to come to the spa.

"Don was in the security business. We were always on the move. He set up systems in stores, warehouses, boats, and private homes. He made a lot of money. We fell in love with Mexico the first time we visited and planned to live in Acapulco. But that wasn't to be. Don had a heart attack just after we built our house."

Tracey felt a wave of self-pity sweep over her. She had to stop. She liked Lara, but she didn't want to tell her too much. At least not yet. She reached for her coffee and sipped it slowly.

"But now, Lara, tell me about yourself and your plans for the future. Do you want to have many babies with Errol?"

"Yes, of course, and I want my babies to have a family. I was an only child who had a few older cousins. They lived in London and I rarely saw them, and when I did we had very little in common. The thing I remember most about my childhood was longing for a sister or brother to play with."

Tracey smiled for the first time. "It was the same for me. I had a lonely childhood until I went to live with Errol's parents."

"I don't know much about that time in his life. Like most men, he has lost all the family photographs and records. He said you were like an older sister to him."

Tracey laughed. "I'm not surprised he lost all the photos. He was an untidy boy. I spent many hours picking up after him.

"Were you adopted by his family?"

"Not legally. My parents were killed in a car crash. Errol's father, Frank, was my older brother. He and his wife, Erika, took me in. So I am Errol's aunt, even though I am only five years older than he is."

"Now I understand."

"I adored him. He was the sweetest little boy. He was two or three when I moved in and quite a handful." Tracey's face lit up at the memory. "That was long ago and it's quite different between us now."

Lara reached for a cookie, broke it half, and took a small bite.

"Tell me about his father. Errol never wants to say much about him."

"When Frank came home from the war, everything changed."

"I've heard some of the stories."

"Erika suffered along with him. She was brave. She married a young ambitious man, who, like so many, went cheerfully off to fight. He came back a distraught stranger. He had given up on life. He was riddled with emotions, but mostly with guilt. He had lived and his buddies were dead.

"I took charge of Errol, but it wasn't easy to pretend that nothing was wrong. I tried to keep him away from his father when Frank's worst attacks came on. Erika depended on me and we became close. I was the daughter she never had. She was the mother I had lost."

Tracey paused, thinking of the sweet-faced young woman who had shouldered so much with her mentally ill husband.

"I have little to remember her by, that's the sad part. All she left me was one necklace that we both loved. Her grandmother received it as a wedding present in the early 1900s, and Erika had worn it at her own wedding.

"It was designed by Louis Comfort Tiffany himself. It wasn't flashy, but it was valuable, though I didn't care about the money. To me it was the memory of Erika.

"After she died Errol took all her jewelry, including that necklace, and sold it. He did it without asking anyone. He said he needed the money. I never understood it. I was heartbroken.

"Later, when I had money, I searched for it. I would have paid anything to get it back."

"What did it look like?"

"It was quite simple. An engraved gold chain with leaves and bunches of pale jade berries suspended from it. It was simple and elegant."

Lara stood up, her body tensed.

"Tracey, please excuse me for a moment." With that she left the terrace. Tracey was stunned. Had she said something to upset Lara?

In a few moments Lara was back with a signature blue Tiffany box in her hand.

"Open it." She handed it to Tracey. "Is this the necklace?"

Tracey's hand shook as she reached out. She opened the box and held up the pale gold necklace, its shimmering leaves set off by the translucent pale green berries.

Tears came to Tracey's eyes.

"See how fine it is, the engraving is so delicate. It is a masterpiece," she said, holding the necklace in different ways so it caught the light.

Lara reached down, took the necklace from her, and put it back in the box.

"You must take it," she said as she handed it to the older woman. "The necklace was meant for you. It belongs to you. If I wear it, wearing it will only bring me bad luck."

Tracey put the box back on the coffee table.

Lara pressed her. "It's yours. Erika meant it for you. Errol should never have kept it. I am so embarrassed for him."

Tracey shook her head.

"If it is mine, then I give it to you. That way, as Erika wished, it will stay in the family." Lara dropped her head between her hands. "I don't want it. Please take it. It will give me so much pleasure to know that I have given you something that you treasure."

Tracey rose, picked up the box, and put in her handbag. There were tears in her eyes. "You are sweet to say that. I know that you mean it, and it will give me great pleasure to have the necklace. Errol is a lucky man to have you. I just hope he appreciates you."

"Oh, Tracey," Lara said with a sob in her voice, "I have so many unanswered questions about Errol. Sometimes I don't know which way to turn."

Tracey bent and kissed her.

"Perhaps, Lara," she said, "I have some of the answers. But for your own sake, it may be better if you never hear them."

Chapter 18

The Big Island
Friday, 1:00 P.M.

"I'm furious! I prepared a list of gutsy questions and she ignored them."

Sonya had to vent her rage at someone. And the closest person was Sabrina, who was frolicking naked in the plunge pool.

They had both been at Donna's 11 o'clock interview with Errol. Sabrina had rushed off as soon as it was finished. Sonya had waited to get the tape from Perry and then come back to the bungalow.

Sabrina flicked a spray of water at Sonya. "Forget Donna and the interview. That's the television business. Take off your clothes and get into the pool with me. It's a dream."

Sonya was too angry to be distracted.

"I don't understand how you can hover there during an interview, playing the goody little makeup artist, patting powder onto the noses of celebrities, and never caring about a word they say. You are one weird creature, Sabrina."

Sabrina grinned. "I hear what I want to hear. Anyway, you were crazy to expect anything but asskissing. Did you really think Donna would rip Errol Swanson apart? Just forget it and enjoy yourself."

Sonya sat on the stone bench beside the pool. Sabrina was right. The interview was over and done with. All she could do was look at the tape and pick out the best sound bites.

She looked at Sabrina's plump, curvy body floating in the water. The makeup artist was as happy as a baby seal. Her short black hair was plastered to her head and her brown eyes were twinkling.

"I love the feel of the water on my naked body. It's so sexy," she said.

Sonya grimaced. "Okay," she told herself, "cool down and join in the fun."

"I guess I'm upset because I dislike Errol so much, and I hoped this interview might show him for what he is."

"I have to give it to you straight, sweetie. Sometimes you're a little too pure for this business."

"Okay, but Donna's good and I just hate to think that she is under Errol's control."

Sabrina started to interrupt, but Sonya stopped her. "I know what you're going to say. That she got her job because she had an affair with Errol."

"So what? She's got her job, you've got yours, and I've got mine. Just let it go."

Sonya bent over the pool and splashed a handful of water toward Sabrina. "Okay, Sabrina. Get off my back. I just want to check one thing on the tape. I'll join you."

"Good. Cut yourself a break."

"I'm glad you are here. You are the only one I can talk to."

"Well, there's always Perry."

"Please, Perry is just Perry," Sonya laughed. "He has his eye on the camera lens, that's it."

As she left, Sabrina called back to her, "Perry can be a good guy to have around. And boy, does he like being around you."

Sonya ignored her.

She sat down at her television monitor. Donna's interview with Errol had lasted eight minutes.

Errol appeared believable and even amusing when he talked about his transition from TV executive to owner of a fashionable spa. But when he got to his background he told downright lies, particularly about his father.

He had told Donna that his father was a successful dentist. But the truth was that a patient had sued Frank Swanson for thousands of dollars for malpractice. His reputation had been shattered and he had closed his practice. Why did Errol lie about it?

Sonya rewound the tape and listened again. She realized Donna had deliberately set up the lie. With a single question, Donna had ignored all of Sonya's research. She had given Errol the perfect way to avoid talking about his past.

Sonya pressed the Stop button. There was only one conclusion. Errol had arranged for Donna to ask only those questions that would show him in the best possible light. Donna had knowingly compromised herself.

Sonya felt numb. Not Donna, the woman she so respected. Where else had Donna allowed Errol to lie? Sonya would have to reread all her notes.

Sabrina appeared in the doorway, naked except for the towel draped around her wet body. She looked happy and healthy, ready for a good time.

"What happened to the plunge we were supposed to enjoy together? And more important, what is happening about lunch? I'm starved."

"Sorry, Sabrina, I need to check the tape again. Get dressed and I'll be ready."

"What's so important about that tape?"

"I am trying to find out if there is a pattern to the way Donna asked her questions. I think she and Errol had some sort of agreement."

"What kind of agreement?"

"I don't know exactly."

"Well, that's your business, Sonya, but it seems to me you have got a bug up your behind about this. Are you sure it's not just because you can't have this story the way you want it?"

"Sabrina, you know me better," Sonya answered with real hostility.

"Yeah? Well, you know me, too, Sonya. I calls 'em like I sees 'em."

At that moment Perry walked through the front door. They stopped talking. Neither one wanted Perry to hear them arguing.

Perry looked at Sabrina, blinked, and said, "You're not wearing something, and it isn't makeup."

Sabrina grinned. "Want to see a makeup artist in the nude?"

"Okay," said Perry. "Drop the towel."

"Not on your life. I have to lose 10 pounds before I pose for you."

"Okay, then, tell me what you were arguing about?"

"Not your business," replied Sabrina.

Sonya said nothing.

Perry insisted. "The two of you have had your heads together since you got here, Sabrina. How about letting your buddy in on it?"

Sabrina flipped her wet hair back from her face.

"All I've got to say is that I've had a plunge and I'm hungry. What about lunch?"

"What about I take you two girls to lunch?"

"Okay. Just give me a minute to slip on my sarong." Sabrina disappeared into the bathroom.

Sonya looked up at Perry. He had understood she wanted to get Sabrina out of the bungalow.

"Thanks. Sabrina doesn't know her way around this place yet, and she deserves a good time. I'm worried about the interview."

"I wouldn't call it a ratings booster," he said "You'll have to beef it up to stop the viewers leaving us."

He walked over beside her and looked at the image on the screen. Sonya thought he was going to play the tape, but instead he put his arm on the back of her chair and looked at her.

"When are you going to eat, Sonya? Do you want me to order something for you? Or bring something back?"

Sonya gave him a hard look. She knew Perry. He was trying to apologize for the way he'd behaved with Joe Robertson last night. She shook her head. "There's yogurt in the fridge. That'll do."

She turned away and pressed the Play button. She didn't glance up when he left with Sabrina.

At last she could concentrate. She would check her notes and see what Errol had said in the preinterview. That was easy. Control freak that she was, she had logged everything.

Rule one was that she started a fresh notebook each day. On the cover she wrote her name, the date, and the name of the story. It was simple. But it worked, especially when she had to check a fact months later.

Rule two was that she stored the notebooks in the top drawer of the desk. That way she could always find them, no matter how frantic she was. For the Swanson preinterview, she had listed her questions. Following each one she had jotted down the essence of Errol's answer.

She had given Donna the same list of questions.

Sonya slid open the desk drawer and saw two notebooks. One for Tuesday and another for Wednesday. But not Thursday's.

Where was it? She'd been busy, but not that busy. Maybe the maid had picked it up and moved it.

Sonya walked around the room, checking the flat surfaces. Then she went methodically from drawer to drawer.

She knew most of them were empty, but she checked them anyway. She had taught herself to use only one corner of a room. That way she knew where everything was if she had to get something in a hurry. Being well organized was essential for a producer. She had learned that from Donna.

Finally, she took her handbag and turned it upside-down on the sofa. No Thursday notebook. Someone must have taken it.

She felt light-headed. She sat down and carefully reviewed her Thursday schedule. After the preinterview with Errol, they had shot the treatment rooms, then gone on the boat with Jackie.

There was Lara's mother. Drinks with Joe and Perry. Then the race to get to the airport before Donna's plane landed.

Sonya remembered that she'd had the notebook at the late-night meeting in Donna's bungalow. But she had been so furious with Donna and Matt, she couldn't recall what she'd done with it.

She remembered searching for her evening bag before she left, but nothing specific about the notebook.

Sonya walked into the bedroom and checked her evening bag, neatly placed on the shelf in her closet. Empty.

She must have left the notebook in Donna's living room. That was understandable. It had been a long day, and she had had two glasses of wine with Perry and Joe.

But if she'd left it, and Donna found it, why hadn't she returned it to her? Donna knew how important a producer's notes were.

"Don't be paranoid," she told herself. "There's a perfectly good reason."

But she'd gone to Donna's bungalow this morning and sat around while Sabrina did Donna's hair and makeup. Donna hadn't said a word about finding the notebook. And Sonya, with nothing to do, had wandered around the room admiring the orchids. If her notebook had been there, she would have seen it.

What she had to do, she told herself, was to go over every minute of that meeting last night. And concentrate on Matt.

He had arrived 15 minutes late, but that was nothing unusual. He made a habit of keeping Donna waiting. At first he had lounged in the armchair next to Donna, getting up once to get drinks. No. Not once. He got up a second time while Sonya was at the window, fighting back her tears.

Right. He had spread out on the sofa where she had been sitting. He could easily have picked up the notebook and put it in a pocket of that safari jacket he was so proud of.

Now she was certain. Matt, had wanted to read her notes and see what Errol had told her. Then he went over the questions with Donna and persuaded her to go easy on Errol.

Errol must have mentioned her interview when he'd called Matt.

Sonya felt relieved. At least Donna knew nothing about the book.

As for Matt, his actions had been despicable, but only to be expected. He would return the notebook to her. And he'd pretend he had the picked it up by mistake.

There was no one Sonya could trust to talk about the stolen notebook. Not Sabrina. Perhaps Perry? Sensible, no-nonsense Perry. No, not even Perry.

There was one person however, who was not part of her world. Joe Robertson. That attractive, lanky park ranger. He was probably waiting for the call she promised to make.

So she would. Only this time she'd make the date away from the spa.

Chapter **19**

The Big Island
Friday, 4:00 P.M.

Frank O'Neill flicked the sand from the black lava step at the edge of the beach. Then he sat, sheltered from the sun under a sprawling banyan tree.

He had walked along the beach to clear his mind before he interviewed Errol. He was uneasy at the thought of it. They had seen each other from a distance here at the spa, but neither had acknowledged the other.

Yet he knew that Errol was aware of him and his relationship with Lara. And that Errol was a jealous and violent man.

Frank watched a crab stepping gingerly across the beach toward him. He picked up a handful of sand and threw it. He missed, but the crab scurried back to its hole anyway. If only he could get rid of Errol so easily.

Errol had been responsible for the downward spiral of his career. Even with his reputation as a writer, he had never regained the ground he'd lost after being fired. That day, Frank's agent had told him that Errol had threatened to destroy his career. Now Frank wondered if his downfall had been Errol's fault, or his own.

Perhaps he never should have given up the professorship at NYU he'd taken after the success of his first book. But he'd been too young to settle into the academic world, and he'd quickly tired of teaching.

Life as a TV commentator was more exciting. And while he was on TV, offers came frequently for lectures and articles in popular magazines. He was on the literary A-list for parties, and he enjoyed that. In fact, nothing pleased him more than to walk up the red carpet with a beautiful blonde. And before Lara, there had been a string of them.

But the moment he was fired, his life had changed. For the first time, he felt like a failure.

Frank told himself that the interview he was about to do was essential; the editor at *The Best* magazine insisted on having Errol's comments in the piece. And more important, for his unauthorized biography of Errol, Frank wanted to be able to claim that he'd interviewed the man in depth.

He wondered how far he could go in asking personal questions without revealing that he was writing a book. Errol must not know about that, or he would use his influence to try to stop publication. His publisher had insisted the project be kept secret as long as possible.

Frank had been surprised when Errol had agreed to the interview, and even more surprised when the spa manager had set it up so quickly. Errol was a game player. He liked to make people wait for his favors.

Checking his watch, Frank saw that it was time to go. He wanted to arrive just a few minutes early; that would start the interview on the right note. He stood and brushed the sand from his trousers.

The front door of the Swansons' home was open when he arrived. The spa manager was standing in the hall as if he was waiting for Frank.

"Mr. Swanson is waiting for you in his study," the manager said. "I'll take you right in. He told me to tell you he will answer any questions you have about the spa." The man emphasized "about the spa" in such a way as to suggest that it was the spa and the spa only that Errol would discuss.

Frank was being warned. He would have to be careful.

Errol was standing at the study door. He put out his hand to shake Frank's as the spa manager ushered him in.

"We'll be just a few minutes," Errol told the manager. "I'll call you when we're finished."

The man nodded and left.

"Please sit down, Frank," Errol said with uncharacteristic warmth as he indicated the chair in front of his desk.

Frank looked around the room. It had Lara's understated touch except for Errol's desk and chair. Both were large and out of proportion to the rest of the furniture. Frank recognized the desk chair as one from the network. It was imposing, in dark leather with a high back, in a traditional office style.

The arrangement was designed to express power and to diminish the person sitting opposite. It was a cliché setup that had become a joke in the news department. Its effect was just the opposite of what was intended. Seeing the furniture again amused Frank. Errol was hanging onto the outward signs of his former power. He must be feeling insecure.

"Would you like a drink?" Errol asked.

Frank couldn't resist; he said sarcastically, "Thanks, I would. A single malt on the rocks would be fine."

Errol went to the bar, poured the drink, then handed it to Frank before seating himself behind the desk, in the supposedly imposing leather chair. Frank smiled to himself. The huge furniture actually made Errol look smaller.

"It's been a while since we last spoke. While you were still at the network, wasn't it?" Errol smiled at him briefly, then narrowed his eyes.

The question hit the mark. Frank felt his old fury return. He took a sip of scotch.

"Well, let's get started," Errol continued. "I hope that you're being well taken care of here. What can I tell you about the spa?"

Frank took out his notebook and began with the obvious travel magazine questions. He already knew most of the answers, but he hoped this would ease him into a more personal interview.

"Tell me something about the service you offer here, and what guests can expect to experience when they stay."

Errol responded at great length with the list of attractions. He also talked about his philosophy behind the spa, and what an inspiration that would be to guests. All without a single mention of Lara.

"Why did you pick this spot for the spa?" Frank asked. "I've been told that other hotels have failed here."

When he responded, Frank detected a change in Errol's tone. His arrogance was showing. "I don't pay attention to what others have failed to do. When I make up my mind, I get what I want."

"Yes, I know that's your reputation. I remember very well from your days at the network . . . and from my days at the network."

"And I'll succeed here," Errol continued, ignoring him. "Now, before we finish, what else would you like to know about my spa?"

He was being dismissed, Frank realized. This was his last chance to talk about Lara.

"Tell me about your wife, Lara," he said, "and the role she's played in setting up the business."

Errol was abrupt. "The role that a wife should play. She's been supportive and helpful."

Frank was not having it.

"I understand that Lara is really the one behind the spa. She's a capable woman," Frank stated forcefully. "It's your money, but her vision, isn't that right?"

Frank saw Errol's body tense and his face redden, and he felt elated. The powerful Errol Swanson was about to lose control.

"Listen," Errol's voice rose, "we're not here to talk about my wife. I've told you of her involvement. That's enough." He slapped his fist onto his desktop. "And that's enough for this interview."

The scotch had done its work. Frank felt emboldened. "No, it's not enough. Let's talk about your wife. About Lara. Yes, we should talk about the beautiful, beautiful Lara. The woman we both love." The moment Frank heard his own words, he knew he'd gone too far.

Errol exploded. "What?!" He sprang from his chair and charged around the desk toward Frank. "Don't you—don't—don't you ever speak my wife's name again, goddamnit. Her name is forbidden to you, do you understand? And don't you ever talk to her again!"

Frank was transfixed. This was the Errol he had heard about, a raging man with a wild, unpredictable, unreasonable temper.

"Do you understand?" Errol was shouting, looming over Frank, gripping the arms of his chair. "Do you understand?"

Errol released the chair and clenched his fists.

"Now get the fuck out of here."

Frank stood and faced Errol, feeling a rush of anger and strength. "Don't you ever tell me what to do! Or what to say. Or who to talk to."

"Goddamn you!" Errol spat out the words. "Goddamn you, motherfucker. If you ever—ever—contact her in any way, I will have you hurt. Seriously hurt." He lowered his voice. "You would not be the first."

Frank knew that Errol meant what he said. He headed toward the door. Errol closed the gap between them and grabbed Frank, swinging him around and gripping him by the upper arms.

"Do you understand, asshole?" He practically screamed it into Frank's face.

"Yes," Frank gasped, recoiling.

Errol held him for a moment more, then released him. Frank wanted to hit Errol so hard the man would never regain consciousness. But he knew that would only cause more trouble for Lara. Without looking back, he walked away.

Frank went straight to his bungalow and sat on the bench where he had waited for Lara on his first day at the spa. She had told him that day that she feared Errol might kill her, and now Frank knew she was right. In a rage, that man was capable of anything.

He couldn't leave her with Errol. He would do whatever he had to. He would get her away from him.

Chapter 20

The Big Island
Friday, 5:00 P.M.

Sonya Iverson stood on the steps of the terrace café, watching Joan Swanson work her way through a thick slice of cake covered with chocolate sauce. Joan sat at a table overlooking the beach, her bright floral muumuu flowing over her body and draped around her feet. Christy was next to her, leafing through a magazine, an untouched glass of cola beside her.

Sonya was uncertain about approaching Joan. It was hard to get a handle on her. She'd been divorced from Errol for years, and he had married twice since then. Why would she, a brilliant business-woman, submit herself to the indignity of paying homage to his third wife's success? That was the question Sonya most wanted an-swered. But she felt that Joan was a troubled woman who could quickly withdraw into herself. She would be easy to upset. So Sonya waited, watching for an opportune moment.

She had met Joan and Christy the night before, just as they ar-rived. Christy had rushed up the steps to the open entrance pavilion, apparently excited by everything. She was slim in her jeans and with her hair soft and free in the breeze, she looked younger than her 39 years. Joan slowly climbed out of the car and stood looking around for a long time. She seemed to ignore the beauty of the spa. Perhaps, Sonya mused, Joan was unwilling to enter a home owned by Errol Swanson.

The manager introduced Sonya to them.

"Sonya's a TV producer, so watch out," he said. "You've got to be careful what you say to the press." Sonya knew it wasn't a joke. The manager was warning them not to talk about Errol.

Then Lara had swept in, greeting them warmly and ushering them off to their bungalow. As she watched them go, Christy unhappily trailing her mother, Sonya sensed the discord between them.

Now, at the café, each seemed indifferent to the other.

Christy turned a page, glanced at her mother, and saw Sonya in the background.

"Hey, come and join us," she called. "Have you been swimming yet? I have and it was wonderful."

Joan hesitated, put down her fork, then waved Sonya over.

"We're waiting for Aunt Tracey to join us," Christy went on, as Sonya smiled a greeting to Joan and sat down. "It's a long time since we've seen her. She was my friend. She took me swimming."

Sonya turned to Joan. "Did you try the pool, too?"

Joan took another piece of cake before she answered. "No, I just had my hair done, and decided to wait a day or two before taking a dip."

"Oh, Mother, don't lie, you never go swimming."

Sonya saw Joan's flash of annoyance. Christy was either short on tact, or she was deliberately trying to hurt her mother.

"My brother's here," she went on, defiantly, obviously determined to irritate her mother. "Do you know that? I called out to him, but he didn't hear me."

"Stop this right now. Remember our agreement." Joan was sharp. "Your brother is dead. He died many years ago. Sonya, please excuse her."

"I don't understand," Sonya said.

"She's obsessed with her dead brother. She imagines she sees him. It's a game she plays. It's embarrassing to us all."

"Yes," Sonya thought, "it's a game they play together. Joan because of guilt, and Christy because she knows it's a sure way of getting what she wants."

Christy gave a harsh burst of laughter, one, Sonya thought, that could quickly turn into hysterics. She was ready to start a scene.

Joan slapped her daughter's hand. "For goodness sake, Christy, stop it. Stop it this minute."

Christy fumbled in her bag for a tissue and sniffed into it.

Sonya saw her chance to get Joan's attention.

"Mrs. Swanson, you know we are doing a story on the spa for the network. I need opinions from some of the guests. You haven't had time to see very much, but if I stopped by, say, tomorrow afternoon, would you mind answering a few questions?"

"Oh, for goodness sake, don't call me Mrs. Swanson—my name is Joan."

"Thanks, Joan. What about the interview?"

Joan hesitated. "I don't know. I've no idea how much I'll have seen by then. We have the opening party at lunchtime."

Sonya could see she was reluctant, and that her reluctance went a long way back. It wasn't the manager's warning last night. Her past dealings with Errol made her unwilling to commit herself.

"Well, let's see how you feel," Sonya said smoothly. "Say I meet you here, about six or so. If we do the interview then, the light would be flattering."

She didn't blame Joan for her reluctance. After all, she was Errol's first wife. It would be strange if she were happy to talk about his third wife and the spa he had built as a wedding present. Sonya caught her eye and smiled, then put out her hand and lightly touched Joan's arm. But Joan didn't respond. "I don't want to upset Errol," she said. "Will Donna Fuller do the interview? Or will you? How does it work?"

"I will do it. It will be a small part of the story. Donna will interview Errol and Lara. I understand how you feel, Joan. I'll make it easy for you. No personal questions. Just mild chitchat about the spa. That's the story we're doing. It's what we call a puff piece. A pleasant story about a New Age spa in a glamorous setting. That's all."

"Okay, I guess so." Joan was still reluctant.

"Thanks," Sonya said with real gratitude.

"Do you want to interview me?" Sonya felt that Christy's eagerness was yet another way to upset her mother.

"Later," Sonya answered, anxious not to get into it.

Christy had already forgotten the question. She saw an aging blond woman who, with the help of a young, dark-haired man, was walking toward them.

"It's Aunt Tracey," Christy shouted, jumping up and knocking over her chair in a rush to greet her. "I knew you were here. I was waiting to see you."

Then Christy turned to the man. "I know who you are," she cried out. "You are my brother Craig. You've been waiting here to see me. I knew it. I knew you'd come. Please, Craig, stay."

"Excuse her, she is confused," Joan called out.

"No harm done," the young man said with a winning smile at Joan.

Tracey took her hand off his arm and gave him a quick nod to leave. Joan's angry shout stopped Christy.

"He is not your brother. Stop it, Christy. Come back here and sit down."

Christy turned back to the table. She looked lost.

Tracey put her arm around her shoulder. "Christy, my dear, his name is Ramos and he works for me in Acapulco. I brought him with me because I've been sick. That's one of the penalties of growing old. You need people to take care of you."

Joan rose. "I'm sorry, and please apologize to Ramos. She has never gotten over the death of Craig. You, of all people, know of her problems."

For a moment Tracey paused. Then she opened both arms and held them out to Joan, Joan walked toward her, tears running down her face. Tracey held her.

"My dear, it has been too long. I'm so glad to see you. I must hear everything that has happened. We must become close, as close as we should have been all these years."

Joan's voice was muffled. She sobbed into the woman's shoulder. "I've neglected you for so long. And you've been sick. Oh, Tracey, life is so brutal." She stepped back and wiped the tears from her cheeks. "Now that I've found you again, I'm not going to lose you."

"She means it," Sonya thought. If Joan gave her word, she would stick to it. She had no doubt Joan was a fighter. In her dealings with Christy she seemed indecisive and even weak, but underneath there were layers of steel.

Tracey linked her arm through Joan's and they walked back to the table. As they approached, Sonya stood and pulled out a chair for Tracey, who, after introducing herself, sat down. "She's a woman of a certain type," thought Sonya. A high-maintenance woman in her designer sweater and skirt with her freshly done hair, makeup, and nails.

Tracey immediately turned to Christy. "My one and only niece, tell me how you are?"

"Is he my brother?" Christy mumbled, slunk into her seat.

"Christy, what am I to do with you?" Joan asked, exasperated. She looked at Tracey and shook her head. "I've tried everything but she still has delusions about Craig. There's nothing I can do for her."

She reached out to take Christy's hand, but her daughter pulled away. "Christy, don't you want to talk to Aunt Tracey?"

Christy was having none of it. "I don't want to talk, Mother. Aunt Tracey, you understand why I don't want to talk, don't you? I want to get away."

Sonya stood up. She'd accomplished what she wanted; it was time to set up an interview with Errol's second wife. "Please excuse me," she said. "I must go to Margot Didot's bungalow. She told me to drop by this afternoon."

"Do you know her?" Joan was surprised.

"Yes. I sometimes do stories on fashion. I've interviewed her several times, and I often meet her at parties."

"I've never met her, but after she married Errol I followed her career. Is she as attractive as she is in photos?" Tracey asked.

Sonya gave Joan a quick glance before she answered. "Yes, she's attractive, but she's also a talented designer."

Tracey laughed. "I know that, I've bought some of her summer dresses. They are great for Acapulco. It may be casual in the day there, but it is quite formal at night."

"I agree, she makes great clothes," Joan broke in. "Margot has made things especially for me when I needed a dress for a special event, and I must say I never looked better."

"She made me a dress, too, when I stayed with her, didn't she, Mother?" Christy broke in.

Sonya smiled. It was astonishing how women relaxed when they talked about clothes.

"Perhaps Christy and I can walk to Margot's bungalow together?" she said.

Before Joan could answer, Christy jumped in. "I know where it is. Margot is my friend. I wanted to stay in her bungalow with her, but there wasn't room."

Sonya looked at Joan for her reaction. The older woman shrugged her shoulders in silent agreement and turned to talk to Tracey. Sonya felt that if she could have taken Christy away for good, Joan would have been more than glad.

Christy's mood changed the moment her mother was out of sight. She straightened her strong swimmer's shoulders and walked happily along the path with Sonya. Sonya was sure Christy was one member of the Swanson family who would talk about Errol. But she hesitated. She had to be careful. Christy was so volatile.

Finally she asked, "You said you know Margot?"

"Oh, yes." Christy spoke quite calmly. "Sometimes when I'm in New York I visit with her. Sometimes I stay in her apartment."

"She sounds like a great stepmother." Sonya was amazed. Margot must be genuinely fond of Christy. She was not related in any

way, and at the beginning of her marriage to Errol, her relationship with Joan must have been difficult.

"Last year she helped me when I had a cancer scare. The doctor
told me I had a lump in my breast and that I had to have it tested.
I told the doctor I wanted to have the test in New York, because I
didn't want Mother to know. Margot set it all up for me. She came
with me to the hospital, Sloan-Kettering, and she held my hand
and told me it would be okay. And it was.

"She took me out to celebrate. We had dinner and then we saw a
play. We had a wonderful time together. And I was so relieved not
to have cancer."

"Did your mother find out about the test?"

"Yes, Margot told her. She said it was better that way."

Christy lowered her voice. "Once, when Daddy and Margot
were living in Chicago after they were first married, I ran away
from home. I needed to see Daddy, but when I got to their place,
he wasn't there. Margot let me come in and talk to her. She was
kind to me. She said she had to call Mother and tell her where I
was because she didn't want Mother to worry. I stayed with her
until Daddy came. Then I had to go home, but I had a wonderful
time with Margot."

"What did your mother say?"

"She thanked Margot for taking care of me. And she said I could
visit Margot any time."

Joan must have been relieved to have Margot take an interest in
her problem daughter. It opened up a part of Margot Sonya hadn't
been aware of.

"Then you know Tomas, too?" she asked.

"Of course I do. He is my brother, I'm proud of him. He is so good looking and he is clever, too. He's a model. I've seen his picture in magazines."

Christy left Sonya's side and ran toward Margot's bungalow. Sonya watched her—a clumsy, awkward woman who behaved like a teenager. If only she weren't so excitable. Christy was hard to understand, harder still to love.

Margot opened the door for them. She gave Sonya a kiss on both cheeks and then a quick hug.

"It's so great you're here. We must get together for a drink and a really long chat."

Next she turned to Christy and gave her a kiss on the cheek. Margot's greeting to Christy was warm, but Sonya saw it was not enough to satisfy the love-starved woman. She was envious of the welcome Sonya received. Sonya sighed. No good telling Christy about the power of the press. She'd never understand.

Margot stood back, a slight figure in black tights and a bodysuit. Sonya had often seen her, but now she examined her more closely. She was a gamine, a delicate, dark-haired beauty with large eyes and a small pointed chin. Errol certainly knew how to pick his women.

"Margot," Sonya said, "after you have seen a bit more of the spa, will you tell me a few of your impressions of it, on camera? Tomorrow? All I need is a quick sound bite."

Margo laughed. "What an opportunity. To talk about Errol's new business venture. I'll be happy to do it. Just tell me where and when."

"How about in the afternoon, say, four-ish? Here in your bungalow, if that's okay."

"Perfect. I'll be here."

"Where's Tomas?" Christy's voice was thin and reedy.

"I'm here, Christy, trying to have a nap." Tomas put his head around the bedroom door and gave her a wide grin.

Sonya saw the delight on Christy's face. "You've got a handsome brother," she said. "Those flashing blue eyes are really something."

"They're just like Daddy's," Christy said.

Sonya left them together and walked to her bungalow, her mind going over the afternoon's events. She was amazed that Christy had such a relationship with Margot. The first two Mrs. Swansons must also be close.

What had bonded them together?

She could think of only one answer—hatred of Errol.

Chapter **21**

The Big Island
Friday, 7:00 P.M.

Tomas walked behind his mother up the stone path to the party. The spike heels of her beige sandals clicked with each step as she moved gracefully in her black sheath dress. As always, she'd taken time and care dressing, and as always, she looked the part of the successful fashion designer. He thought of the chinos and T-shirt he had put on, deliberately dressing down so that he could escape into town as soon as he had spoken to his father.

Margot stopped before a pool that was fringed with ferns and full of lazily floating carp. "Stay calm when you speak to your father," she said. "Remember his violent temper. Once he loses it he becomes a monster. He doesn't care what he says. Or does."

Tomas put his hand in his pocket and felt the gun. "Stop worrying," he said. "Let's go to the party. I'll get you a drink and then see Dad."

Tomas was fuming at the indignity of having to make an appointment with his father. He was the man's son and should be able to drop in and talk at any time. Errol no longer had corporate responsibilities; he had plenty of spare time.

He arrived early, as he knew his father was a fanatic about punctuality. Standing at the door, he knocked vigorously. He wanted to send a clear signal of his determination, independence, and strength.

The spa manager opened the door.

"You can go in," he said abruptly. "I'm leaving."

Tomas walked into the study; the TV was blaring but the room was empty. This was the first time Tomas had been in this room, and he stood admiring its understated décor. Only Errol's desk and leather chair proclaimed his power. They were huge and placed so that he could look to the door and the courtyard. Tomas could see no family photos, not even one of Lara.

He waited almost 15 minutes before his father arrived. When Errol entered room, he said brusquely, "Okay, I am here. What do you want to talk about?"

Tomas wasn't put off. He moved to meet his father in the center of the room and put out his hand. Errol took it and squeezed it hard, as if to test his son's grip. Tomas was startled by this ferocity, but accepted the challenge and responded with equal vigor, turning the contest into a greeting.

Errol moved away and sat behind the desk. "Sit there," he said, indicating the chair facing him. "What do you want? Are you in some kind of trouble?"

"No, no trouble."

"Then what? Did your mother send you here to ask for money?"

"I came because I wanted to see you," Tomas replied. "I think it's time we talked. You're my father, and we have no contact."

"And, so? I ask again, what do you want?"

Tomas took a breath. He had known this would not be easy, but he had hoped for some interest from his father.

"Dad," he began and watched Errol's jaw tighten at the word. "Dad," he said again, "you think of me as a kid. But I'm an adult, and I want a real relationship with you. I want to tell you what I've been doing, what my life is like today, and I want to know about you."

His father stared at him in silence.

"You probably know," Tomas continued, "that I'm doing well as a model. I'm making a great career for myself. I have more work than I can handle."

Errol shrugged his shoulders as if to say "so what."

"Dad, you taught me how to get ahead and how to handle business. I'm grateful. You're my inspiration. I have to credit a lot of my success to being your son. It's your genes that drive me."

Errol smiled at him. "Don't be so sure of that, Tomas."

"Of what?"

"My genes. I don't see my genes in you. Look at what kind of man I am, and what kind of man *you* are." He put his head back and laughed. "I don't consider you a man at all."

Tomas was seething, but Errol went on. "You're a faggot. I don't know who it was your mother screwed, but I've never believed that you were a son of mine."

"That's just plain stupid," Tomas exploded. "You know it and so do I."

Errol's tone was icy. "I had this out with your mother a dozen times."

"Yes, I know how you had things out with her. You hit her. She always made excuses, but I know where the bruises came from."

"She's lucky I stayed with her as long as I did, and you're lucky that I pay for your education."

"All that's past," Tomas replied. "This is between us. You lost one son, do you want to lose me, too? I hoped to make a new start with you. But I was wrong."

Errol laughed. "You were wrong."

Tomas put his hand in his pocket and felt the gun. Then he walked over and turned off the TV.

"Someone else is your father, faaaggot." Errol drew out the word in derision.

Tomas pointed the gun at him. "I don't care what you say about me. But apologize about my mother. She was faithful to you and you know it."

Errol laughed again. "You'll never shoot me. You have none of the Swanson strength or blood. You are a faggot and what you do for sex disgusts me."

Tomas stepped closer. "And what *you* do for sex disgusts me."

For the first time, Errol paused. Tomas could see that he had touched some nerve in the man. He took advantage and pressed on. "You don't think I know, but when I was little I heard you and Mother. I could hear you begging her to do things to you. Things that only whores would do."

"You don't know anything about your mother and me."

"Once, when I was small, I saw the sex toys in your closet. I didn't understand what they were at the time. But I learned. You wanted my mother to use them on you. And she refused."

"You little shit. You cocksucker," Errol hissed.

"Yes, you were the tough man who hit my mother. The strong man who terrorized everybody who worked for you. But the other side of you was a man begging to be whipped and humiliated. You disgusted me, and you disgusted my mother."

Tomas lowered the gun. It was true. He had nothing but loathing for his father. He wanted only one thing now—to get away from him.

But Errol wasn't finished. "Go ahead. Work as a model. Support her when her business fails, because her business is going to fail. Just remember this—neither of you will get anything from me for as long as I live."

Tomas went to the door. He looked back at his father and started to speak again. But he knew it would be no use. Suddenly tired, without thinking, he put the gun down on the table by the door and left.

They'd both said things that could never be taken back. Tomas and his mother had an enemy now. How had Errol put it? An enemy for as long as he lived.

Sonya accepted a glass of champagne from the waiter and walked to the side of the terrace that overlooked the pool. Floating on the water were hundreds of orchids woven together to form the letters L and E. It was spectacular, a scene right out of an Esther Williams movie.

On the other side of the room were the buffet tables. Perry was already there, carefully loading his plate with oysters.

"Hi. Oysters are quite a change from a medium-rare steak," Sonya said as she walked to him.

He grinned at her. "I'm just starting," he said. "After this, I'll tackle the lobsters."

"What about you, Sonya?" Lara moved between them. "Would you like something now?" Lara had curled her hair; the blond ringlets fell, framing her face. Her diamond earrings flashed almost to her shoulders and her pale silk dress dipped to a deep V between her swelling breasts. She looked more like a sex symbol than a businesswoman. Who was she trying to impress, Sonya thought, Errol, Frank, the dozen or so travel editors who had arrived that afternoon?

"No, Lara, I'll wait a little, thanks," she said. "The caviar is what's tempting me. But I think I'll get a refill of champagne before I start." She smiled at Perry and left him with Lara, his eyes focused on her bare neckline.

Sonya left her half-full glass of champagne with a waiter and went toward Frank O'Neill, who stood alone at the bar.

Frank saw her coming and greeted her. "Still working?"

"Well, Frank, I guess at an event like this, work never stops. You must find it that way, surely."

He paused before he answered, "I guess so. But tonight I am here to enjoy myself."

"Are you getting plenty of material for your magazine article?"

"Right now I have other things on my mind. Anyway, the article is just 800 words or so. Should be simple." he said.

"Have you interviewed Errol yet?"

His face tightened. "Yes, I got more than I need, and then some. What did you get?"

"It was okay, the usual Errol Swanson stuff." Sonya decided to change the subject. "It's interesting, don't you think, that Errol's three wives and two grown children are here? I'm surprised there hasn't been much in the way of fireworks among them."

"I think that Lara has set the tone," Frank said. "She is calm and has everything under control."

"Really?" asked Sonya. "I'd say it was Errol who has control here. He wants all of us to think that Lara is in charge, but I'm not convinced." She waited to see how he would react.

"You work at the network, you know what he is like," Frank said with a touch of irony in his voice. "But you don't know her the way I do. Lara will get her way with Errol Swanson."

"Lara always gets her way with me. But that's none of your business." Errol's Midwestern drawl came from behind them.

Sonya turned to him, but Frank remained facing the bar. "I'm talking to you, O'Neill." Errol grabbed Frank's arm and turned the man to face him.

"You will look at me when I speak to you," he said. "Now get your ass away from my bar. You've had enough to drink. I want you out of here in the morning. First thing. You understand?"

Errol released Frank and turned to Sonya. "I can't stand rude drunks. Sometimes you have to be tough with them. Sorry, honey, if I upset you." He patted her on the shoulder and walked to a group of editors who had just come up the path.

Sonya turned to Frank. "You okay?"

"Yes. Don't worry, I know how to take care of myself. I could have hit him, but I didn't want to upset the party."

"You did the right thing. It's best to forget it."

"I'm not going to forget it. I'm having a drink and then I'll go back to my bungalow." He looked over his shoulder at Errol. "And not to pack. I'm not going anywhere—not tonight, not tomorrow." He took the scotch the waiter handed him. "Good night, Sonya. I'll see you after breakfast."

Sonya watched him walk away. He was a brilliant man who'd been unjustly treated. She hoped his hatred of Errol would not destroy him.

Tracey sat in a chair near the pool and thanked the waiter as he placed her plate in front of her. She smoothed the pale green tablecloth with her hand as she watched Christy walk toward her. Her plan was working. Christy was overjoyed to see her. Coming to Hawaii had been the right decision.

"Why do you always wear white, Christy?" Tracey asked as they settled down to eat.

"I'm too thin," Christy said. "I've always been too thin. White makes me look fatter. You told me that when I was little."

Tracey laughed. "You remember that!" She was delighted.

Christy had come alive, eager to go over the stories of the swimming carnivals Tracey had taken her to. They bonded as if they had never parted.

"You should never have stopped swimming, Christy. You really were championship material."

"When you left, there was no one to take me," Christy responded. "Saturdays were the busiest day in the toy store. And Daddy was working, too."

"What about Craig? Couldn't he take you?"

"He did sometimes, on the bus. But after a while, he stopped because he wanted to go to football practice. He had a friend, and the friend's father used to drive them."

Tracey closed her eyes. It seemed impossible that both parents could be so uncaring about their daughter. Neither one had stopped to consider that their daughter needed help from them and not just a psychiatrist.

"So what did you do on the weekends?"

"I watched TV."

Tracey felt a wave of bitterness. She could have continued to care for her niece on the weekends. It would have fit easily into her life. But Errol had made it impossible. He had stubbornly refused to let Tracey have anything to do with his family because she was living with a married man.

"Get rid of that guy, and you can see the kids again. You are a disgrace to our family. You are behaving like some kind of trailer trash whore." She could still hear the rasp in his voice as he growled the word "whore." She had hated being cut off from the children—but she had loved Donald.

"Why did you stop coming to visit us?" Christy asked, as if she had read her aunt's thoughts.

Tracey hesitated, then said, "Because of a disagreement I had with your mother and father." Tracey looked at Joan, who sat near the buffet table with Margot. She wondered how differently all their lives would have turned out if she had confronted Joan and Errol years ago.

"It wasn't a disagreement," Christy said sharply. "It was because you had an affair with a married man. Mother didn't want me to see you."

"You're right," Tracey admitted.

"You should have insisted," Christy exploded. "Didn't you know you were the only friend I had?"

Tracey put her hand over Christy's. "I am sorry, but I could do nothing. I missed you terribly, I thought of you every Saturday, and wished we could spend time together." She felt tears in her eyes. "Sometimes, Christy, I picked up the phone to call you. But I knew if I spoke to you, it would only get you into trouble."

Christy pulled her hand away. "Is Ramos your boyfriend now?"

Tracey brushed her question aside. "I've told you, he helps me run my home."

But Christy wanted more. "Is he a Mexican?"

"I'm not sure, Christy."

"You should know. He works for you."

"Sometimes it's better not to ask where people come from. Often they don't want to say the truth, so they lie."

"Is Ramos married? Does he have any children?"

Tracey laughed, making a joke of her question. "Really, Christy, do I detect a romantic interest?"

But Christy took it seriously. "The doctor says I mustn't have boyfriends. It would just upset me too much. Ramos is nice. I would like him to be my friend. Just as he is yours."

"Have you spoken to him?"

"Yes, in the garden. He told me a lot about the plants. He says he does your garden in Acapulco, and it is beautiful. If I came to Acapulco and visited you there I could see it." She made it a question, not a statement.

"Of course you can come. We'll go out and see the sights and have a really good time. And I'm sure Ramos will show you my garden."

Tracey told herself that her plan was working. But it was better not to rush. Christy was fragile. She had to get used to the idea of coming to Acapulco. Then they could see what the future held.

"Do you really mean it?" Christy leapt up and gave Tracey an awkward hug. Tracey filled with pity. Christy's life was so empty.

"Is Ramos here now?"

"No, he didn't want to come. And your father wouldn't want him here. Tonight is for family."

"I know. I know," Christy said. Her mood changed. She went to the edge of the pool.

"I want to swim," she shouted. She bent over and pulled up one of the orchids that floated on the surface. "I want to swim with the orchids," she screamed as she threw the flower to the ground.

Joan moved quickly despite her size. She grabbed Christy's arm, but Christy was not to be subdued so easily.

"I'm wearing my swimsuit under my dress. Why can't I go in the pool?"

Errol strode over. "For God's sake, Joan, get control of her," he snapped. "I won't have her act out one of her scenes now."

Christy turned away from them. "I hate you, I hate you," she shouted, and ran into the darkness.

Chapter **22**

The Big Island
Saturday, 8:45 A.M.

Errol Swanson was dead. Tied to his bed and murdered.

Sonya Iverson felt the hair prickling on the nape of her neck. She leaned on the stone wall outside the Swanson home and swallowed hard to control the horror sweeping over her. Next to her, Perry put his camera on the ground and wiped the sweat from his forehead.

"Perry," Sonya said, "he must have been killed while we were with Lara on the terrace. The murderer could be anyone here. Any member of his family. The staff. Frank O'Neill. Jackie. Anyone at all. My God, it's awful."

"Swanson had it coming. I'm not going to pretend I'm sorry." Perry's voice was gruff. He looked at his watch. "If Lara has called the police, we'd better get this tape to Donna."

"You're right. I'll take it straight to her. The spa is crawling with press and I want to get a jump on them. Word of this will spread in a few minutes."

Sonya straightened up as Perry bent down and slid the tape out of the camera. "Put it in your bag."

"Right. I don't want anyone to see it."

"I'll go back to the terrace and pick up the tripod and the rest of the gear I left there. I'll join you at Donna's in a few minutes."

Once again, Sonya felt thankful that she had Perry with her.

She hitched her bag higher on her shoulder and walked quickly to Donna's bungalow.

As she went, Sonya remembered how much in control of herself Lara had been at the morning's shoot. If she had shot Errol, then she was certainly a cool killer.

It was odd that Lara had not seemed surprised to see Errol tied to the bed. Perhaps she had been the person who put the bullet through her husband's head.

As for Errol's other two wives, both of them probably had a motive for murder. Money. Hate. Revenge. But one thing was certain, Errol's murder would make the spa story the lead in the Donna Fuller program on Tuesday night. So much for the puff piece that Donna and Matt wanted.

When Sonya reached Donna's bungalow, the anchor was sitting in the garden. She glanced up, then stood quickly and took Sonya by the arm. Sonya knew the shock she still felt must show on her face. Before Donna could voice her concern Sonya reached into her bag, pulled out the tape, and handed it to Donna.

"Errol Swanson's been murdered," she said.

"Murdered? How?"

"He was tied to the bed and shot. Through the head."

"Do you know who did it?"

"No. We just discovered the body. We were shooting with Lara when Christy came to tell us he was dead. We went to his bedroom and saw the body. Perry rolled tape for a few moments before Lara threw us out."

"What did you get?"

"Perry's not sure, Donna. Lara was frantic, trying to untie his legs and arms."

"You mean she disturbed the body?"

"Yes."

Donna took the tape from Sonya and walked into her bungalow. Sonya could see no sign of distress on her face, she was pure business, and Sonya admired her for it.

"Call Matt and tell him to come here."

Sonya followed her into the living room, pulled out a chair, and sank into it. She got out her cell and dialed Matt's number while Donna rewound the tape.

"We just got a few seconds right at the end," Sonya said.

And there it was, in Perry's perfect focus, a wide shot of Swanson on the bed, then a tight shot of his blood-streaked head. Perry had even managed a close-up of Lara struggling to undo a scarf that bound one of his feet to a bedpost. Finally Lara's hand came up and signaled them away.

"Whatever you say about Perry Dalton, he gets the picture." Matt's voice came from the doorway. "I just met him walking back to the terrace. He told me what happened, and that you were here." Sonya closed her cell.

"Take a look at all of it, Matt." Donna signaled him to join her at the monitor.

She replayed the tape. "Look. He's lying on his back with his feet and hands tied with scarves of some sort. His blood is all over the sheets and pillows." She stopped the machine. "We can't run this. But we have to tell New York about it. It's early afternoon there. The executives will want to have a conference about how to handle it."

Matt squatted down beside the monitor, rewound the tape, and watched again.

"Yeah, you're right, it's gruesome. It's a pity we can't run it. But we've got plenty of tape of Errol. We'll manage to put a story together for tonight's network news."

"Do you think the network will want to go live with Donna?" Sonya asked.

"Sure I'm sure. We have to be fast. With the time difference, we'll have to go on air at one-thirty our time. Sonya, you work with Donna. I'll call New York, then book a satellite feed with the local affiliate."

"Donna, surely we'll get extra time for this," Sonya said. "How about two minutes instead of the usual minute and 15? After all, he was president of the network for 10 years, and then went on to head the conglomerate. It's a good story."

"No," responded Matt. "A minute, a minute 30. Donna will do a live intro. That's enough."

Sonya started to argue, but Matt interrupted. "It shouldn't take you long to get it together, that is, if you've finally got around to logging your tapes."

Matt couldn't resist taking a dig at her.

"I've logged the important ones," Sonya responded, ignoring Matt's attitude. "It's no problem. I'll just have to go through Donna's interview with Swanson and get a good sound bite to end the piece."

Sonya reflected on the Swanson interview and the mysterious disappearance of her notebook. Could that have had anything to do with the murder? What could Swanson have said that was so important? Was there some family secret he revealed? Who could she trust to talk about it? The last thing she wanted was to go to the police with her story.

Donna broke into her thoughts. "We'll work here with Perry. Go get all the tapes and your notes from the bungalow, Sonya. Be quick about it."

Donna sounded almost like her old self. She reached for her laptop and flipped open the top. "Errol Swanson was a bastard," she said as the laptop booted up, "but he was also a brilliant businessman."

Sonya started out the door, but Donna called her back. "Sonya, I want the piece to reflect what he did for international journalism."

International journalism, Sonya wondered, as she walked to her bungalow. Errol Swanson's only influence on international journalism had been to close bureaus and cut staff.

Once again, Donna was avoiding the truth about Errol Swanson. He was dead. What hold could he still have over her?

When Sonya returned to the bungalow she found Matt in the garden, speaking on his cell phone. As she approached, he put his hand over the receiver and mouthed "Get coffee." She brushed past him, pretending she didn't understand.

Inside, Perry was setting up the editing bay they would need to cut the piece.

"Give me five minutes to get this hooked up and I'll be ready to work with you," he told Sonya as she walked to the desk.

She put down the tapes. "I'm going to log Donna's interview with Swanson. Then I'll find the video we need. We'll get it done it in less than an hour."

"Okay, then I'll set up for the live shot with Donna. I guess you need the usual sea-and-beach background?"

Sonya managed a smile. "What else in this Hawaiian paradise? This place of contrasts. On the one hand, serenity and joy, and . . ." she deliberately paused, "on the other hand, murder."

"That's enough, Sonya." Donna looked up from her typing. "Keep it focused on what an important man Errol was. This spa is one of his legacies."

Without responding to Donna, Sonya continued, "We could even do the live shot on the terrace where we had Lara this morning."

As she said it, she shuddered. Only an hour had passed, but it seemed a lifetime since they had stood there impatiently watching Christy as she wandered through the water, her white dress trailing behind her.

Sonya's thoughts raced.

Could the disturbed woman have pulled the trigger and killed her father? Could her voices have told her to do it? Surely not. Christy must have gone to see him at the house and found his body. But why didn't she call anyone? Why just walk away? Could she have seen something? Did she know who the killer was?— perhaps her own mother? Joan had made no secret that she was not happy with Errol.

And Lara's mother? The woman was crazy with jealousy of her daughter. She had the freedom to wander in and out of the Swanson home. She had the opportunity. It was possible. Margot? Sonya found that hard to believe, but there were rumors that her business was doing badly. Had she come to the spa to borrow money from Errol and been refused? And Tomas? The boy loved his father, just wanted to get close to him. Surely the only reason he'd kill him would be to protect his mother. Or Tracey? That was difficult—who knew how far back her animosity with Errol went?

It was obvious that Christy knew something—and that she was unhappy about what she knew.

"I don't believe Christy killed her father," Sonya said, half to herself, as she sat beside Perry.

"No," he replied as he rewound tapes. "I've got my money on Frank O'Neill. Swanson treated him brutally, and O'Neill was pretty close to Lara before she married."

"Yes, I was with him when he had that scene with Errol last night."

"He hated Errol Swanson, I can tell you that. And he has been crazy for Lara for years."

The phone rang. Sonya answered.

"Donna, it's Lara Swanson," Sonya called. "She wants to speak to you."

Sonya shook her head at Perry. He understood not to talk so that Sonya could concentrate on overhearing Donna's end of the conversation.

Donna took the phone and turned on her sympathy. "Lara, we are stunned. It is monstrous. I am so very sorry. What can we do to help? I can only imagine how difficult this is for you. To lose Errol in this way. My God.

"Errol had enemies, of course. But this . . ." her voice trailed off. Sonya realized Lara had broken in.

After a few moments Donna continued, "Lara, you should call your attorney immediately."

Donna paused for Lara's reply.

"No, certainly not, Lara. We will not run the tape. You have my word on that." Sonya and Perry exchanged glances. She saw that Perry had his doubts.

"We could run a little of it," he mouthed silently.

"As for handing it over to the police," Donna continued, "I have to check with the lawyers in New York. You know, freedom of the press. Legal issues, and so forth."

Sonya was frustrated at not being able to hear Lara. But she guessed Lara's aim was to make sure the network handled Errol's murder as positively as possible.

"Yes, Lara. Yes, I'll come and talk to you," Donna said. "Just give me half an hour to check on things here. And don't worry about the story."

She hung up and turned to Sonya. "I've almost finished the script. We'll go over it together quickly and then I'll do the voice track. I want to get to Lara as fast as I can."

It was unlike Donna not to share what Lara had said.

"What was Lara's reaction?" ventured Sonya.

"What you would expect," was the answer. "Now let's get back to work."

Donna started typing. When Matt came in, she said, "If I persuade Lara to do an exclusive interview with me, it would do her a big favor, don't you agree?"

"It would also give us a strong promotion for the Tuesday show," Matt answered. "We have to start thinking about handling Lara. The network will want to show her in a favorable light, and I agree with that."

"Of course," replied Donna.

Sonya looked at them in alarm. "Don't forget, she might have killed her husband. At the very least, she must be the one who tied him to the bed."

"Why do you say that, Sonya? What proof do you have?"

"I overheard them arguing about something, and it made me wonder if there were things about their relationship that might be hidden, sexual things."

"Stay away from that," Donna insisted.

"Well," said Matt, "if she murdered him, then an interview with her could only help ratings. But at first we'll go easy on her."

"Do you really think Lara could have done it?" Perry broke in.

Sonya could hardly believe that. Perry had interrupted a conversation between Donna and someone else. It was totally out of character for him. The thought of Lara being accused of murder must be upsetting him. Sonya remembered his obvious liking for Lara's professionalism when they were working on the terrace. Perhaps he was even more taken with her than Sonya had realized.

She intervened before Donna could object to his interference. "No, Lara is too clever to have done it with a pistol. My guess is that she'd use poison." Sonya laughed, then, realizing she sounded slightly hysterical, stopped.

"Matt," she said, changing the subject, "we'll need extra crews to cover this. Have you arranged anything?"

"Naturally, Sonya. I've contacted our affiliate station here. The master control there is standing by for the tape of Donna's story. They'll feed it to our guys in New York so it can be played after her live introduction."

"And the extra crews?"

"One crew is on the way here to cover the police—and Lara's press conference, if she decides to give one. Let's consider what else we'll need. Sonya, let's go over the video you managed to shoot in the two days before we arrived."

Matt's demeaning attitude again. There was no relief from it. During the years since he had become executive producer of the *Donna Fuller Show,* Sonya's usual tactic had been to ignore it.

"Basically," she replied, "we have a lot of background shots. The volcano erupting, the treatments in the spa, the chef, the boat, the bungalows, the pool. We'll need more interviews. Most of the family and guests only arrived last night, and I had some interviews scheduled for today."

"The best things to have would be comments from Errol's family, and that may not be so easy," said Donna.

"I don't know if anyone will keep our appointments for this afternoon, but I'm supposed to meet with both ex-wives. The daughter, Christy, is disturbed and may not make sense, but since she was the one who discovered the body, I'll give her a go after I'm finished with her mother.

"That leaves the son, Tomas, and Tracey, the aunt. Right now I'd say we'll get the best stuff from Margot Didot, the second wife. She's a cool lady, totally controlled. She was doing yoga when I went to her bungalow yesterday. She didn't have a hair out of place. But, more important, she relished the thought of doing an interview. She's got an agenda for sure."

"What kind of 'agenda'?" Matt said sarcastically.

"I can't put my finger on it, but my instinct tells me that she came here looking for something from Errol, probably money. I just wonder if she got it before he was murdered."

"We can't go on your instinct. Forget it. Just get on with the interviews we need." Matt opened his phone and dialed as he walked back into the front garden.

Sonya turned to the monitor, put on the headphones, and started listening to the tape of Donna's interview with Errol Swanson. The sound of his voice nauseated her. The clichés he uttered were so bland. She wondered again why Donna hadn't pressed him to say something more interesting. She listened and then replayed it.

"Donna, how do you like this bite for your piece?" She raised the volume so Errol's voice filled he room. "My life has begun anew here in Hawaii. I've left behind the pressures of the business world and found real peace and happiness."

"It's okay. Just the sort of thing we need." Donna pressed a key and started printing her script. "It is certainly ironic."

Sonya walked across the room and picked up the pages from the printer.

"Would you like me to come with you when you see Lara?" she asked.

"Heavens, no," Donna jerked out a laugh. "Lara is furious with you. She says you had no right to force your way into the bedroom to shoot video of Errol on the bed. In fact," she continued before Sonya could reply, "Errol told Lara last night he was angry about the preinterview you did with him. Just stay away from her, do your job, and stop interfering with the direction of this story."

Donna turned away and left the room.

Sonya sat stunned. Errol was furious with her? Well, he certainly hadn't shown it while she was doing the interview. He must have gotten mad when she hadn't shown up at the swimming pool later that night. What an ego the man had. It was true the world was better off without him.

Chapter **23**

The Big Island
Saturday, 9:15 A.M.

Margot Didot stood in the middle of the bedroom and flipped the narrow chain of diamonds that circled her wrist. She had brought the bracelet to wear to the opening party at noon. But now Errol was dead.

She had hoped Errol would see the bracelet and remember the love and joy they shared when Tomas was born. He had given it to her in her flower-filled hospital room just after she had taken Tomas into her arms and begun to nurse him. How happy she had been.

"Thank you for my son," he said as he bent to kiss her. "He's what I wanted more than anything else. You gave me a new life when we married, and now you have given me a chance to start over as a father."

Her world was golden then. A luxurious apartment in Chicago. A baby boy. And above it all, Errol's love. She started each day waking up beside his strong warm body, knowing she would have his support always.

She flipped the bracelet again and watched the brilliant stones flash over her wrist. Then she took it off and put it in its red suede case. How naïve she had been to think Errol would have noticed.

When he had first fallen in love with her, Errol had catered to her love of diamonds. First were the earrings, the pendant, the choker, and then the bracelet. She knew a huge part of his generosity came from his pleasure at doing business with the dealers. He spent hours discussing the quality of the stones, the different cuts and sizes. In a few years he considered himself a expert. Margot would sometimes see him at a party, looking at a woman's ring and giving her his assessment.

He had fallen in love with Margot at a party in Paris. The event, hosted by the wife of the American consul, was for a group of visiting American businessmen. Margo had said a firm, "No, not this time" when she was first asked. She'd spent enough evenings talking to homesick men and looking at photos of their kids.

But the consul's wife had begged. "I'm really desperate, I've got eight men and only two women so far. The men may not be so bad. They are all in the media, so they've got to be able to talk about something other than wheat and electronics."

Margo had given in, insisting it was the last time.

"I'll sit you next to the best of them," the consul's wife said. "His name is Errol Swanson, he's divorced with, I think, two kids, and he's rumored to be shooting to the top. He works in Chicago now, but the buzz is that he'll end up in New York."

At the party, to Margot's amazement, Errol didn't bring out photos of his kids. He did mention the divorce, saying it was quite amicable. But mostly he listened. He seemed fascinated with the idea of seeing more of Paris.

Errol took Margot home and when he dropped her off, he asked her to have an early breakfast with him the next day. She had refused, not wanting to see him again. But he had insisted, and at last she agreed to a quick cup of coffee at the corner café. She shrugged her shoulders and tried to push the memory of that morning away. If only she had trusted her instincts and not given in to him.

The breakfast was an unexpected success. He seemed much more sophisticated and comfortable than he had been at dinner. Margot canceled her plans. They began spending evenings together. They ate in restaurants she liked and spent hours walking hand in hand through the narrow streets of the Left Bank. Errol postponed his flight home and stayed with Margot for the weekend.

She went with him to the airport in his limousine. He left her with passionate words of love, but when she said good-bye to him, she meant good-bye. It had been a fleeting, magical moment, one that was not to be taken to heart. He was a divorced businessman with a wife and children. She was a young apprentice designer enjoying a free life in the world's most glamorous city. It was not to be.

But he had called her when his jet touched down in Chicago and told her he would be back the following weekend. And he was, for two weeks. Margot's attraction to him grew. She let him move into her small apartment. It had once been a stable, and she had decorated it simply, making the most of the huge beams that had been there for centuries. Errol admired it all, even the stylish Art Deco sculptures she had combed the city's flea markets to find.

"The pieces are like you, elegant and sensual," was his comment.

Every night at sunset, they walked along the banks of the Seine, while he told her about himself.

"I never allowed myself time to play. I married too young and for the wrong reasons. I didn't know how to live, and I didn't know what romance was. That's what you are teaching me."

Some days he did the marketing and they cooked dinner together in Margot's tiny kitchen. Errol loved it all, lying in bed with her, listening to the children playing on the cobblestone path outside, weeding and watering the flowers she had planted in her window boxes, gossiping in his bad French with the maid who came to clean.

One evening, after they had walked through the Luxembourg Gardens, Errol took Margot window-shopping on the Rue St. Honoré. She had admired a pair of diamond earrings in the Cartier Jewelry window.

"Look, they are shaped like a four-leaf clover. How chic, and how lucky. They are so French."

"No, they're not. They're as Midwestern as I am," he had laughed at her.

A day later, when she dipped into the healthy breakfast of yogurt and fruit he had insisted on preparing, she spooned out the earrings. She laughed at him. But she'd made up her mind, if he asked her to marry him, she would accept, even though it meant moving to the States and all but abandoning her career. How credulous she had been, marrying a man she knew nothing about.

And now Errol was dead. Tied up and shot on the bed he shared with Lara. Margot laughed. That was appropriate. There was justice in the world after all.

She thought back on the evening before. Tomas had refused to go to the casual dinner on the terrace.

"The party will be more than I can stand. I want to talk to my father, but I'm not going to stay. He has humiliated me enough."

She had watched him, tanned and muscled in his favorite jeans and vest, as he phoned the concierge. First he requested the names of clubs in Kona, the nearby town that was the center of nighttime activity. Then he ordered a taxi.

Margot hadn't argued. She thought it better if he were not there. She simply asked him to escort her to the party before he left. Even in these days of women's independence, she didn't like arriving alone.

She felt nervous about the evening, but it had to be done. She had to speak to Errol and persuade him to give her the money he owed her without a lawsuit. It would be easier to ask him to meet her if Tomas weren't there.

Errol had agreed to have coffee with her in the morning, before the official opening of the spa.

Now, none of that mattered. Errol was dead and her money was now part of his estate. So be it. The money was rightfully hers and she would get it eventually.

But Tomas knew nothing of his father's death. She must wake him and tell him. She must be with him when he learned that the man could never hurt him again. She walked through the living room and knocked on his door. She had given him the front bedroom so he could come and go without disturbing her.

"Tomas, wake up. I have news."

She knocked again, then swung open the door. Tomas wasn't there. The room looked exactly as it had when the maid had left the night before: the bed turned down, the gardenia laid against the embroidered pillowcase, the curtains drawn against the light.

Margot walked across the room to the wall of built-in closets and pulled open the door, but even as she reached for the drawer, she knew the gun was gone. It had been there the day before. Tomas had shown it to Christy, and Christy had laughed. He was like a young boy, trying to impress his sister.

Margot had reminded him to put the weapon back in the box and place the box where the maids couldn't see it. Obviously, he had not.

Margot shivered. She was icy cold. She had to get out of the room before she fainted. She walked into the garden and stood in the sunshine, feeling it spread warmth and life into her body. She took a deep breath and looked around. And there was her son, sprawled on the lounge, his body hot and sweaty, his face dark with his morning beard.

He must have been very drunk. That was not like Tomas. But that did not matter. What mattered was that he was safe. Relief flooded through Margot. She sat on the bench and put her head down between her hands to stop herself from sobbing. When she looked up, Tomas's face was grim.

"It's all right, I know he is dead. I was there." His voice was flat. "I took the gun, but I swear, Mother, although I wanted to kill him, I didn't do it."

Margot sprang to her feet and looked down at him.

"Why, Tomas? Why?"

Tomas got up and grabbed her arms.

"You have to ask me that? After all he did to you? After what he did to me? For God's sake, Mother, I am 19 years old, the age he was when he first married. He should treat me as an equal, talk over my plans as any father does with his son, be proud of what I've achieved. Instead, he drives me away, just as he did with Craig. I hate him, Mother, and I'm glad he's dead."

Margot felt the earth slipping away beneath her. She collapsed against Tomas.

"Tell me what happened," she sobbed.

Tomas put his arm around his mother and led her inside. "Last night, I went to his home. I wanted to discuss my career, my plans for the future, investing my money. He said he wasn't interested, that I was your son, not his."

"Tomas, for God's sake, why did you stay?" Margot screamed at him. "You know he is evil. You should have walked away."

Tomas told her everything his father had said. He told her about threatening Errol with the gun.

"All he did was laugh."

"My God, Tomas."

"Mother, I wanted to pull the trigger. I wanted him dead and out of our lives. I wanted to pay him back for everything he did to you. But I couldn't. He deserved to die for what he did to you, to me, to Craig and Christy. But it wasn't up to me to kill him."

Margot shook her head. "Oh, Tomas, if you knew how many times I wished I'd never married him." She sighed.

"I left the gun on a table near the door. I didn't want to bring it back here. It was as if I was afraid I'd run into you and have to tell you everything Errol had said. And I couldn't do that, not last night; it just hurt too much." He paused. "I wasn't thinking straight."

"What did you do?"

"I got my taxi and went to Kona. I had a wild time—I danced and drank, going from club to club with a crowd of guys. I tried to forget his abuse, but I couldn't. And the more I drank, the worse it got."

"And this morning? What happened? Did anyone see you coming home?"

"I don't know, Mother. I got here about seven and realized that I had to get the gun back. So I went back to the house and let myself in. It was easy, someone had left the front door ajar. The gun was gone. The bedroom door was open. I looked in and saw him lying there, dead. His head was covered in blood. And the gun was there, lying near his foot on the sheet."

Margot swallowed hard. "Where is it now?"

"I picked it up, put it my pocket, and left as quietly as I could. I went to the rocks near the airfield and threw it into the sea. I picked up some shells and threw them too, so that if anyone saw me they would think I was playing around."

"What about the box?" Margo walked into the bedroom.

"It still has some bullets in it," Tomas said. "I'll throw everything into the sea."

Margot called. "Come lie down. You've been up all night drinking. People will assume you have a hangover and are sleeping it off.

"I'll get rid of the box and the bullets and I'll arrange to get us out of here as fast as I can."

Chapter **24**

The Big Island
Saturday, 10:30 A.M.

Sonya walked in silence down the path to Joan Swanson's bungalow. Perry was behind her, camera in one hand, tripod in the other.

Sonya still stung from Donna's rebuke. She understood that she had to get the job done and make Errol look like a good guy.

"Someone hated that man enough to murder him, but I have to convince the world he's a good," she raged. "What's happened to Donna, the respected journalist?" Sonya laughed bitterly to herself. It seemed that everyone had a price after all.

"Okay, if that's what you want, Donna," she told herself, "I'll just ask Joan three standard questions about the murder and we'll run one of the dumb answers she gives. It may leave viewers unsatisfied, but it won't upset anyone."

But she wouldn't stop thinking. It was the first time Donna had spoken so sharply to her. It was also the first time she had seen Donna to lose her cool. Yes, Donna knew something and she was hiding it.

Sonya tried to give Donna the benefit of the doubt. She must have gotten instructions from the 19th floor.

Still, if she'd decided to do what the executives insisted, she had to agree it was the right thing.

It was, after all, Donna's show. Her name was on it. And she was responsible for its success. *Donna Fuller Show* ratings were always near the top.

She had received the network's vote of confidence just two years ago, when it was decided that her program would run twice a week, rather than weekly. Friday nights had been added to the regular Tuesday slot and each night was a full hour.

Though Matt Richards would never admit it, Sonya knew she made a real contribution to the show. She had a talent for gaining the confidence of those she interviewed. She could get them to talk, share confidences, reveal themselves. That was golden for a producer. And she had solved the murder of Harriett Frankin. That had not been easy.

Now she had an opportunity to prove herself. If she could solve this murder, it would be good not only for Donna's show, but for her own career. Sonya told herself that she might have to ask dumb questions on camera, but when the tape stopped rolling, she would ask what she wanted. That was the way to do it. And she had to do it fast.

Errol's murder would draw an international spotlight. The handful of press here for the opening was nothing. Today's flights would bring in dozens of reporters, photographers, and cameramen. Every aspect of Errol's life was going under the magnifying glass.

Sonya already knew everybody here, and she could spend the day using that knowledge to the best advantage. Tomorrow there would be too much competition. Yes, she would work fast—and do it her way.

Start from the beginning. She remembered the argument she had overheard, between Lara and Errol. What was he begging Lara to do? There had been rumors about Errol's sexual eccentricities. Sonya had put that down to the kind of gossip that always follows famous people.

Still, it might be true. She had once interviewed a psychologist who wrote a book about powerful men who needed to be humiliated. Day to day they might be monsters, but in bed they needed to be beaten. For some it was a way of freeing themselves from guilty feelings. And Errol had lots to be guilty about.

Who had tied him to the bed and left him helpless? Probably Lara. But there might be others here at the spa who knew of his needs. After all, his first two wives were here. And Donna—it was a loosely kept secret that she had had an affair with Errol.

Perry interrupted her thoughts. "Does Joan know we are coming?"

"Yes," Sonya replied. "I called and persuaded her see us. She was nervous, so I told her she would have to answer only three simple questions. And that's exactly what I'm going to do—on camera."

She turned around and looked at Perry. "It was strange in a way. She had nearly refused an interview yesterday, but today agreed practically at once. I think she is anxious to prove she has nothing to hide."

Joan was waiting for them in the living room. She smiled as she opened the door and ushered them in.

"Excuse the mess, it's my daughter Christy at work."

Sonya looked around the room in amazement. Clothes were

thrown over the sofas and chairs, shoes piled on the floor, and cosmetics strewn across the coffee table.

Joan saw Sonya's face.

"Christy is a collector," she said. "She buys and buys clothes, yet she can never make up her mind what to wear. She brought too much with her and then put everything out so I could help her choose. That's never a good idea. She argues with my suggestions and then wears something completely different. But that's often the way with mothers and daughters."

"I know. I was a difficult daughter, too." Sonya laughed gently. "I see that you have a real eye for what looks good on television."

Joan was carefully and simply dressed in a blue blouse that dipped into a deep V that flattered her big bust. Her hoop earrings elongated her neck, and her hair was combed back from her face, showing the perfect curve of her high forehead.

"Thank you. I have always heard that blue was right for the camera. Would either of you like some coffee?" she asked. "I ordered a large pot so that Christy could have some when she came back from her swim."

"That's very thoughtful, Joan, I would like coffee. It's one of my vices."

Though usually he did not accept an offered drink, Perry also took a cup and sipped it as he set up the lights.

"Wow, that's hot," he said. Then, ignoring the plate of fresh fruit, he reached for a muffin. "These look good." He took a bite. "And warm, too. You're lucky. Mine were cold. It must have just arrived. No wonder we didn't see the room service waiter."

Joan said, "How do I look on your monitor, Mr. . . . . Mr. . . . ."

"Perry. Just call me Perry"

"Oh, Perry. How do I look?" She continued, "I wore blue because of Errol. He's the one who made me television-savvy."

"You look great," Perry said.

"Shoot me from the left side, please. It's a better angle for me. And please be gentle with the light."

"Don't be concerned, Joan, Perry's an expert with lighting. He's Donna's favorite cameraman. When Perry shoots anyone, they look great. Especially women. He likes women." Sonya looked at Perry with amusement. "Are you ready to go?" He nodded. Sonya began.

"Tell me how you feel about the murder."

"I'm devastated, as everyone is. It is a great blow. We live in such a violent world. To see my child's father dead causes me great pain."

"Have you any idea who might have done it?"

"No, none at all. Of course not," she added with a hint of indignation. "But, you know, Errol was a strong man who rose to a position of great power. And strong men make enemies. Though I know little about his life today. We were divorced so many years ago."

"Who brought you the news?"

"When I called to order my breakfast, the girl on the phone seemed upset and told me something dreadful had happened, but she wouldn't give me any details. When the waiter brought my tray, he told me about the murder."

Sonya leaned forward, took off Joan's mike, and smiled at her. "Thank you, that was just what we want. As I explained, we are just doing a short piece for the network news."

Joan got up and refilled Sonya's coffee cup. "That was easy.

Though I was surprised when you asked me if I knew who the murderer was."

"It's fairly routine to ask if someone has 'an idea' of who might have done it. But you answered beautifully. Is Christy here?" Sonya continued, wondering if Joan's difficult daughter would answer a few questions.

"She went for an early swim and hasn't come back yet." Joan poured herself more coffee.

Sonya hesitated. Did Joan know that Christy had seen her father's body? Sonya thought not. If she had known, she would never have been so comfortable talking about the murder.

"She loves to exercise, doesn't she? And she's very fond of Margot Didot. When she walked me down to Margot's cabin yesterday, she stayed to do yoga with her."

"When Christy visits New York, she always sees Margot. Once or twice, she's stayed at Margot's apartment. Christy is quite fond of Tomas, too. She loves to have a brother."

"It's unusual, that you all get along so well."

"Well, I was not bitter about the divorce. I was as unhappy as Errol was in our marriage, perhaps even more so. I was so close to my family and had their full support. And the divorce was a tremendous release. I started doing what I really loved, working full-time in the toy business."

"Why did you decide to come to the spa opening?"

"It was a special request from the new Mrs. Swanson. She said it was important for us and for our children to forget the past and create a circle of love in this beautiful place."

Sonya thought that as philosophical as it sounded, each of the family members must have had a stronger reason for being there.

Joan's, she was sure, had something to do with the toy stores she was so fond of talking about.

Joan continued, "Also, Christy wanted very much to come. Despite the way her father ignored her, she's always loved him. Just after Margot and Errol were married, Christy ran away to them. Margo took her in and treated her well. It is hard to express how grateful I was."

Sonya looked at her, unconvinced. She sipped her coffee slowly.

"I need this," she said, holding up the cup. "I still haven't got over the jet lag from New York."

"I understand," Joan replied. "I was up at six this morning and so was Christy. As soon as the sun came up, we went for a walk together. It is so beautiful and fresh then. I'm afraid the heat during the day exhausts me. But Christy is always full of energy. She went off for a swim and I came here for breakfast."

Sonya looked at the breakfast tray on the dining table. The eggs and butter were not yet congealed on the plate. Sonya glanced at her watch. It was 10:45; either Joan had waited a long time to order breakfast, or she was hiding something about her morning schedule.

"If you've finished your coffee, you'll have to excuse me; I must call my lawyer in Chicago and give her the news."

Perry started to pack his gear. Sonya rose and followed Joan to the door and into the garden.

"It really is cooler in the early morning before the heat of the day. That's the time to be out and about," Sonya said as a hot breeze blew her hair from her face. "Thank you again."

But Joan wasn't listening. She was looking along the path at Margot Didot, who was striding along in a loose, dramatically printed cover-up. A striped plastic bag stuffed with a beach towel hung over her shoulder.

"Margot, isn't it terrible," Joan called. Margot looked up and almost ran toward the gate. Joan opened it and stepped forward to greet her.

To Sonya's surprise, they embraced. Then Margot lifted her face from Joan's shoulder and Sonya saw the tears in her eyes.

"Yes, I heard early this morning. They phoned me."

"Where is Tomas?"

"Asleep. He spent the night on the town in Kona. He knows about his father, but I told him to go back to sleep if he could. He got in very late. I just couldn't sit still after I heard the news. I decided to go for a swim, but found that I needed to walk."

"Yes," said Joan with sympathy. "I went for a walk early."

"Oh," Sonya thought, "it appears everyone was away from their bungalows at the time Errol was killed."

Margot glanced over and saw Sonya.

"Oh, no," she said immediately, "I can't give you an interview now. I'm shocked, so shocked that such a dreadful thing should happen, just as Errol and Lara were so happy together."

Sonya answered, "I understand. We can do it when you are feeling a little better, but I hope it will be possible to meet this afternoon as we arranged."

"Come in for minute," Joan said, seeing Margot's discomfort with Sonya.

"Just for a minute. I need to get back to Tomas. I saw the police examining the grounds outside Errol's house. The police will want to interview us all. And I don't want him to face them alone."

Margot turned to Sonya, as if she were making an effort to

apologize for her lack of enthusiasm. "Call me later and I'll let you know about the interview."

"Thank you, I will." Sonya stepped aside and let her pass.

She took a good look at Margot's face as she walked by. It was rigid, the face of a terrified woman.

Chapter **25**

The Big Island
Saturday, 10:30 A.M.

Frank O'Neill walked into the courtyard of the Swanson home feeling better than he did most mornings. Last night he had drunk little—a few light beers with a scotch for a nightcap. He'd had a surprisingly good six hours of sleep. He was glad, for this was a time when he needed to have a clear mind.

The heavy pine tree branches sheltered the courtyard from the sun. It was cool and serene, impossible to believe that a few yards away Errol Swanson lay murdered, blood soaking the bed he had shared with Lara.

The moment he'd heard, Frank had phoned her, but the operator told him she was not taking calls. He refused to leave a message. He had to see and talk to her.

He felt that not even her husband's murder would prevent her from doing what needed to be done. Not his Lara. She was getting on with it, calling lawyers and network executives.

He also knew those executives would not be happy that he, a high-profile ex-employee, was at the spa. There was no doubt he had reasons to murder Errol. Let them try to prove it.

Frank ran up the steps to the entrance. Surprisingly, there was no policeman on duty at the door. As he peered through the window, he could see the yellow tape cordoning off the short hallway that led to the closed door of the master bedroom. He tried the handle, but as he suspected, the door was locked. He knocked, then stood back from the door and looked around the courtyard.

Lara had taken a group of the press around her home last night. He had felt odd being near her and unable to say a private word, but he was glad he had taken the tour. He had only been in Errol's study before and the tour gave him an idea of the layout of the whole house. The terrace with the statue of Buddha was at the front, next to the ocean. All he had to do was to clamber over a few rocks to get to it. From there, he could see what was going on inside.

When his foot slipped, he tumbled onto the hard floor of the terrace. He checked himself over, stood up, and looked into the blue eyes of Jackie Olsen, Lara's friend and assistant. He had first met her when she visited Lara from London.

She leaned forward and kissed him on the cheek. "That's a graceful way to make an entrance."

"Oh, Jackie, what a relief that you're here. Tell me, how is Lara?"

"As well as anyone could be. What are you doing here?"

"I have to see Lara."

"Right now, that's impossible. She's in shock. And she's worried. With all the press here, think how Errol's murder will damage the spa."

"You can never tell," Frank said. "The name will be all over the place."

"I guess so. But whatever happens to the spa, for Lara's sake I'm glad he is dead."

Frank was surprised at Jackie's frankness. "I agree, you know that."

Together, they walked to the table and chairs that were set in the shade of the house.

After a pause, Jackie said, "I'm afraid that his sexual habits will come out in the press. You know that he was tied to the bed when he was shot."

Frank replied, in a matter-of-fact tone, "The story's all over the spa. It will be headlined in the tabloids, you can be sure of that. Did Lara tie him up?"

"Yes. She hated what he wanted from her, but she agreed this morning."

"What happened when the police arrived?"

"She called me before she called them, and I insisted she not do anything until I arrived. When I got to the bedroom I found Christy struggling to untie him."

"That was a mistake. She was tampering with evidence."

"Luckily, I stopped her. She stood there in her wet dress, mumbling something over and over again. Lara had covered Errol's face with a towel, so I couldn't figure out if Christy knew her father was dead, or if she was so shocked she couldn't face the reality of it."

"Have you spent any time with Christy?" he asked. "What do you think of her?

"Yes, I've had some time to watch her since she arrived. She's very sad, and now she's got to face her father's murder." Jackie paused. "I got her out of the room as fast as I could. She had blood on her dress, and I told her that she should go to her bungalow and change before the police arrived."

"That was smart, Jackie. But I think we will all be involved before this is over."

"I told her that she should say as little as possible. I told her that Lara and I would stand by her."

O'Neill stood up impatiently and looked down at Jackie. "I don't want to wait. When can I see Lara?"

"Frank, she's had quite a time with the police, and then with Donna Fuller. Fuller just left, and Lara's agreed to give her an exclusive interview."

"Really? I am surprised that Lara said okay to that. Is it the right thing to do?"

"We think so. Lara wants to get the facts straight from the start. She's given a full report to the police, and she'll just repeat what she said to them."

Frank pleaded, "Let me see her. You can't lock her away from me."

"Frank," Jackie said, "I'll ask her if it's okay for you to see her for a couple of minutes while I'm there. But don't ask her any awkward questions, and try not to push her too hard."

"Jackie, you know me better than that. I could never do anything to hurt Lara. I love her."

"There's something else. She is being watched now, and so are you. After all, you had a motive. Your relationship will come out sooner or later, especially because there is no way Lara can prove she was happily married."

"I hear what you're saying. But right now, I want to see her."

Jackie left; a few moments later she signaled him to follow her.

Lara was propped up on the sofa in her office. She was wearing a pale green robe; under it Frank could see the swelling of her pregnancy. He started toward her, then stopped, dismayed at how pale and distracted she was.

"Lara," he started to say, but she interrupted.

"Frank, I'm all right, just let me rest."

"I'm sorry to see you in pain," he said. "I'm here for you, whatever happens."

Jackie took him by the arm. "I told you she must rest, we have to think of the baby," she said. "We are worried about the baby."

"Remember," Lara whispered as he left, "there is always tomorrow."

It was better than Frank had hoped. In her way, Lara was making a promise to him. Now that Errol was dead, they could be together.

He needed a drink, and walked up to the terrace restaurant. Sonya Iverson was there, sitting by herself and nursing a mug of coffee.

Frank was pleased to see her. It would be good to chat.

He knew Sonya well and felt he could confide in her. He'd met her years ago, when she'd interviewed him for a story on best-selling authors. She had asked intelligent questions and treated him with respect.

He pulled out a chair and sat down beside her. "Well, you're the expert. Tell me who did it."

She gave a quick laugh. "Your guess is as good as mine. Everyone here seems to have a motive . . . and that includes you."

Frank motioned to the waiter and ordered a coffee. "Well, in fact, I've just been told I'm likely to be a number-one suspect, and my motive is jealousy. I've been in love with Lara for years. I asked her to leave Errol and marry me. She refused. You'll find it hard to beat that for a motive."

Sonya thought for a moment before she replied. "I'd say both you and Lara should be ruled out. She's too smart to tie her husband to the bed and then have her ex-lover come and shoot him. I mean, really!"

She glanced at him to get his reaction before she continued. "No, I have the feeling that this murder is much more complicated than that. My gut tells me the motive for it is buried in the past."

Frank conceded. "Maybe you're right."

"Yes, maybe I am," said Sonya. "I've been going over the Swanson family history. Tracey interests me. She is Errol's aunt—his father's sister, and the oldest member of the family."

Frank was starting to enjoy himself. He asked, "What's her motive?"

"Revenge." Sonya didn't hesitate. "Errol treated her badly. She fell in love with a married Jewish businessman. He never divorced, so they lived together. Errol wouldn't have anything to do with them. He said it was because the guy was married, but everyone knew it was because he was Jewish."

"I see your point. But surely that's all long forgotten. Who's next?"

Sonya gave him a shrewd look, then said, "You know a lot about Errol, don't you? I'd guess you're writing a book about him."

"What makes you say that?"

"It adds up. This is how I see it. An author with a grudge shows up where he is least expected and probably not wanted. He has a reputation for research and an analytical mind. What else could he be doing but writing a book?"

Frank patted her hand. "Okay, you're right," he said. "I'm writing a biography of Errol Swanson, and I'm counting on you, as a fellow journalist, to keep that quiet. I want to tell the truth about that sonofabitch. And to do it, I've spent hours researching him and his family."

"Then maybe you can share something with me." Sonya paused. "I don't want to use it, I'm just curious. Tell me about Errol's father. Why was Errol so secretive about him? Was it something he did in World War II? From what I've heard, he suffered a lot."

"Yes, but so did a lot of other guys." Frank refused to be sympathetic.

Sonya pressed him. "I read that Errol's father was in the battle for Okinawa. That was about the worst, wasn't it?"

"Yes, the Japanese were determined to hold onto that little hellhole. They knew the Americans planned to use it as a base to attack the rest of Japan. They made a last desperate stand. The fighting was fierce. The island was riddled with caves where the Japanese troops hid, coming out at night to attack."

"I know it was grim." Sonya was thoughtful. "I once did a story about a family from there. They told me the people worshiped the emperor and that 75,000 committed suicide rather than be taken by the Americans."

"Yes," said Frank, "and thousands more took to the caves, hiding there for weeks. They were a big problem."

Frank hesitated again, but Sonya insisted. "Tell me what had this to do with Errol's father."

"Well, from what I gathered, Swanson and his unit entered one of the caves. It had been raining and the cave was flooded. When the American soldiers turned on their lights, they saw, floating in bloody water, the bloated bodies of some 50 Japanese soldiers who had ripped open their stomachs in a mass suicide."

"My God, Frank, how awful."

"The Americans were horrified. They slowly turned their torches to examine the rest of the cave. Standing on a ledge was a small group of women with sacks on their backs. Apparently they'd come to bring food to the men. The women screamed in terror and Swanson lost it. He opened fire and killed every one of them."

Sonya sat silent. Frank looked away. Finally she spoke. "No wonder he was mentally ill. What he did must have haunted him. What happened? What did the brass do to him?"

"Well, he had committed multiple murders, but of course he was under enormous stress. They put him in the hospital and after a while quietly discharged him. But the incident was noted on his report."

"So that's the secret Errol was intent on hiding?"

"Yes," said Frank. "The father never forgave himself, and neither did Errol."

"So only a few family members know the secret?"

"I can't be sure," Frank said. "Tracey must, since she lived with him and his parents. Maybe Joan knows. But I'm sure Lara doesn't."

Sonya took a deep breath. "Thanks. You did me a favor, Frank. That story clears up a lot. It helps me understand why Errol became such a tyrant."

"I'm putting the story in my book. Now it's your turn to share some information, Sonya. What do the police think?"

"Not much at this stage, as best we can tell. They're doing some interviewing. They're photographing the body, checking for fingerprints, and searching for the gun—all the expected things. But the real work starts later today. The A-team is flying in from Honolulu. That's when the inquiry will really begin."

She glanced at her watch. "Donna's got a live shot at 1:30. With the time difference, that will put her on this evening's network news. I'd better run, Frank. She'll want me in her bungalow to see that it is all going according to plan."

Frank looked at her keenly. "What's wrong?" he said.

"Nothing, really. But better than most, you know television and the network shit. I guess it gets to me sometimes."

"Don't trust anyone," he said. "They'll get rid of you on a whim. Remember what happened to me."

Sonya gave him a strange look. He had put his finger on what was bothering her.

Chapter 26

The Big Island
Saturday, 10:30 A.M.

"It can't be, but it must be. There is no getting away from it." Tracey Swanson was distracted, talking to herself as she dialed her lawyer's phone number in Chicago.

She listened anxiously as the phone rang again and again. When the voice mail system clicked on, she almost cried in disappointment. "Oh, Roger," she said, "Errol has been murdered, and poor Christy found the body. Ramos brought her to me. She doesn't want to go to her mother. I don't know what to do. Please call me the minute you get this message."

Roger McCoy was the only person she could talk to freely. He would know what to do. Tracey was fond of Christy and wanted to be part of her life, but Joan was her mother. And her mother had to be responsible for her.

Tracey had tried to call Joan at the bungalow, but she'd had to leave a message. She said that Christy had come to her, exhausted and distraught, and that she had put her to bed.

Joan had never called back. When Tracey had asked Christy for her mother's cell number, Christy said she didn't remember it. Tracey was hesitant about asking the manager if he had seen Joan. She didn't like the man and she was afraid of raising suspicions.

Christy needed help. Tracey sighed. Seeing her father lying murdered on the bloodstained bed had traumatized her. What was the name of Christy's doctor? What drugs was she taking? Had she taken them on schedule? Without medication, Christy was an unknown quantity.

Tracey walked back into her bedroom, where Christy lay sprawled asleep on the bed. The linen bathrobe she had put on after she showered had opened and Tracey saw the red blush of sunburn on her thin legs. Her body was angular, and her face, which as a child had been soft and round, was now raw-boned. Her nose was too long, her jaw too square, and her eyes too deeply set. There was little about Christy that was attractive. Of the twins, Tracey thought, Craig had had the good looks.

Christy turned in her sleep and smiled one of her rare smiles. For a swift moment, Tracey saw the funny little girl she had once been. Then, just as swiftly, the smile vanished and the little girl was gone. Tracey bent and kissed the top of her niece's head. They had had good times together.

Tracey walked to the chair and picked up the white dress Christy had worn that morning. She took it into the bathroom, filled the basin with cold water, and put the dress in to soak. Then she went to her wardrobe and chose a white skirt and blouse that Christy could wear when she woke. Now there was nothing to do but wait.

When the phone rang, Tracey picked it up quickly, frightened that it might wake Christy. She knew it was Roger even as she lifted the receiver.

"Tracey?" he asked, in his slow, calm manner.

"Oh, Roger, you got my message?" she breathed in relief.

"Yes, and I am concerned about you. Getting close to Christy was the reason you went to Hawaii, but that doesn't mean you should take responsibility for her. Tell me exactly what has happened. Errol was murdered?"

"Oh, Roger," Tracey whispered, "it's dreadful. Everything was going so well, and now Errol is dead. Ramos heard about it first. He'd been out for a walk and when he stopped at the office to check on scuba diving rates, they could talk of nothing else."

"Where was Errol killed?"

"He was still in bed. Lara had left early to work with a TV crew that's covering the spa. Apparently someone got in and shot him around eight A.M. Christy found the body and told Lara, and they all went to the house and found him."

"Christy found the body? That's strange. What was she doing in her father's bedroom at eight in the morning?"

Tracey sighed. "Oh, Roger, if only I knew. She seems to believe that she is responsible for her father's death. But she couldn't possibly have shot him. Where would she have gotten a gun? And where would she have learned to fire it?"

"It does seem unlikely," he agreed. "She's probably hallucinating."

"I'm sure she is," Tracey interrupted. "I feel so sad for her. Last night we had a party and I had a long, happy talk with her. She was completely at ease with me. We were talking about her coming to Acapulco for a visit. This morning she was almost incoherent."

"You said Ramos brought her to you?"

"Yes, he told me he found her in my garden, mumbling something over and over again. She looked dreadful. I took her in and told her that I would call her mother to come and get her, but she refused. She didn't want to see her mother. So I ran a bath for her and put her to bed. Roger, I gave her one of my Valiums to calm her down, and now she's asleep."

"That's okay, Tracey, but don't give her any more tranquilizers. You don't know what other medication she is taking. Did you call Joan?"

"Yes, and left a message. We've gotten quite close here, and my guess is that she feels Christy is safe with me."

"Did Christy give you any reason for going to see her father? It's puzzling that she was the one who found the body."

"Last night she had an argument with him. It was really quite silly. The pool was afloat with dozens of orchids. It was spectacular. Anyway, Christy decided she wanted to swim, but Errol stopped her. She got upset and ran off, saying she hated him."

"That doesn't sound like a motive for murder."

"Of course not. She loves her father. She would never harm him. All she wants is his approval."

"So you think she might have gone to him to apologize?"

Tracey thought for a moment. "Yes, it's more than likely. Ramos told me he saw her walking with her mother early in the morning. Joan may have said something to Christy about her behavior. That may have triggered her visit."

"Now tell me about Joan. You said you've grown closer?"

"Yes, we've had two long chats. It seems ridiculous that we haven't gotten together before this. She says her business is her life. She often works twelve hours a day, but enjoys every moment. She loves checking with the stores each day and visiting manufacturers to find the latest trend. She told me her father was a tyrant, but that the toy business was the greatest gift he could have given her. It saved her sanity, for Christy has never ceased to be a problem."

"And will continue to be a problem," Roger added. "You said Christy was mumbling something when she came in. Have you an idea what she was trying to say?"

"I thought it was something like, 'we know he's dead, we know he's dead.' But Ramos disagreed. He said it was just gibberish."

"Considering her condition, you can't put much faith in what she says. As you say, it could be hallucinations. Anyway, leave that for the police to investigate. Have they interviewed you yet?"

For a moment Tracey was surprised at the question, but then realized that, of course, the police would interview everyone.

"No, not yet. Surely they will interview Lara and the maids before they come here."

"Probably. Tracey, since Swanson was such an important man, they will bring experienced detectives from Honolulu. This will be a high-profile case, and I am sure the police will pursue every angle. Errol Swanson was a man with a bad reputation and many enemies. Any one of them could have killed him. The murderer doesn't have to be a member of the family."

He paused, then said in a softer voice, "Please understand this question, Tracey. I am thinking of your own good. Where were you at the time the murder was committed?"

"Here in my bungalow, Roger. You don't think I murdered Errol, do you?" Despite herself, she felt hurt at his question.

"No, I don't. I'm just anticipating what the police will ask you. Were you by yourself?"

"Yes, as I said, Ramos woke early and went for a walk." She heard Roger start to comment, and interrupted him. "There is nothing wrong with that, Roger. The early mornings are exquisite. And they are cool, the coolest part of the day."

"Yes, yes, of course," he responded with a hint of impatience. "But going for a walk alone doesn't make much of an alibi. Where is Ramos now?"

"I told him to go scuba diving. I wanted some time alone with Christy." She paused, the added, "I need to persuade her to go back to Joan. It has to be her decision. I would hate her to think I rejected her." Then she added lamely, "And anyway, why shouldn't Ramos enjoy himself? After all, that's what we came for. To relax and have a good time." Roger had made her feel guilty; perhaps she was too free with Ramos.

"No, having a good time is not the reason you are in Hawaii," he reminded her. "You went to see Christy. To find out how she was and see if you wanted to get close to her again." He spoke firmly. "When I visited you in Mexico, you had serious doubts about making the trip. When you did decide, it was with the assurance that Ramos would be with you. Now, on the morning your nephew is murdered, Ramos left you alone."

"Roger, for heaven's sake, he just went out for a few hours. You didn't expect him to be with me every minute of the day and night."

"I did, Tracey. He came to look after you, not to go scuba diving."

"But, Roger . . ."

He interrupted her. "Tracey, I am worried not just about Errol's murder, but the position you're in with Christy. Why hasn't Joan called you? Could she be involved in the murder? I think you need help—from a friend and a lawyer."

"Roger, I can handle this. In fact, I have an idea of who the murderer is, so I'll be wary." She said it lightly, but in the back of her mind she was wondering if she could be right.

"What do you mean? You know who murdered Errol?" The sharpness of Roger's tone stilled her thought.

"Call it a woman's intuition. It's just that. Really, nothing more." She tried to calm Roger, despite her growing feeling that she was right.

"Who do you think it is?" he came back.

"I don't want to accuse anyone; I'll let you know if and when I am certain."

"Tracey, that settles it. I'm coming. Now listen to me—until I arrive, stay in your bungalow and avoid people, especially the press. Believe me, once this news is out, dozens of reporters and cameramen will pour in and they'll all want to talk to you."

Tracey hesitated. Should she tell him about the interview she had promised Sonya Iverson? If she didn't he'd find out anyway, that was his way. She said, "Roger, I promised the producer from the *Donna Fuller Show* that I'd tell her my impressions of the spa this afternoon. It couldn't do any harm. She's charming and I'd hate to go back on my word."

"Cancel it. Use any excuse. Tell her you've been ill and need to rest. That's the truth. And Tracey, if you really know something, or even suspect something, go to the police."

"Oh, Roger, please, don't be ridiculous. I told you it was just woman's intuition."

She could tell by his silence that he was angry. Then, in his usual calm voice, he said, "Just do what I say. And when Ramos comes back, tell him to call me immediately. I want to talk with him. And for God's sake, keep him with you."

Chapter 27

The Big Island
Saturday, 11:30 A.M.

Sonya pushed herself into the middle of her plunge pool and floated on her back. She picked up a gardenia that drifted by and caught it in her fingers. If only everything was as sweet at the spa as that delightful fragrance.

But it wasn't, and she had to face the facts.

The story that Frank O'Neill had told her about the brutal massacre of women on Okinawa had left her horror-struck. It explained so much. Not just the reason for Errol's cruelty, but why the network executives had protected him.

The shame of knowing that his father had gunned down innocent women in a moment of panic had shaped Errol's life. He must have hated his father, but his hatred must have been tempered with compassion for what the man suffered.

Errol must have lived with the constant worry that someone would find out what his father had done. Trying to first live down the shame and then conceal it had made Errol a hard, cruel man.

It had cost him two marriages and three children. It had made him a tyrant in business.

Now it would probably all come out in the coverage of Errol's death or in Frank O'Neill's book. And then what?

Sonya shook her head. It would take time to understand all the ramifications of Errol Swanson's life and death. And right now, time was something she didn't have. At noon she had to be at Donna's bungalow to prepare for the live shot an hour and a half later.

"Move over, I'm coming in with you." Sabrina's voice floated through the air. "I'm hot and sticky and exhausted."

Irritation swept over Sonya. Her solitude had been shattered.

"Where have you been and what do you have to report?" she called back, keeping her voice as pleasant as she could.

Sabrina ran out naked, then, holding her nose, jumped into the pool.

"What a lovely splash I made," she said gleefully when she surfaced. Then she dipped her head back in the water to get her hair out of her eyes.

"I went to check out the spa facilities for making us girls beautiful. I was impressed. Lara spent big bucks. It's all as good as the best in New York. Right up to the minute."

"Did you try anything?" Talking about anti-aging treatments was not what Sonya wanted to be doing, but Sabrina was a good friend.

"No, I didn't have much time, but I learned a lot about this place."

"Yes?" Sonya was interested again. "Who told you what?"

"You get right to it, don't you?" Sabrina giggled. She was always happy when she was gossiping. "Whenever you want to get the skinny on a place, talk to the people who serve the food and make the beds. They know everything. They always have a story to tell, and they are usually eager to tell it."

Sonya knew Sabrina's sense of drama; she was building suspense.

"Okay, you win," Sonya gave in. "You've got me hooked. I'm interested."

"The big story is that the spa is built on sacred land. It has an ancient curse on it. That means that anything built here will go bust. The spa is doomed to failure."

"That's hardly news, considering Errol was murdered this morning."

"Perhaps not to you or me," Sabrina was jovial. "But to the Hawaiians, it's different. They don't like hanging around where an ancient curse might strike again. If one more thing goes wrong, Lara may find her Hawaiians walking out. They're discussing it already. She'll be left with very little staff and you and I will be cooking breakfast."

"Anything more?" Sonya was impressed.

"How about this? Can you believe that Tracey Swanson, that nice blond old lady, brought her lover to the spa? And our murdered host was furious about it. In a rage, I was told."

"That bearded, good-looking guy who never stays around long enough to say 'hello'? He's Tracey's lover?"

"That's him. One of the girls saw him putting his arm around her and kissing her the morning after they arrived."

"How do you know all this?"

"Lara belonged to some sort of cult in England. Jackie was one of the leaders and she took Lara under her wing. That's when they became such good friends. They followed the guru's teaching or something like that. In fact, it was his philosophy that Lara used in building this place."

"Yes, I've heard that."

"When she opened the spa she asked some of her friends from the cult to come work for her. They all hang out together, watch what goes on, and pass the information along."

"They all understand Lara's philosophy," Sonya laughed. "That's why they're here. You could call them Lara's underground support system. Do you think they're watching us right now?"

"Could be," Sabrina teased, "but they like you. Of course they wanted me to give them some info in return. I told them there wasn't much to say about you."

"I don't know whether to be flattered or angry."

"In this case, flattered," Sabrina laughed.

Sonya flicked a spray of water at Sabrina before climbing out of the pool. "You mean there are more skeletons hidden in the Swanson closet?"

"Nothing would surprise me. But that's all I found out—for the moment. I'm glad you're the producer, not me. I wish you luck sorting it all out."

Sonya was beginning to do just that. Nothing hung together yet, but she knew it would soon become clear. "Be patient," she told herself. "It's only been a few hours since the murder."

Donna was working at her laptop when Sonya entered her bungalow. She didn't look up or greet her, so Sonya sat at the desk, put on a headset, turned on the playback machine, and started logging a tape.

Her back was to the door and she didn't hear Donna rise and lock it. When Donna placed her hand on her shoulder, she started.

"Take off the headset, Sonya," Donna said. "I want to talk to you."

Sonya did as she was told. She didn't want to talk, she just wanted to get on with her work. She was angry with Donna, and the more professional the relationship remained, the better, as far as Sonya was concerned.

"You think I treated you unfairly at the meeting this morning, don't you?" Donna asked.

Sonya thought for a moment, then answered slowly and deliberately, "I believe we can't continue to do a puff piece on Errol Swanson. The world press is about to descend on us, and they will explore every facet of his life. To conceal anything we know would be foolish, and harmful to your show and the network."

Donna stood back. "You are right. You know I was against doing this story. I fought against it as long as I could. But Errol was still powerful and the executives on the nineteenth floor insisted. I don't think the executives realized that Errol was a changed man. From what Lara told me this morning, I believe he was verging on serious mental illness. Lara was becoming increasingly frightened by his behavior."

"I see," Sonya said. "I didn't realize you resisted so strongly when you were asked to do this story. Frankly, Donna, I thought you'd agreed for personal reasons."

Donna nodded. "I can understand that. I suppose it was because of the gossip about my having an affair with Errol when he was splitting up with Margot." She paused, then said calmly, "That's true."

Sonya didn't know how to reply. She was embarrassed for Donna.

After a moment Donna continued, "While I admit to the affair, I swear that's not the reason I got my show. I also acknowledge that Errol was helpful to me at times. But I hope the value and quality of my work speak for themselves."

Donna paused. Sonya could feel her humiliation. Donna was a proud person and must be hurting badly.

"I understand, Donna," she said.

"I want you to know, too, that I had nothing to do with taking your notebook. When you interviewed him, Errol thought he had revealed too much about his father. Matt decided to check your notes, so he picked up your notebook that first night we were here. He saw no harm in it, he was merely protecting the privacy of a director of the company."

"Where is my notebook now?"

Donna bent over and opened the bottom drawer of the desk. "Here it is. I owed you an explanation and an apology."

Sonya took the notebook and let out a sigh of relief.

"Oh, Donna, I am so glad you told me. I was so concerned about you. I just didn't know what to think."

"Well, now you know the truth. I hope you won't suspect me of murdering Errol." Donna's laugh was half sob. "The Swanson spa may be the most beautiful place on earth, but I think there is something evil about it."

She reached out and touched Sonya's cheek. "I want to assure you that I will tell the whole story to the police when they question me. And you must do the same, too. I will ask them to be discreet, but that is all."

Then she got back to business. "Let's go to the terrace and rehearse the live shot. I told Sabrina and Perry I would be there about now."

Sonya didn't like the pressure of live shots. She didn't even like the name. And in this case, reporting on a murder, the words seemed ironic.

When they arrived the truck was set up and in sync with the satellite. Perry was working with the lighting; he asked Donna to stand in the place he had marked with tape.

She did so lightheartedly. "Here? This is my mark?"

Sonya thought she seemed relieved. Some of the pressure was over.

Sonya looked in the monitor while Matt listened on a headset. He spoke to the producer at the network. "Okay, she's here. Let's go with the rehearsal. Do you have her story tape cued?"

They waited for the reply from New York; after a moment, Matt looked at Sonya. She called to Donna, "The anchor introduction will be a simple one. Your cue will be, 'Here, from Hawaii, is Donna Fuller.' You will do your introduction and Master Control will roll the tape with your story. We are ready for the rehearsal. Three—two—one—cue."

Donna looked into the camera, her face solemn and her voice grave. "Errol Swanson was murdered here today in his home in one of the most beautiful spots on the island. He was surrounded by those he loved and those who loved him. But the world is not always as it seems. Nearby a volcano erupts and here, a murderer roams free."

Sonya looked at her with admiration. Donna knew how to the get to the heart of it. She was a great storyteller.

Chapter **28**

Tomas Swanson had never felt so free. An updraft lifted him high and he soared over the ridge. Then he floated down, circling the palm trees that lined the lagoon.

He was flying, gliding effortlessly through the air with the curve of the world below him. A soft breeze caressed his body and with it went his anger and frustration. He had found his peace, his serenity.

The manager of the spa had told him of the hang gliding school.

"Mrs. Swanson loves it; she's making it a part of the spa's activities," the man had said. "She was on the way to becoming an expert before she got pregnant and had to stop. She said for her, it was a Zen experience."

He grinned at Tomas. "But not everyone is so spiritual. The guys say they get the same rush as when they surf 20-foot waves."

Tomas had discovered he was a natural. At first he went up with an instructor strapped at his side. After a few runs, he flew solo.

"It's risky," the instructor told him. "But then, it always is. It's meant for people who like to live on the edge."

It was true—the risk heightened the experience. Tomas was exhilarated, cut off from the world, and at the same time mindful of his body and every movement he made.

"I'll be what I am," he told himself as he dipped to skim over a sand dune. "My father is dead. I'll have no more of the agony of wanting him to accept me. I'll live the life that is natural to me. I'll march in gay parades if I want to. I'll do anything I like."

He caught another updraft, turned, and floated back to the lagoon with its rim of palm trees. In two hours his time with the glider would be up. He would have to go back to the spa and his mother, but now it was impossible to think of coming down to earth.

"Mother will encourage me to be myself," he told himself. But would she? In her way, she was as materialistic as his father. She had always tried to manage his life. Power and control—that's what his parents were about.

Margot had pressured him this very morning. She wouldn't leave him alone for a moment. She fussed around the bungalow in her irritating way, telling him, as she so often did, that everything had to be perfect before she could leave. He had gritted his teeth in frustration.

He had gone into his bathroom to shower and shave, locking the door to keep her out. Her pale face and thin, nervous hands could not follow him there.

He stood under the shower and let the hot water pour over his head and down his body while he waited for her to go. He felt his muscles loosen and relax. But when he closed his eyes he saw his father's head, lying on the bloodied pillow.

Tomas flexed his fingers and felt the gun again in his right hand. He had been a fool. He should have had more confidence in himself and not gone begging for his father's approval. He should have realized what a damaged human being Errol was.

When, at last, he unlocked the bathroom door, she was still there, sitting on the bed waiting for him. She was wearing one of her own designs—a bright, printed beach cover-up. Beside her was one of the spa's giveaway string beach bags. The box that had held the gun was packed in it.

She held up the bag and said, "Here it is, the evidence that is about to disappear."

"Mother," he said. "Put the box in another bag. I can see the shape of it clearly."

"I wrapped it in a sarong to hide it, but you're right. I've got a stiff plastic beach bag. I'll use that."

He went over and dutifully kissed her hair. "You are wonderful. Just be careful. I can't imagine they will search the bungalow. But you're right to get rid of the box."

"You get into bed and sleep," she said with the baby lisp she'd used when he was a child. "I'll tuck you in and kiss you good-bye."

He accepted her kiss, then lay on the bed. But the events of the past 24 hours kept crowding back. It was useless trying to sleep. He got up, and made coffee. While it was brewing, Tomas walked around the bungalow. Lying on the desk was the flyer on hang gliding. He called the number, booked the glider for three hours, and arranged for their car service to pick him up.

After 20 minutes, his glide ended effortlessly at the bottom of the grassy hill. It had been breathtaking; he never wanted to stop.

Just one more go, he told himself, and he would return to the spa, to Margot. But now everything would be different. He would find a new way of life, his way of life. Errol's murder had changed everything.

When he arrived at the bungalow, he paused outside the glass door and looked at his mother. She was sitting on the sofa. She had changed into her favorite outfit—black pants and a T-shirt. Her body was a dark, narrow streak against the gold-beige of the sofa. She was stitching a piece of needlepoint. He could see by the quick jerkiness of her movements she was upset. His heart leapt with love for her. She looked frail, almost ill.

She sprang up as he slid open the door, her needlepoint falling heedlessly to the floor.

"I told you to stay here until I got back." Her voice was shrill and harsh. "Where have you been?"

"Stop it, Mother. I've been hang gliding. I had to get away from the spa, to be by myself and decide what to do."

"Why didn't you leave a message? I've been worried out of my mind."

He put his hands out to hold her, but she twisted away from him.

"Calm down," he said. "How could you think for a minute that I wouldn't come back? That I had deserted you?"

"You should have left a message," she said. "The police have been here to question me. It wasn't easy to admit that my son had disappeared a few hours after his father was murdered."

"The police have been here?" He stopped to think. It was natural enough. They would need to question everyone at the spa, and the logical place to start would be with members of the family. "What did you tell them?"

"The truth. I said you'd been partying all night and I left you lying in bed when I went out. When I returned, you were gone. I was terrified, Tomas. It just isn't like you to walk out and not tell me where you're going. I had no idea where you were, and on this day of all days."

"You're being ridiculous." He went to the bar and poured her a small glass of cognac. "Now sit down and drink this. It'll make you feel better."

He got himself a beer, snapped off the top, and took a long drink.

"There was no need for you to sit here by yourself. Why didn't you go to Joan's?" he said. "She's a friend and good one. She'll always listen."

"I did see her. She was calling her attorneys to tell them of Errol's murder and ask them what to do. He still has a share in her toy business, and she is in terror that it will go to Lara. She was in no mood to deal with my problems."

Her face hardened. "You're the one who should have been here for me. You landed me in this mess and then walked out and left me to face it."

Tomas knelt beside her and caught both her hands in his. "Now stop worrying and be realistic. The police have to question everyone. You were his second wife, so you have to be high on their list. That's what it was about."

Suddenly she was sobbing, deep, wracking sobs that shook her whole body. She took her hands from his and buried her face in them. "Tomas, the police were here because they found the box."

Tomas stood up. He felt as if she had kicked him in the stomach.

"The box?" he said in disbelief. "The box that held the gun?"

"Yes," she said. "That box."

"How could they find the box? You told me you knew how to get rid of it—and the bullets."

"The bullets were easy, I just let them slide down the side of a rock and sink into the water. But the box was wood and I was sure it would float. I tried to pull it apart, but it was too solid. I thought of breaking it with a heavy stone, but I was scared. Someone might have seen me."

He couldn't look at her.

"Oh my God, what an idiot I was to listen to you. I should never have let you do it."

Margot lifted her head and glowered at him.

"You mean what an idiot you were to leave the bungalow. I came back to ask you what to do, but you had left. You left, when I told you to stay. That's the kind of idiot you are."

"Okay, okay, okay. I'm an idiot." Tomas fought to control his fear. She was right. He should never have given in to the urge to get away from the spa. He should have been there to protect her. To protect himself.

"What did you do with the box?" he asked as calmly as he could.

"I hid it beneath some thick, low shrubs in a small hollow near the marina. I looked around to make sure no one was watching me. Then I pretended to admire the view and pushed it under the branches with my foot. I thought it was well hidden. But the police found it when they were searching for the gun and came and questioned me."

"How could the police have known it belonged to you? It didn't have your name on it." Tomas spat out the words.

"Tomas, I left your granddad's papers in it. I totally forgot about them. The police were here moments after they found the box." She pressed her hands against the sides of her head as if to block out the memory. "I can't believe this is happening, and it's all my fault. I should have kept the box here. The police had no reason to search this place. I just didn't think straight.

"I'm sorry, so sorry." She wrapped her arms around herself and began to moan as she swayed back and forth. Tomas ignored her.

"Just tell me what you told the police," he said fiercely. "What reason did you give for hiding the box? How did you explain the missing gun?"

"I told them that the box was mine, that I'd brought it and the gun to Hawaii. That the last time I'd seen it was when you showed it to Christy yesterday. Then, after I heard of Errol's murder this morning, I checked and found the gun was gone. I was frightened for both you and Christy and decided to get rid of the box. That's all. I swear that's all."

"Did you tell them about our conversation this morning?"

"No, I only told them that you'd been partying all night, came in late, and went straight to bed."

She was telling the truth, he knew. But he also knew she was holding something back.

"Mother," he said, "why did you give me the gun? And why did you insist on my bringing it here?"

Her voice dropped. "I wanted to be as tough as I could with Errol. I had to force him to give me the money. He knew I wanted it for the business."

"You didn't plan to murder him?"

She paused, then said, "Only to threaten. My business is doing badly, much worse than I told you."

"But your accountant said Errol had to pay you every penny he owed you." He felt like a little boy again, trapped in his parents' arguments.

"And so he did. The money is legally mine. Errol owed me my share of property we bought together when we were first married. We decided to sell it, and as Errol was such a good businessman, I let him handle the sale. He refused to give me the money. He said I'd have to sue him to get it."

"How could you let him get away with it?"

"I was stupid. I trusted him. Even though we divorced I thought he believed in me and my talent. That he wanted my business to continue. But he didn't. He wanted to destroy it."

Tomas saw the muscles taut in her face, the nervous twitch of one eye. She was close to collapse.

"Your father could afford the best and the most expensive lawyers," she went on. "They found ways of delaying the payment, and they'd have done it until my business went under. Of course I could have sued, but the case would have gone on for years, and the end result would have been the same. The simple truth is, Errol wanted to ruin me, and he has all but succeeded. Once the police really start investigating me, they'll find I had a strong motive for murdering him."

He filled with compassion for her. She was a victim. His father had used his power and money to torment her, and she hadn't had the resources to escape from him.

"Mother," he said. "What do you want me to do?"

"Why do you ask? You know what you have to do. Go to the police and tell them everything. But, Tomas, before you go swear to me that you didn't kill your father. I have to know that."

She was right. He had to go to the police. He'd already made up his mind. It was the only thing to do. But why did she want to extract a denial of the murder from him? He'd already told her what had happened that morning.

He took a deep breath and let it out in a gasp. "Oh, Mother, for God's sake, stop playing games with me. You gave me the gun and insisted that I bring it here. You swear to *me* that you didn't kill my father."

Chapter **29**

The Big Island
Saturday, 2:00 P.M.

"It's obvious our beautiful blond widow knows nothing about lighting." Perry was irritated. He didn't complain often; he liked the challenges his job presented. But Lara's demand that the statue of Buddha be beside her for her interview gave him big problems. The sun was directly overhead and the shadows it cast were harsh and unflattering.

Sonya studied the picture in the monitor. "I'll get Jackie to sit in for Lara. She's fair and about the same height. That should make it easier to set up the backlights. We have to be ready to shoot the moment Lara comes. She won't give us much time."

Sonya walked up the steps to the Swanson house and reappeared shortly with Jackie, who was dressed somberly in navy pants and shirt. She was no longer just the captain of the marina, she was the spokesperson for the spa.

"You've been with her all morning? Is she okay?" Perry asked as he adjusted Jackie in Lara's chair, and then checked her on the monitor.

"What would you expect?" Jackie put up one hand to shield her eyes. "But she's dead set on doing this interview. She feels she has to salvage Errol's reputation, whatever the cost."

"Donna sent Sabrina to do her hair and makeup. Is Lara happy with her?" asked Sonya.

"Sabrina is a godsend." Sonya heard real relief in Jackie's voice. "Lara insisted she had to wear black, but she looked like hell in it. Ashen, completely wiped out. Sabrina asked her what Errol's favorite color was. When Lara said pink, Sabrina whizzed into the closet and came out with Errol's favorite dress.

"That did it. Lara is wearing the dress and Sabrina is hard at work with a 'pink palette,' as she calls it."

Perry looked at Sonya and grinned. Jackie caught it and said, "Please, Perry, no matter how good Sabrina makes her look, no tight shots. She's been through too much."

"Of course," Sonya replied for Perry. "We'll keep the lighting as soft as we possibly can. But, as I said, we could get a much prettier shot inside."

"For her, other things are more important. Lara wants the Buddha in the shot because it represents her philosophy. She needs people to understand that even though a horrendous crime was committed here, it is still a spiritual place.

"She is committed to sharing her philosophy with others. For Lara, it's important to reach out to the world and provide a path to the giving and accepting of love. For her, the Buddha will be a silent symbol that says there is still love even where there has been violence."

"I understand, Jackie. Perry will do his best, and we'll stay away from the tight shots," Sonya assured her.

"Thank you. I know the interview will go well. Lara is so positive about everything she touches, it makes me happy just to be near her," Jackie replied.

"Errol's murder must have devastated her," said Sonya. "Just think, if it hadn't happened, at this very minute we would have been enjoying the party."

"Yes," said Jackie, "and we mustn't forget for a minute that she is pregnant. That baby is doubly important to her now."

Sonya nodded in agreement. The baby was important—in more ways than one. It surely would affect the amount Lara would inherit. Sonya wondered about the terms of Errol's will. Lara would have signed a prenuptial agreement, but with the child she would have a stronger claim on his estate.

She glanced at Jackie and saw her frown. It was time to change the subject.

Jackie apparently thought so, too. "Have either of you seen Tomas, Margot's son?" she asked.

"No." Sonya and Perry both shook their heads.

"I got a call from her an hour or so ago. She was worried. She wanted to know if Tomas had gone out in the boat. I called down to the marina, but no one there had seen him. Apparently Margot had gone for a walk, leaving Tomas sleeping in bed. When she got back an hour or so later, no Tomas, and no note. At first she wasn't concerned; she presumed he had gone for swim. But after another hour passed, she decided to call around and see if she could find him. She says he has never behaved like this before."

Perry looked up from tightening the screw on the leg of the tripod.

"I did see him," he said. "But it was early this morning. Tomas was standing on the cliff, picking up stones and hurling them into the ocean. He seemed to be having a good time. He was wearing jeans, so I guess he wasn't going swimming." He thought for a moment. "Do you think I should call Margot and tell her?"

"I'll do it after the interview," Jackie replied.

"Have you seen Joan this morning?" Sonya asked.

"Come to think of it, I did see her early this morning. She was sitting on a bench, apparently lost in thought. I thought it was rather odd to see her out so early. It must have been about seven-thirty."

"Was Christy with her?"

"No, she was alone."

"Have you seen her since Lara discovered Errol's body?"

Jackie shook her head, then said, "I think I can see Sabrina in the study with Donna. That must mean Lara's makeup is done and she is ready for us."

Sonya walked up the steps to the study and looked in.

"Yes," Donna said, "we are ready to start. Lara is more fragile than I thought. We'll have to make it quick."

"Donna, she's crazy to insist on having the interview on the terrace. It's hot and the lighting is awful."

Donna nodded in sympathy. "I know. But I want to get a few minutes on tape, and it's the only way she'd do it. So let's work fast. Tell Perry not to fuss with the reflectors, just get the job done as best he can."

When it came to lighting, Perry the perfectionist, couldn't resist. Before he went back to the camera, he made one last adjustment of the backlight, then glanced at Donna as if to excuse himself. Donna exchanged looks with Sonya, shook her head, and rolled her eyes.

The moment Lara appeared at the top of the stairs, Jackie went to help her. Lara smiled at her.

"Don't be anxious. I'll get through it. I have to. I have to save everything we worked for." Lara took Jackie's arm and Jackie led her to the green canvas chair Perry had set near the Buddha.

"The pink was the right choice," Jackie said encouragingly. "It gives you strength."

But strength was something Lara obviously lacked. "She looks thinner," Sonya thought, almost as if she had lost weight in the few hours since Errol died.

Lara looked up at the group that surrounded her. "I feel better now that I am near the Buddha."

Sonya motioned to Sabrina, who nodded and immediately moved to Lara. With a lightly powdered brush, she began to touch up the blond woman's face. Lara sat up and lifted her head to help Sabrina work.

Sabrina looked back at Sonya to indicate she was finished.

"You look fine, Lara," Sonya assured her. "Ready, Perry?" He nodded, but Sonya noticed he was already taping. "Good for Perry," she thought, "you never know when you might get something to use." She was sure he'd had the camera running from the moment Lara came out of the house.

"Donna, the tape is rolling," said Sonya.

After a pause to be sure Lara was comfortable, Donna started in her calm, soothing voice. "This must be the worst thing that has ever happened to you. Tell me how you are managing to cope."

"This is the most terrible day of my life. Errol and I planned it to be such a celebration. Not just of the opening of the spa, but of our life together. The spa was my dream, and Errol fulfilled it for me. We wanted it not just for ourselves and the family we planned together, but for a world of troubled people."

"Your philosophy is important to you, isn't it?"

"Oh, yes, very important. It is why I wanted this spa. Here I want to establish a center from which the family of man can go out into the world and *love*. For Errol and me, this was to be a place where perfect love could be achieved. This Buddha is a symbol of that." She paused, looked at the statue, and continued, "Now Errol is gone, but he has left this beautiful place for us all."

What Lara was saying would work well in the story, but Donna was anxious to move on before Lara became too tired. With the next question, she got to the heart of the interview.

"Where were you when Errol was shot?"

Lara paused, then answered carefully, measuring each word. "It must have been when I was on the terrace arranging the flowers for the party. Your crew was working with me. We were enjoying ourselves in the beautiful morning."

"And now, what are your plans?"

"That is an easy question to answer. I will go on. That is what Errol would want me to do. I want to raise our child here in the tranquility of this glorious place. It will become a haven for all his life."

"Are you receiving a lot of support?"

"Everyone here has been extraordinary. Many of our staff became our friends as we worked together. There is nothing they would not do to help me." Lara shifted in her seat. She was getting uncomfortable. Sabina slipped in quickly, patted her forehead and nose with a tissue, then dusted it with a light coating of powder.

Donna examined Sabrina's work. "You are amazing, and you look beautiful. I am so glad you wore that pink dress." After a few seconds' pause, she added, "Have you any idea who would commit such a dreadful crime?"

"No," Lara said, "how could I? Of course we were close as man and wife, but I knew so little of his business world. People tell me he had many enemies. Perhaps he did. He was a man of great strength and power. But I know that he was a good man, a man who I loved and respected."

"And your baby? Do you know if it is a boy or girl?"

"A boy. My child will be a boy." Lara smiled. "He will bring joy to us all and help us to forget this dreadful morning." She was struggling against her fatigue, and it was obvious she couldn't go on much longer. Sonya thought, "Donna will have to push."

"Will you name him Errol?" Donna pressed.

"No," Lara replied with vigor. "I will give him a Hawaiian name. Perhaps Ailani. That means 'high chieftain.' He will be the one who ends the curse some Hawaiians say is on this land."

Lara sank back into the chair, looking exhausted. It was obvious she had no more to say. Donna leant forward and put her hand on Lara's knee.

Sonya signaled to Perry to stop taping.

"Thank you, Lara," Donna said. "I know what it must have cost you."

"Cost her?" The shrill voice came from the house. "It will cost her nothing. She will inherit all his millions. She planned it that way. Now she will have the control she wants."

A quick glance from Sonya, and Perry started to tape again. He turned the camera toward Margaret Halstead. Jackie moved fast; she put her arm out and took hold of Lara's mother as she tried to run to her daughter. Margaret struggled fiercely in Jackie's strong grip.

"Liar," she shrieked, "she's a liar, every word she said was a lie."

Jackie slapped the old woman across the face.

"Stop it," she said. "You are overwrought. You must calm down before you make yourself ill. The shock has been dreadful for all of us."

"Oh no, not for Lara," the old woman said. "She got rid of Errol because I said I would tell him about her first baby—my granddaughter, who lives on this island. Lara got rid of her, too. She put her up for adoption. But I know where she is, and I will tell."

Lara tried to stand up, but then, shaking, fell back into her chair.

"Oh, Mother," she cried, "you know I am not the sort of woman who would lie to my husband. Errol knew everything about my child. He understood. That child is well taken care of. She lives with devoted parents. She will have whatever she needs. What's past is past."

"I was at your side when she was born, that little brown girl," the older woman shrieked.

Lara looked at Donna and shook her head. Her voice quavered. "I'm sorry. My mother has never recovered." She stopped and put her hands up to cover her face.

"Sabrina," Jackie called, "please take Lara upstairs and help her into bed. I'll be there as soon as I've taken care of Mrs. Halstead."

Sabrina bent over Lara, put an arm around her, helped her to stand, and led her away.

"Honey," she said, "I can fix your makeup in a jiffy. But please don't let those tears stain that beautiful dress."

That was Sabrina.

Chapter 30

The Big Island
Saturday, 2:30 P.M.

Sonya's cell phone rang just as she and Donna crossed under the pine trees in the Swanson courtyard. Sonya glanced at her. "Excuse me," she said, "I can't imagine who it is." She flipped open the phone.

It was the police. They wanted her at the spa's main building for a preliminary interview.

When Sonya told her, Donna said, "Don't be concerned. You've got nothing to hide. Just tell them what happened."

"Okay," Sonya agreed. "It seems such a long time ago since we found Errol's body." She looked at her watch. "But it's only six hours. I can't imagine they've cornered the murderer already."

"I wouldn't be too sure. The detective in charge, Al Shannon, is a sharp man. My guess is that he resents the forensic team that's coming from Honolulu. He wants his report to be right on. Maybe he's aiming for a promotion."

"That's natural enough. Errol Swanson's murder must be pretty big as cases go on the Big Island," agreed Sonya.

"At least in modern times. Don't forget the chief who put the curse on the place."

Sonya was surprised that Donna knew about the curse. "That wasn't murder, though. The story I heard was that the chief was betrayed by his son, swam out to sea, and was drowned, rather than being captured." She paused and thought about it. "Well, yes, I guess you could say it was murder."

Donna stopped at the path leading to her bungalow. "It's fascinating how the story of that curse has lingered through time. It's probably influenced the lives of generations of Hawaiians."

She smiled and patted Sonya on the arm. "Well, I guess those superstitions are part of their culture. But we'll soon put these islands far behind us."

The sergeant had told Sonya that Detective Shannon would be in Lara Swanson's corner office. But when she arrived it was the spa manager, not the police, who was waiting for her on the steps to the entrance.

"They phoned and said you were on your way," he said with an obsequious smile. "Mrs. Swanson wants me to look after you. Would you like anything to drink?"

"A cup of hot black coffee would be marvelous," Sonya breathed. "I think I could get it down in one gulp."

"I'll have it brought immediately," he said as they walked across the open veranda to the glass wall of offices.

She didn't reply. The manager, who had been so curt to Lara when Sonya first arrived with Perry, had done an about-face. Now he was singing Lara's praises. It was embarrassing. She nodded her thanks and walked quickly into the office.

A large urn of glorious green orchids stood on a pedestal at the side wall. Once again Lara had used the orchids' colors to decorate the room. The walls were a light, clear green, the furniture was a satin charcoal lacquer, and the accents were in the mysterious deep red that formed the heart of the flower.

Detective Lieutenant Al Shannon introduced himself and his assistant, Peter Toshi. Shannon motioned Sonya to a chair, then sat behind Lara's curved lacquered desk. Toshi settled at the side, notebook in hand.

Shannon was a tall, heavy-set man with thick black hair and a ruddy complexion. He reminded Sonya of a young Ronald Reagan, another man whose easy manner hid a biting ambition. Donna was right. Shannon wanted to solve the case.

Shannon came straight to the point. "Tell me exactly what you were doing before Christy Swanson came across the beach and interrupted you."

"We were shooting the decorations on the tables. Lara's staff had prepared them earlier and we were taping Lara doing the finishing touches. There was nothing unusual going on."

"What time did you start?"

"I'd say right at eight. I got there with Perry, my cameraman, at seven-thirty to decide on camera angles and to set up lights. Lara arrived, as I said, just before eight."

"Coffee, sir." The young girl who stood at the door with a tray gave Shannon a frightened nod when he told her to put the tray on the desk. He ignored her. Leaning forward, Shannon poured coffee and placed a mug in front of Sonya.

"So you had the camera rolling continuously?"

"Well, not exactly. We don't work that way. We roll on a shot and when we finish it, we pause and wait until we've set up the next shot."

"How did Mrs. Swanson seem to you when she arrived? Was she nervous or anxious?"

"No. Not at all. In fact, just the opposite. I remember thinking how calm she was. She listened to what we wanted and then focused on doing it." Sonya paused and thought back. Yes, Lara had been surprisingly calm.

She added, "Most people show a few nerves before the camera, but she was the exception."

Shannon turned to Toshi. "Make a note for me—total control."

Sonya gave a light laugh. "Not really total control. I was directing her, after all; it's just that she was able to do what we asked, and quickly."

"Yes, I understand," the detective responded. "Now, which way was the camera pointing when you were photographing Mrs. Swanson?"

Sonya paused.

"Most of the time we were shooting into the café, with the garden and beach behind us."

"Then Mrs. Swanson was the only person who could see what was happening outside the café?"

Sonya paused. "Well, yes, I suppose so."

"Why do you hesitate?"

"Well, during a shoot, I watch the on-camera person closely. I don't remember her stopping and looking up as if she had seen something."

"But you agree there is a possibility that she could have seen someone on the path that leads to her home without you noticing it? Or even signaled to someone that it was okay to come through?"

"Yes, of course it is possible. I'm concerned about the video, not what's happening around me."

"Hmm." Shannon looked at his watch. "Did she leave you at any time during the shooting?"

"No, it wasn't necessary. She had two maids standing by to help her. We got what we needed quickly and then decided to do the reverse shot."

"So you would say for about 5 or even 10 minutes, anyone, man or woman, could have gone up the path to the Swanson house and you wouldn't have noticed?"

"Yes, as I said, I was busy watching Lara in the monitor."

Sonya felt a wave of anger. He was trying to make her feel guilty. And he had no right. She had simply been doing her job.

"Do you know the writer, Frank O'Neill?"

"Yes."

"So if you had seen him on the path, you would have recognized him."

"Of course. I don't know him intimately, but for a while he worked at the network. His was a Sunday program, so I didn't run into him that often, but I knew him."

"He was very close to Lara Swanson before she married. Did you ever see them together?"

Sonya was tempted to say a sharp "no" and forget it. But the truth was, she had seen them together, in a small Italian restaurant near the studio.

She told the story as simply as she could. But Shannon wanted more.

"Tell me what you thought then. Did you think they were particularly close?"

"As far as I remember, I looked at Lara and thought how beautiful she was. I could understand why any man would fall in love with her."

"Did Frank O'Neill look as if he were in love with her?"

"I don't remember."

"You don't remember, but you thought that she was so beautiful any man could fall in love with her?"

She wasn't going to lie. Frank had been so obviously in love with Lara. Sonya gave a light sigh and shrugged her shoulders.

"That's the only time you saw them together."

Sonya put her head back and closed her eyes. "Yes, I think so. But then they may have been at parties together. I just don't recall."

"Have you spoken to O'Neill since you've been here? If so, what did he give you as the reason he came?"

Sonya picked up the mug and sipped the coffee. It was lukewarm and bitter, left over from breakfast. The staff was already slacking off. Maybe some of the Hawaiians had already walked out. She took another sip. She had to think what to say. She had given her word to O'Neill that she wouldn't mention he was writing a biography of Errol. She put down the mug and said, "He said he was doing several projects, including a story for a travel magazine."

"He didn't mention the book he was writing on Swanson?"

"Yes, he did. He told me about it, but asked me to keep it quiet. That was only natural. It's obvious he wouldn't want the Swansons to know about it."

"He has done a lot of research on Swanson. Do you think O'Neill was planning to blackmail him?"

Sonya almost burst out laughing. "Oh, no, for heaven's sake, that's not Frank O'Neill. He's brilliant, a highly respected journalist. He doesn't need to blackmail anyone."

"Did O'Neill mention to you that he visited Lara Swanson after her husband was murdered? If so, what did he tell you?"

It had been obvious to Sonya that Frank had come from Lara, but he hadn't mentioned it to her.

She shook her head firmly. She wanted to stop this line of questioning. Shannon was way out of line suspecting Frank. But Shannon continued, "Were you at the network when Errol Swanson fired O'Neill?"

"Yes, I was," replied Sonya.

"Was there a reaction among the staff?"

Sonya nodded. She remembered the shock waves that had spread through the building when the staff heard the news the following Monday morning.

"There was talk of a petition of protest, but Errol was too feared and it fizzled out."

The e-mail that had been sent to the staff had said simply, "Frank O'Neill was under contract to the network. He was let go with his contract fully paid."

"Let's go back to the shoot on the café," Shannon said. "You admit it is possible that Christy Swanson could have walked past you on her way to her father's home, murdered him, and then gone down to the beach without you seeing her."

"Yes," Sonya said reluctantly. "But Christy didn't murder her father."

"How can you be so sure?"

"It's just my instinct."

Shannon raised his eyebrows, smiled, and ignored her statement. "When did you first see Christy on the beach?"

"I didn't notice her until my cameraman zoomed in on the beach. He told Lara that Christy would be in the shot and suggested she get her out of the way."

"I see," he replied. "Now let's talk about the dinner last night. Did anything unusual occur? I understand there was a scene between Mr. Swanson and his daughter. Did you see that?"

Sonya was cautious. "I know that his daughter, Christy, wanted to swim, and her mother and father seemed to object. But I did not hear the whole conversation."

"And did you notice anyone missing—anyone you might have expected to attend? Like Frank O'Neill?"

"Look, Detective, I didn't have a guest list," Sonya said with force. "I did see the family, Frank, and a few members of the press, of course. Beyond that, I didn't notice. And I can't speculate on who should or should not have come."

Once again the detective turned to Toshi. "Make a note to find out more about the dinner."

Then he continued with Sonya, "Now, about the discovery of the body."

It was inevitable that he would ask about that, thought Sonya. She dreaded having to tell what she had seen.

"I would like you to tell me the position of the body as you saw it."

"His hands and feet were tied to the bedposts."

"And Mrs. Swanson started to untie one of his legs?"

"That's right, and she told Christy to help." Then she added, defensively, "It must have been humiliating to Lara. She wanted to get him untied and get us out before we photographed him."

"You didn't help Mrs. Swanson in any way."

"No, we were there for just a minute or two. She asked us to go and we left."

"We'll need to go into this again later with you and your cameraman. We also want to see some of your tapes."

Sonya said nothing. He knew as well as she did that that was not her decision. There were legal questions about giving reporters' material to the police. Matt would have to call the nineteenth floor about that.

Shannon leaned forward with his arms on the desk.

"One other matter before we wind up. I hear you lost a notebook containing an outline of your interview with Errol Swanson?"

Sonya looked at him in disbelief. "How did you know about that?"

"I can't say, you know that," he said. "Is it true?"

The phone rang. Toshi mumbled an apology and picked it up. He put his hand over the receiver. "It's the sergeant. He says Tomas Swanson is here. He wants to talk about the gun."

Shannon showed no surprise. "Tell the sergeant to keep him there. I'll see him as soon as I'm finished here."

He turned back to Sonya. "Is it true?

"Yes, it's true. The book contained all the notes I'd taken that day, not just the ones on the Swanson interview."

"And that was Thursday?"

Sonya paused. "Yes, it was Thursday. Apparently I left the book in Donna's bungalow after a late meeting on Wednesday."

Sonya felt that she sounded like such a lightweight, leaving her notebook behind, but she had said enough.

"When did you discover it was missing?"

"The next day, about lunchtime, I went to check my notes and found it missing. Donna gave it back to me."

"Did the notebook contain comments about Errol Swanson that might have upset the family?"

"I can't judge what would have upset them. I only wrote down what he said. That's all."

With that, Shannon let her go. On her way out, he added, "Ms. Iverson, we'll need to talk again. In the meantime, if you think of anything more, let me know." He gave her his card.

Sonya walked away, trying to figure out who had told him about the notebook. Not Perry, not Sabrina—she had deliberately not told them. And even if Sabrina had overheard something, she would not have gone running to the police.

Only one person could have told the police about her notebook. Matt. He was trying to protect someone. Probably himself.

Chapter 31

The Big Island
Saturday, 2:50 P.M.

The news that Tomas had been held for questioning for the murder of his father spread quickly. Sonya heard it while she was waiting for Perry at the terrace café. They were due to interview Tracey in 10 minutes.

Tracey had at first sounded reluctant to do the interview, then, after a discussion, had asked Sonya to come early. Sonya had dressed with Tracey in mind. She was wearing a beige sleeveless shirt and matching slacks. Tracey was a neat, fastidious woman and it was imperative that the interview go well.

Jackie walked in with none of her usual swagger, sank into a chair, and ordered an espresso.

Sonya went over to her. "What's up? You look as if you've had a nasty shock."

"I have," she said, pulling out a chair for Sonya. Sonya waved to the waiter for coffee.

"Tell me," she said.

"Lara heard from the police that Tomas has confessed to throwing the gun that killed Errol into the ocean," Jackie said slowly.

"Did he admit to the murder?"

"No, but he said the gun was his. He says he left it on the hall table after an argument with his father last night. He told the police that to cool down he went into town, where he visited some clubs and spent the night partying in Kona.

"When did he come back to the spa?"

"This morning. He had sobered up and decided he'd better retrieve his gun. When he didn't find the gun in the hall, he went into the bedroom. He told the police he found Errol there, already dead."

"What about the gun?"

"He says it was lying on the bed so he picked it up and left. He went to the top of a cliff and threw it into the ocean. He refuses to say more until he hears from his mother's attorney."

Jackie blinked several times, then took off her glasses and wiped her eyes. She reached out for her coffee.

"Are you all right?" This was the first time Sonya had seen Jackie so emotional.

Jackie paused as the waiter brought Sonya's coffee. He filled Sonya's cup.

"Grown here in Hawaii," the waiter said. "The best in the world."

Sonya nodded and smiled politely. Then, as he left, she repeated the question. "Are you all right?"

Jackie lowered her voice almost to a whisper. "Yeah, I'm okay. It's just that we like Tomas. Lara said all he wanted was some attention from his father, and she's sure that's what the argument must have been about. She asked me to go to Margot and see what we could do for her. Margot was sitting in the dark, the lights out and the blinds drawn. She said there was nothing Lara could do. She had left a message for her attorney and was waiting for his call."

Jackie massaged the back of her neck to ease the tension.

"Sonya," she said, "Margot was so calm it was frightening."

Sonya sipped her coffee. Margot was a complete control freak. Sonya had seen her in action at her fashion shows. Now events were completely out of her control. It must be driving her crazy.

"Why did Tomas have a gun? And why did he take it when he went to see his father?" Sonya asked.

"Margot won't say, and if the police know, they aren't saying."

"He arrived only a few hours before the party. He can't have gotten the gun here. He must have brought it from New York, and that sounds as if he could have planned the murder."

Jackie shook her head. "I can't believe it."

"Tomas didn't kill his father," Sonya said with conviction. "He's just 19, a sweet kid. Talented, with a rich life ahead of him. He wanted his father's love, but I don't believe he wanted it enough to pull the trigger on him."

"I agree with you." Jackie's voice was unsteady. "And so does Lara."

Sonya glanced at her watch. "I have to interview Tracey right now, and I don't want to be too late. I'll see what I can find out when I get back. Matt, my executive producer, is handling the police, and he'll have all the details. Where will you be? I have a lot more questions I'd like to ask you."

"I don't know where I'll be, but call me on my cell. Leave a message if it's busy, I'll get right back to you."

The day's events had obviously caught up with Jackie. Sonya put her hand on her shoulder and gave it a sympathetic squeeze.

Sonya joined Perry at the café entrance and walked with him to Tracey's bungalow. She knew Tomas could not be the killer. Only yesterday she had watched him in the pool, tossing a ball with Christy. He was in the deep end, and she in the shallow, but after a while Christy had insisted they change places. Tossing the ball to her in the deep end, he made certain each time to place it easily within her reach. Christy squealed with joy when she caught it. Tomas cared for Christy. He was kind and gentle.

She and Perry reached Tracey's bungalow in silence. Sonya stepped forward and pushed against the garden gate to open it for Perry, but it didn't budge. She tested the lock, but it still resisted.

"I think it's jammed shut," she said. Perry put down the camera and looked over the top of the gate.

"It's wedged shut with a piece of wood. Someone doesn't want us to come in," Perry grunted. "But they're here. Listen to the music."

Sonya felt a shiver of fear. There was a murderer loose. Who was Tracey afraid of letting in? Surely Ramos was strong enough to protect her.

Perry teased her as usual. "Does she know we're coming? Did you check with her, 'Ms. Control'?"

It was his standard joke, but this time Sonya welcomed it.

"Oh, Perry, of course I did." She kept her voice half stern, half joking. "I called her half an hour ago to confirm it. She said Christy was with her, and they were in their swimsuits by the plunge pool, but that she was all made up for the interview. She could slip into a dress and be ready in five minutes. Probably they can't hear us over the music."

Sonya took a deep breath. "Hello," she shouted, "it's Sonya. I'm here for the interview, but I can't get in."

There was no reply.

Perry put down the tripod, put two fingers in his mouth, and gave an ear-piercing whistle.

"Hello, anyone there?" he shouted.

Ramos slid open the front door and walked to the gate. His patterned Hawaiian swim trunks showed his lean strong body and his tanned skin. His manner was easy, but he kept his eyes down, avoiding Sonya's. His beard was thick and his face expressionless. It was impossible to tell what he was thinking.

"Sorry about that," he said. "But you're early. I didn't expect you until three-thirty. Tracey must have mixed up the times."

He pulled out the wedge of wood. "Tracey's attorney, Roger McCoy, suggested this," he said. "He told me he wanted the place made secure."

Sonya watched him lead the way into the bungalow, moving like a jungle cat, his body tense, each foot carefully placed.

As Sonya walked into the living room, she glanced into the bedrooms. The main one—Tracey's—was open, the bed made but pillows crumpled as though someone had rested there. The door of Ramos's room was ajar but she couldn't see inside. From the back garden she heard the rumble of Louis Armstrong singing "Mack the Knife."

"Tracey loves jazz, and Armstrong is one of her favorites. She must be playing it for Christy," Ramos said.

Sonya turned to Perry. "I thought we might do the interview by the pool," she said. "But if Christy is splashing around it will interfere with the audio. What do you think?"

"I'd rather do it there. The back garden is in shadow and that will make the light more flattering."

Sonya walked in her usual brisk way across the living room, motioning to Perry to follow. The door to the garden and pool was closed. She pushed it open, letting Perry step through ahead of her.

"We're just coming to look for a good spot for the interview," she called.

But Perry shouted, "Oh my God. Christy, what are you doing?"

As he put down the tripod and started to swing the camera off his shoulder, Sonya pushed past him. The two women were in the pool. Christy was holding onto Tracey, as if trying to pull her out of the water. Tracey's body was limp, and Christy was having difficulty getting a good grip. She managed to get Tracey's head above water for a moment, only to have it slip back in.

"No, stop it," Sonya cried, throwing her bag off her shoulder. "Let me get her out." She grabbed Christy's hair and jerked her away from her aunt. Then Sonya slid into the pool and reached for Tracey. She put her arm around Tracey's neck and, keeping her head above the water, pulled her over to the steps.

Ramos was waiting for her. He lifted Tracey out of the water and laid her flat on her back. He put his finger to her neck and felt the pulse.

"I can't tell," he said. "All I can do is try to get her breathing." He yanked Tracey's mouth open, held her nose, and breathed heavily into her mouth.

"I'll call an ambulance," Sonya said, scrambling out of the pool.

"I think she's already gone, but I'll give it a last try." Ramos rolled Tracey's head to the side and started pumping her stomach. Water spurted from her mouth. But Tracey lay still.

"She's dead." Ramos's voice was grim. He stood up. "She and Christy were playing in the pool. She must have had a heart attack."

Sonya looked at Tracey. She was fully made up for the interview, with mascara, eye shadow, blush, and her usual coral lipstick. Her fine blond hair, drenched, was so thin that Sonya could see her scalp.

Sonya realized in an instant that Tracey had not gone into the pool willingly. Even with Sabrina's expert hands, that fine soft hair would take 40 minutes to be styled. Tracey had been forced into the pool and murdered. Sonya had no doubt about it.

"I don't think it was a heart attack." She straightened up and looked Ramos directly in the eye. "I think Tracey was pushed into the pool and drowned."

"Who would do that?" He waited for an answer.

Sonya said nothing.

Ramos continued, "I don't know what happened. I was in my room reading. I didn't come out until I heard your whistle. If anyone pushed her in, it must have been Christy."

"I didn't, I didn't," Christy screamed. Staring, her face distorted, flushed with her wet hair straggling across it, she shook her fists in a wild frenzy. "She was my aunt. I wanted her to come and live with us in Chicago. She promised we would go swimming together, like we used to do."

She turned toward Ramos, her thin angular body tense with fury. Then she rushed at him, crazed, and with all her force she pushed him into the pool.

"You die, too. I hate you, I hate you."

She whirled around and forced her way through the heavy bushes beside the bungalow.

"Perry," Sonya gasped, "I'm frightened. Let's go after her." They ran through the living room and paused at the gate to see which way Christy had gone.

"There she is." Perry pointed. Christy was running up the cliff that loomed over the waterfall.

"Christy, stop, stop," Sonya shouted. "I understand. I'll help you."

But Christy either didn't hear or didn't care. She reached the top of the cliff, where she paused and looked across the stretch of blue ocean as if saying a last good-bye. Then she dived in a clean straight line toward the black rocks below.

Sonya stopped at the edge, breathless, her heart pounding. She looked down at Christy's body where it lay on the rocks with the waves gently lapping over her.

Then Perry was there, panting, behind her. Amazingly, he had his camera on his shoulder. He put the viewfinder to his eye and zoomed in on Christy's body.

"Is she dead?" Ramos's voice was grim as he joined them.

"Yes," said Sonya, "yes, she's dead." She struggled to control her anger. "Who are you? What right had you to accuse Christy like that?"

Her heart began to pump wildly. She wanted to batter him with her fists, to get revenge in some way for what he had done to Christy, to Tracey, to Errol. To his family.

Ramos showed no emotion. He merely turned and walked away.

Chapter 32

The Big Island
Saturday, 9:00 P.M.

Sonya slipped her bag off her shoulder, threw it onto the sofa, and headed for the bathroom. First a shower. After that maybe a hot cup of chamomile tea and a few yoga stretches. Then perhaps the memories of the day would slip away and she could nap before she had to meet Donna again that night.

She turned on the shower and let the hot water pound her shoulders. She sighed with pleasure. The blessing of water relaxed her whole body. Nothing worked better.

The bungalow was calm. Sabrina was out chatting with the staff. Sonya should have peace at least for an hour or two.

The phone rang. Not her cell, thank God. The spa line. That meant she wouldn't have to get out of the shower to answer it. She put her hand out of the shower and picked up the phone.

"Yes," she said abruptly, trying to keep her stubborn red curls out of her eyes.

She didn't recognize the voice. "I'm sorry to inconvenience you, Ms. Iverson, but Detective Shannon suggested I call you."

"Yes." She kept her voice hard.

"Ms. Iverson." His tone was pleasant, low. She caught the hint of a Midwestern accent. "My name is Roger McCoy. I've been Tracey Swanson's lawyer and friend for many years. I have just arrived from Chicago. I wonder if you could spare me a few moments to talk to me about Tracey's death."

She agreed immediately; he could tell her more about Tracey's relationship with Ramos. "I can tell you just what I told the detective," she said, turning off the shower. "I only met Tracey briefly, I know little about her."

"But the detective told me that you tried to save her life. You pulled her out of the pool."

"Yes, that's true. Give me 10 minutes. I'm in a bungalow named Hibiscus."

"I'll be there in 10 minutes. Exactly."

Sonya dried herself quickly and put on fresh jeans and a shirt.

She saw Roger McCoy's silhouette through the glass door as he pressed the buzzer. He was a tall, powerful man.

He glanced around as he walked in. "Thank you for seeing me," he said. "Tracey called in great distress this morning. She told me Errol Swanson had been murdered and that she knew who the killer was. I was extremely concerned about her and decided to fly here in my company's plane. When I called from the plane to speak to her, the operator connected me to Detective Shannon. He told me that Tracey was dead, but only gave me the barest details. He did tell me that you were there." McCoy looked into Sonya's eyes. "So I've come to you."

Sonya said, "I'll help any way I can."

Then he said, "I'd like to know where Tracey died."

Sonya went to the wall and flipped a couple of switches. The blinds slid up and lights lit the pool and garden.

"The layout of her bungalow was the same as this. Tracey was drowned in a pool similar to this one."

McCoy walked to the window and stood looking out. His silence was so deep that Sonya hesitated to speak. When at last he turned to her, she could see he was struggling with grief.

"Tracey's death ends a chapter in my life," he said. "Her partner, Donald Simpson, was my friend. She was everything to him. When he died, I did my best to look after her."

"I am so sorry." Sonya's sympathy was genuine. "Sit down and let me get you a drink."

McCoy chose a chair with its back to the pool and asked for scotch. When he took the glass from her, Sonya saw that his hand was shaking.

"Tell me about it, every detail, if you don't mind."

She did immediately.

When she finished, he said, "It was clever of you to realize that Ramos was really Craig Swanson. He was wounded, along with a dozen or so other guerrillas, fighting with the Zapatistas against the military in Mexico and Guatemala."

"Is that when Tracey took him in?"

"Yes. His legs were badly injured. She got him into a good hospital, and when he was discharged, he came and stayed with her."

"She looked after him without telling his parents? Why?"

"He begged her not to. The situation at home was terrible. Errol was abusive. Craig had been bright, ambitious, and good at school. He was studying political science and was fascinated by the struggles in Latin America. Like many young kids, he was an idealist. He rejected Errol's values, then took off, saying he wanted to live a more meaningful life."

"But why didn't he ever go back, especially after his injuries?"

McCoy frowned. "It was complicated because of his guerrilla activities. Tracey asked me to check around; both the Mexican and the U.S. governments have files on him. Craig Swanson, or Ramos, as he prefers to be called, has quite a history."

"I see," Sonya said softly. "That kind of history would have made things worse with Errol."

"Exactly. The one thing that hung over him was the guilt of abandoning Christy. He told Tracey that it haunted him."

"How close was he to Tracey?"

"Very close. She had no one else. We talked about her moving back to Chicago, but we both knew she could never leave Mexico, for that would mean leaving Ramos."

"So whose idea was it to come to the opening of the spa? Tracey's or Ramos's?" she asked.

McCoy finished the rest of his drink.

"Tracey planned it all. Her dream was to reunite the twins. At the back of her mind, I think she hoped that Ramos would take responsibility for Christy, perhaps even bring her to live with them in Acapulco."

Sonya brought ice cubes and the bottle of scotch to the coffee table, refilled McCoy's glass, then sat beside him.

"You could say it was all accidental," Sonya said. "Ramos couldn't have planned the shooting—after all, it wasn't his gun. My guess is that when he and Christy found Errol tied to the bed, their father must have shouted at them to get out. It would have been traumatic for Christy and Ramos couldn't handle things. He overreacted." And then some, Sonya added to herself.

"What should have been a reunion became a disaster. Errol's legendary temper contributed to his death."

"Yes," Sonya agreed. "Then Ramos had to find a way to cover the murder."

Sonya imagined how Ramos must have panicked when he realized what he had done. "He must have told Christy to go for a walk on the beach," she continued. "Then he slipped into the shrubs and watched. He saw Christy come back with Lara, waited until his sister came out again, and that time, he followed her. Then he took her to Tracey."

Sonya leaned forward, resting her head on her hand.

"Christy was tragic. No friends, so little family support. The only thing she achieved in life was winning a few swimming races when she was a girl. And then her family clamped down on that. She became the family scapegoat."

McCoy nodded. "Tracey told you?"

"Yes, last night at dinner."

He got up, walked to the window, and studied the pool.

"When Tracey told me she knew who the killer was, I told her to go to the police. She refused. That's where I made the mistake. I should have called them myself. When Ramos phoned me, I foolishly told him what Tracey had said. I had no idea I was tipping off her murderer."

"You couldn't have known he would kill her. He must have been afraid that she would expose him. Perhaps he couldn't stand the thought of the aunt he loved betraying him."

"Perhaps," McCoy said thoughtfully. "But Ramos might have another motive for killing Tracey. When he came to live with her, Tracey made a will and left most of her estate to him. But she told me this week she wanted to split her money between the twins. In other words, Ramos would get only half the amount he was counting on."

"Did Ramos know she planned to change her will?"

"I'm sure he did. Tracey confided in him. She had no one else."

"And poor Christy," said Sonya, "killed herself not because she was guilty, but because the brother she desperately longed for betrayed her."

With that McCoy rose. "Thank you, Ms. Iverson, for sparing me the time. It's helped me to talk with you about it. Now, sadly, I must go and begin arrangements for Tracey's burial. I think she would have wanted to rest in Acapulco. She loved it there."

"And thank you, Mr. McCoy," Sonya responded. "You've helped me understand it all."

McCoy shook her hand and held it for an instant. "When you do your story, please be as gentle as you can."

She stood at the door and watched him walk down the path, tall and straight, the moonlight turning the gray in his hair to silver.

Then she went to the stone statue in her garden.

For a minute she stood in silence. Then she whispered, "Whoever you are, wherever you are, please take care of Christy."